She was trapped in the Gothic labyrinth

Katarina sidestepped a gridwork of jointed beams and went deeper into the room. The music played on, calling her.

Then she heard it—a soft scrape. A brush of cloth on stone. A footstep. She spun around too quickly, and her flashlight tumbled from her fingers . . . falling into the hands of a shadowy figure, visible only in silhouette.

"Who are you?" Katarina asked.

"Someone who has watched your every move." His voice was low, with a sexy Latino accent.

Katarina felt excited, hypnotized, drawn to this man who stood wreathed in darkness. "What are you doing here?"

"Living in isolation, hoping that one day you would join me. And you have."

"I . . . I heard music. I thought it came from down here."

"It did. You were meant to hear it."

Back away, Katarina's instincts warned her. But she couldn't. And then the shadowy silhouette came closer, exposing her phantom of darkness.

ABOUT THE AUTHOR

Puppets is an amalgam of Jenna Ryan's love for the Phantom of the Opera, ghost stories, dark places, dark moods and the feeling she used to have as a child that "marionette puppets looked frightening, like people with strings attached to their hands and feet." According to Jenna, "I'm really still a child at heart."

Books by Jenna Ryan

HARLEQUIN INTRIGUE

88–CAST IN WAX
99–SUSPENDED ANIMATION
118–CLOAK AND DAGGER
138–CARNIVAL
145–SOUTHERN CROSS
173–MASQUERADE
189–ILLUSIONS

Puppets

Jenna Ryan

Harlequin Books

TORONTO • NEW YORK • LONDON
AMSTERDAM • PARIS • SYDNEY • HAMBURG
STOCKHOLM • ATHENS • TOKYO • MILAN
MADRID • WARSAW • BUDAPEST • AUCKLAND

To Miss Henderson, Mr. Hartel and Mr. Wende, my favorite teachers, who all encouraged me to write.

To my parents and my sister. And to my aunt, Alice Malcolm, one of my very favorite people.

Harlequin Intrigue edition published December 1992

ISBN 0-373-22205-X

PUPPETS

Printed in U.S.A.

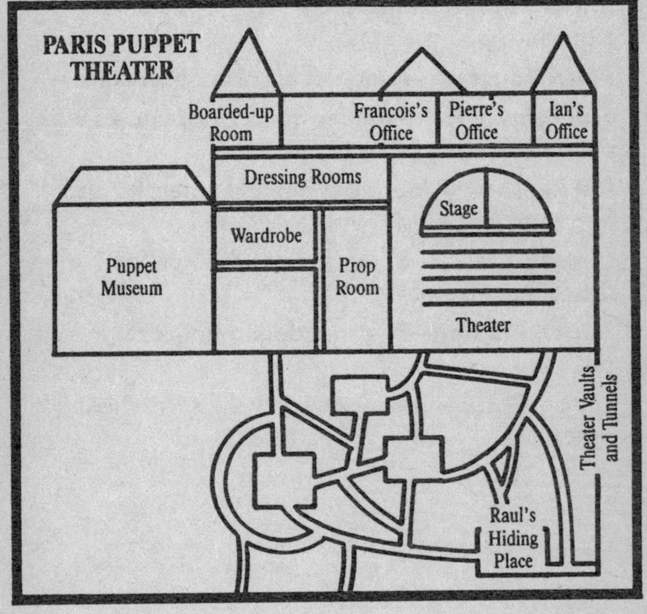
PARIS PUPPET THEATER
Boarded-up Room
Francois's Office
Pierre's Office
Ian's Office
Dressing Rooms
Stage
Wardrobe
Puppet Museum
Prop Room
Theater
Theater Vaults and Tunnels
Raul's Hiding Place

CAST OF CHARACTERS

Raul Sennett—He lived in darkness and isolation in an underground lair.

Katarina Lacroix—She was lured by him to the vaults beneath the Paris Puppet Theater.

Philip Gordon Hambleton—He, too, wanted Katarina.

Pierre Fousard—A man of bizarre obsessions.

Francois Lupier—His fascination for puppets was unnatural.

Ian Renshaw—Manager of the theater; he also had another deadly job.

Claudia Clercy—Set designer who stumbled upon the real murderer.

Babette Toulon—A prima donna both onstage and off.

Louise Grant—She alone knew the secret hiding place.

Prologue

Today I'm a teller of tales. Tomorrow, who knows? I live in the vaults beneath the Puppet Theater, but no one knows exactly where. Sometimes I go up and wander through the streets of Paris, but not so much now as when I was young.

Now I will tell you a story, and maybe when I'm finished, I'll be wiser than I am at this moment.

It wouldn't take much to make me so, unfortunately. Wisdom has never been my strong suit.

My story takes place in the Puppet Theater and Museum, but a good portion of it unfolds down here, in these lightless subterranean chambers that I know better than anyone in Paris.

Indulge me now, if you will. Hang cobwebs and shadows in your mind. Think darkness and danger, too, and tales from another time. Maybe some of those tales are true. Or maybe they are just pertinent to the one I'm about to tell. When it's over you can decide this for yourself. At least I hope you can. Because, you see, my story isn't finished yet. It isn't done.

And so we shall witness the finale together. Who knows, maybe we will both be shocked by the outcome.

In the meantime, travel with me, please, into the darkened recesses of other people's minds, to a world of wood and cloth and string. The magic threads will connect people and puppets, like dots in a children's book. But first, we must journey to the city of New Orleans. . . .

Chapter One

Her name was Katarina Lacroix. She was a pretty girl, a nine-year-old Creole with green eyes and black-brown hair that fell to her waist in a single thick braid. She was too thin, or so her aunt kept telling her. But after five years of living with Aunt Didi and Uncle Denis, Katarina had learned to ignore them both.

Most of the time they were too busy fighting to notice her, unless Uncle Denis was drinking. Then Aunt Didi would put on her slinky red dress, the one that looked like dyed snakeskin, her spiky red heels and her gaudy jewelry. She would drench her skin with French perfume, slam out of their sweltering New Orleans apartment and head straight for whatever bar was playing the loudest Dixieland jazz.

"Take care of the kid," she would shout at Denis as she left. But he was too in love with his bottle of bourbon to notice anything Didi said.

"Your uncle, he's gonna miss you, Kati. Maybe I should phone and tell him where you got to."

Luther Dumaine limped onto the balcony of his shabby second-story apartment off Magazine Street. His kindly black face was creased and worn from seventy-three years of hard bayou living. His hair was curly and white, and his dark eyes, dimmed by time, were infinitely gentle whenever he looked at her. He took care of the props at the run-down

Garden District theater that Uncle Denis managed. He was nice, he was alone and he was Kati's very favorite friend.

Meticulously, Katarina licked all traces of powdered sugar from her fingers. Luther made great chicken gumbo, but it was his *beignets* she loved best. They were so fresh that when she pinched the edges they stuck together, so hot that she always burned her tongue.

"He'll make me come back if you call," she said, hunching her thin shoulders in determination. "I won't go back, Luther. I hate it there. I'm gonna leave soon. Run away." Proudly she puffed out her tiny chest. "I got ten dollars and thirty-two cents saved up."

"Well now, you be getting mighty rich there, little miss. Just where would you be going with all this money?"

Luther eased himself into a rickety wicker chair, and for a moment Katarina stopped chewing. Her wiry body stiffened. Luther was old and the heat of a steamy New Orleans summer only made his arthritis worse. He needed to leave, too. Could she save enough for both of them to go away?

She pressed her lips together, listening to the wail of a saxophone and beyond that the boat sounds from the river. Sad music, like the blues.

Katarina shuddered and pulled a wrinkled picture from the pocket of her shorts. "I'll go to Paris," she answered Luther, scrunching the picture in her hand. "Papa was born there. He used to tell me about it when I would go to bed. Someday he would take me there, he promised." She lowered her eyes, wadding the picture tighter in her fist. "But then he died and he never got to take me. But I'll go anyway. I'll get to Paris, you'll see."

Luther nodded, pursing his lips. "And what will you do there? How will you live?"

"I'll..." She stopped, frowning slightly. Then her eyes landed on the hand-painted puppet stage Luther had built back when his hands didn't hurt so badly, and she brightened. "I'll be a puppeteer, like you are."

"Like I was, Kati." His eyes glistened in the faint light that rose from the noisy street below. "Anyway, you don't gotta be going all the way to Paris to be a puppeteer. You already know how to do that kind of magic here."

Katarina shoved the picture back in her pocket. "I still want to go there," she insisted. "Get away from them."

Luther turned affectionate eyes on her. "You can go anywhere you want to, you know that, too. I showed you how."

"You mean just pretend I've left." She darted a sulky glance at the stage and the puppets that lay beside it in a seemingly impossible tangle of string. "Maybe I'm too old to pretend anymore."

Luther shook his grizzled head. He levered himself out of the chair with difficulty and came over to her.

Summer nights were full of rich smells in this part of the city. Fried bananas, bougainvillea, memory of the sun on worn-out roofs and every kind of spice in the South. There was the smell of the river too, and sometimes, like now, the sweet smell of rum and rice. But Katarina loved the way Luther smelled best. Like paint and varnish and sawdust. Like his puppets.

She felt his gnarled hand on the back of her head, turning it so that she stared at the miniature theater. "See the magic, Kati," he said solemnly. "You got the eyes to find it. All you got to do is keep them open and looking."

Her fists unclenched slowly. With one small hand she reached out to pick up a crumpled puppet. "Marie Laveau," she said, then grinned when she heard Luther's disapproval.

"Don't you go messing with no voodoo queens, little miss," he warned. "You gotta choose your ghosts carefully. Some, they be watching all the time, making sure no one's trying to steal their souls away."

"But I'm only pretending." Katarina held up the dark-haired puppet, separating its delicate strings one by one.

"I'll make this one me, send her to Paris in my place." With her free hand, she pushed a golden-haired marionette at Luther. "You can be the prince who comes to carry me off to his castle."

Luther chuckled, lowering himself to his sore knees. "If that's what you want," he agreed. He always indulged her in play. "You're the one with the magic eyes. Remember, Kati, the bad things don't exist here. This world's under your control."

Fifteen years later.

IT WAS A grotesque night, wild, uncontrolled. Mardi Gras. Every costumed creature Katarina had ever imagined swarmed past the small group on the street. There was noise everywhere. It was pandemonium and she was trapped in the middle of it.

Curious ghouls with brightly painted eyes and mouths pressed closer, angling for a better view of Davide Montreau who was sprawled on the pavement where he'd collapsed twenty minutes ago. Semiconscious now, his face was whiter than the vampire rock star whose mask he'd donned for this, the final night of Carnival.

Katarina stared at his chalky features, his glazed blue eyes, his limp mouth. He was dying, and there wasn't a thing she could do about it. Her husband of four long, troubled years was not responding to whatever the paramedics were doing. He would die, just like her parents had twenty years ago. Just like Luther had last month.

"We're losing him," one of the paramedics muttered under his breath. Funny how she could hear that so clearly when a thousand brass bands played away in a rude blast of noise behind her.

More masked bodies bumped against her. She smelled champagne and French cologne. Davide's eyes went from glazed to glassy.

"Looks like a junkie," someone wearing a clown suit and tinseled pink hair stated. "Let's get back to the parade."

A wave of dizziness swept through Katarina's body. She felt like one of Luther's wooden puppets. *Not real.* She swallowed the pain in her throat, focused her eyes—and almost choked. Davide wasn't breathing!

The older paramedic looked up. There was no sorrow for her loss in his hardened gaze. "What was your husband on, ma'am?" he asked. Uncaring fingers closed Davide's sightless blue eyes.

Katarina pushed the heavy braid over her shoulder, too numb to react, much less think. "I don't know. He said he didn't do drugs."

"Uh-huh."

Clearly the man didn't believe her, but Katarina was beyond caring. Two deaths in five weeks; so much grief. It wasn't fair.

Someone led her to a waiting ambulance. Things must be done, a calm voice told her. The signing of papers, that sort of thing. Total dispassion in the man's voice. But then, his life hadn't just fallen apart.

Trumpets blared cheerfully to Katarina's left. There were people in costumes everywhere she looked, laughing, dancing, celebrating. Papier-mâché floats drifted past. No reality tonight, she thought grimly. With one horrible exception. Davide was dead. Help me, Luther. This world is *not* under my control.

Katarina closed her eyes. It was time to leave for Paris.

Chapter Two

"This is a story of darkness, a tragic tale of love and the magic of a time long past. So come, let me tell you the legend. Let me take you back through the centuries, to an age when every shadow held an untold secret, when myth and mystery abounded and Giovanni Verrone's exquisitely crafted puppets were all the rage on the boulevards of Paris."

Exquisite...

The word seemed to float through Raul Sennett's feverish brain as he stood hiding in the cool, stone corridor of a fourteenth-century Paris theater, staring at a woman who might well be a figment of his imagination.

Her name was Katarina Lacroix. Her long, dark hair was thick and full of waves. She had green eyes and ivory skin and features that could have been sculpted by a French master. A tour guide by day and performance "puppet" by night, she was beautiful beyond belief. Not so much on the surface—although she was very pretty—no, it was something else that drew him to her. This lovely creature possessed a quality he could not explain.

Did he dream up this walking vision, he wondered, this woman who called out to every one of his senses? He knew he had a fever but he couldn't be that far gone.

Raul pressed his forehead against one of the smooth stone columns, carefully, so he would not be exposed. She was a temptation, but this was not the time to be seen. He should go back to the vaults below the theater.

But he had to find something first to bring down the fever.

He glanced up. It was important to find a remedy, yet on a more personal note he wanted to hear Katarina's soft, New Orleans accented voice. And so he would hide here a while longer and listen as she told the story of Giovanni Verrone, creator of the now-famous Paris Puppet Theater.

"Tragedy, my friends," Katarina said with a dramatic sweep of her arm. Raul heard the layers of her colorful peasant costume rustle against her long legs, and risked another glance around the column. Heavenly eyes, the color of a misty sea. He pushed damp, dark hair from his face as she continued.

"For Giovanni, this magnificent theater wasn't enough. He was a handsome man, but very lonely. A broken soul, forever trapped in a web of darkness. His puppets were his only friends, and you must believe he loved them with a passion that bordered on obsession. Or absurdity." She gave her fascinated group an eloquent shrug. "This you can decide as the legend unfolds."

There was a trace of melancholy on her lips and sorrow in her voice. Raul smiled faintly. She was a performer all right, just like the other twenty or thirty actors who did double duty here. Entertainers on the stage of the Puppet Theater each evening, shepherds of tourist masses through the adjoining Puppet Museum each afternoon.

They were one and the same, the theater and the museum. The only real difference was that here in this world of gilt and glass showcases the puppets were made of wood and cloth and string while in the theater, on that six hundred-year-old stage, the puppets were people pretending to be marionettes. Every night these puppets came magically to life. This was Giovanni's legend, more or less, dramatically embellished and presented to a mesmerized audience.

People as puppets were not a common concept, even in the Paris theater. But it didn't seem to matter. The theater was always full. Who could resist watching human puppets act out a tragic love story that had supposedly taken place in this building six full centuries ago, or listening to the ghost story of Giovanni Verrone, who was still said to roam the dark passages beneath the theater.

"Giovanni made his first mistake when he fell hopelessly in love with one of his marionettes," Katarina was saying softly. "He called her Mignon and wanted to give her life. But, of course, even a great puppet master like Giovanni couldn't manage that. And so his world grew more obscure, the boundaries became blurred by his deepening despair."

She motioned toward a huge mural that covered one of the stone walls. Cracked now and faded, the painting, with its dark Gothic overtones, had been done sometime during the Renaissance by an unknown artist. In the center stood Giovanni and beside him a beautiful, dark-haired woman in a rose-colored taffeta gown. Broken strings dangled from her wrists and fingers, and in her hair were twined shimmering strands of gold thread.

Katarina touched similar gold threads in her own hair. "And then," she told the crowd, "a miracle. As often happened in that magic time, Giovanni's wish was granted." She indicated a black-cloaked figure in the mural, a silhouette only faintly visible in the dusky light. "Late one night Giovanni was visited by a shadowy Italian merchant who appeared suddenly in the vaults below the theater, which had become Giovanni's home.

"'I offer you a bargain,' the merchant said to him. 'The fulfillment of your deepest desire in exchange for this theater that you own. But be warned, my friend. To desire is one thing; to have and to hold, something else. Only through her limitations can you control your precious Mignon. Puppets possess no will save that which you give them. But humans...' He shook a bony finger at Giovanni. 'These beings do not so easily submit. They are real. And to face reality is the greatest risk of all...'"

Raul stirred in the shadows, rousing himself with an effort. It wasn't safe up here, his brain reminded. He must leave.

To face reality is the greatest risk of all...

The words pounded in his head. It hit painfully close to home, and he groaned in his throat. All the twists and turns of his current situation aside, the facts were clear, irrefutable. He was no ghost. To live in the underground vaults was a matter of necessity, nothing more. That was his reality.

He cast one final longing glance in Katarina's direction. He wanted her badly, more so now than when he had first seen her three weeks ago. But he had to go back.

He pushed off from the stone column, and almost staggered into the wall behind. Another mural, another part of the legend. Mignon's escape.

His dark eyes focused on the somber blend of texture, form and color. These were the night shades, dark and intriguing. He would have to come up again and listen to Katarina tell the rest of the tale. But for now the false ghost would return to his underground lair, to search for the answers he would need if he ever intended to rejoin the real world above.

"*MON DIEU*, what a day this has been. Forever and forever it goes on. Soon we will all become puppets who dance at the master's command." Babette Toulon removed the obligatory gold threads from her black hair, sighed, then smiled at her reflection in the vanity mirror.

One mirror in a dressing room shared by three actresses. Riots had started over less.

Katarina unbound her own gold-laced braid and at the same time wriggled out of her layered petticoats. She'd been working at the Puppet Theater for a month now, and she still hadn't gotten used to Babette's constant complaints—or anything else about the woman who played Mignon.

"You are quiet today," Babette observed. She lifted a bottle of red wine to her lips and swallowed with a deliberately loud sound. Wiping her mouth with the back of her hand, she smiled smugly. "Perhaps there is trouble in paradise? You and Philip have had a falling out?"

Katarina managed to control her tongue. Philip Gordon Hambleton was one of the company's performance puppeteers and a prime investor in the current production. He was also the most beautiful man she'd ever met. His maternal grandfather was a titled Briton. His father, though not of aristocratic stock, was also extremely wealthy. Philip was charming, rich and he had hair the color of spun gold. He was a dream come true, and Katarina definitely preferred dreams to reality these days.

With determination, she blocked out the memory of Luther's and Davide's deaths. She'd been in Paris for three years now. She should be able to deal with these thoughts.

Tossing her heavy hair over one shoulder, Katarina pulled on a pair of old jeans and an oversize black sweatshirt. Magic would help the hurt, the magic of Giovanni's legend.

"So quiet today," Babette said again. She twisted around in her chair, her chin resting on the side of her fist. Her black eyes shone with undisguised malice. "Maybe I choose a bad topic. Maybe you would rather discuss more bloody matters. After all, you are new here. So many things our lovely puppet, Vignette, does not yet know about this place. Should we talk about Giovanni's ghost instead, or try to unravel the mystery of Claudia's death? You have heard about the murder? That a woman from wardrobe was killed in cold blood?"

"You're a ghoul, Babette." Louise Grant, an outspoken British actress who played the puppet Verona onstage, strolled into the dressing room, tugging the gold threads from her curly auburn hair. "No one wants to talk about an unsolved, six-month-old murder. It makes them nervous."

Babette took another long drink of wine. "The police do," she said, and ran her tongue lightly over her wet lips.

The sun had begun to set. Its lulling rays spread out over the Opera Quarter, flooding the cramped room with golden light. The smell of powder and cologne hung in the air. Katarina braided her hair loosely, opened a bottle of soda and stretched out on the shabby settee, propping her bare feet up on the arm. But she couldn't help being curious about a murder that no one here seemed anxious to discuss. "Do you know what really happened to this woman?" she asked Louise.

"Yes," Babette answered.

"No," Louise corrected. "Claudia Clercy, who was head of wardrobe, died in the room where many of the old sets are stored. That's all anyone knows about her death."

Katarina brushed several strands of hair that had escaped their braid from her face and swallowed a mouthful of soda. "Maybe Giovanni's ghost did it," she suggested.

"Perhaps," Babette agreed, surprising Katarina with her acceptance of a remark that was not meant to be serious. "Ghosts exist, of course. Maybe they kill as well. But I say it was the architect who did it." She slashed her red fingernails across her throat. "He was her lover. And he comes from Spain." She spit the last word out as if it were profane. "Señor Raul Sennett. He was hired to restore this beautiful theater to its original grandeur, but I knew he would be trouble. They found him over the body, savoring the kill as you say. It is no surprise to me that he has vanished. For six months the police have searched for him. They talked to his family, searched his home in Barcelona.

He will not go there. He is in Casablanca or Marrakech for sure.''

It sounded to Katarina like Babette was sure of many things, including Raul Sennett's guilt.

Louise lowered her lanky body into a hot pink leather chair. One leg dangled carelessly over the chrome arm, but her expression remained tight, serenity masking irritation. ''Your opinion only, Babette,'' she repeated calmly.

Babette sent her a cold smile via the mirror, plucking fitfully at her black curls. ''His fingerprints were all over the knife and we all know about the big fight they had not two hours before she died. I say he did it. So do the police.''

Katarina shoved back the sleeves of her top. It was hot in here and the topic was less than pleasant, but then, so was her curiosity sometimes.

She watched the sun's rays play across the plaster walls, then asked Louise, ''Why don't you think Raul Sennett killed her?''

Babette sniffed. ''Because Louise liked his sexy smile and his dark eyes and his long brown hair. I think he is arrogant and impossible.''

''And sexy,'' Louise murmured.

Babette's eyes narrowed. ''Raul Sennett is a murderer.''

She tipped the wine bottle back again. Katarina heard the slosh of claret and suddenly wished someone would change the topic of conversation.

She sighed and closed her eyes, ignoring the sniping female voices that bounced off the dressing room walls.

''That's right, little miss. Shut it out. . . .''

Luther's soothing voice came back to her. Why couldn't the people you loved live forever?

''He is sexy, I do not deny that.'' Babette broke into Katarina's thoughts, her tone fierce. ''But he killed Claudia. She was my friend. I will see Señor Raul Sennett punished for what he has done, and then I will spit on his grave.''

Having delivered that icy promise, Babette tossed the wine bottle aside and reached for the emerald green jacket that matched her silk trousers. "I am going to Fouquet's," she announced. "Monsier Ian Renshaw, the most-charming manager of this theater, has invited me to an early dinner." Despite her anger, she managed a lofty smile. "So if I am late for the performance tonight, you will know why. *Au revoir, mes amies.*"

It was amazing how she could make the French word for *friends* come out sounding like *peasants.*

Katarina watched the actress flounce through the door, then she crooked her forearm over her eyes to block the setting sun. She had no energy to move from the settee. She would just lie here until it was time to turn into a puppet again.

"Are you coming to Chez Marcel?" Louise asked, cheerful enough now that Babette was gone. "There'll be a lot of us there. Without Miss Attitude around, we might even have fun."

"Probably," Katarina agreed, not stirring. "I might come later."

She felt a tap on her arm and lifting it slightly saw that Louise's layers of costume had given way to a pair of red jeans and a baggy blue sweater.

"Don't fall asleep," her friend warned. Grabbing her leather knapsack, Louise headed for the door. "Chez Marcel," she called back. "Dinner and drinks and tons of good gossip."

"About the disappearing Raul Sennett?"

"He didn't do it."

"So you said."

"But only me, more's the pity. Half an hour, Kati. We'll be waiting."

Katarina winced. Only Luther was allowed to call her Kati. But how could she explain that to one of the few people here that she could call a friend?

The theater fell silent around her, a great soundless tomb, empty now as it usually was between the hours of five and seven p.m. Sun on her face, memory of a thousand long departed performers and thoughts of Giovanni and his beloved Mignon soon had Katarina sliding into a drowsy half slumber.

It was a delicious state, full of blurred pictures. She thought dreamily of Mignon, the puppet and the woman. Magic threads woven into her hair had given her life. Poor Giovanni. His control over her was gone, vanished, like the architect accused of murdering Claudia Clercy...

Katarina woke with a jolt. What a weird thought to have in the middle of a floaty half dream.

Shaking the cobwebs from her head, she linked her fingers and stretched her arms straight up. Her eyes found the face of her watch. 5:45 p.m. If she was going to join her castmates, she'd better do it now. She had to be onstage in full Vignette makeup and costume at eight o'clock.

She slid from the lumpy settee in one smooth motion and wandered over to the closet. She stared at the mess inside that was all Babette's doing, made a face and prayed her sneakers were near the top.

Katarina weeded through a mountain of ruined silk, old tapes, black aerobic gear and gym bags.

Shoving away stray strands of hair with the back of her hand, Katarina took one last look for the elusive sneakers—and spotted them. "Sure," she muttered. They would be right at the back, and stuck behind the water pipe no less.

She crawled into the closet, tugged the sneakers free, then started out. But something made her pause suddenly and stop moving. She tilted her head to one side. Did she hear music? In a closet?

The smell of perfumed clothing filled her head as she knelt there listening. She definitely heard classical music.

She studied the cracked pipe with interest, glanced around, then inched closer, pressing her ear against it. The soft sound of flute and drum keeping time came from somewhere below the theater, from the vaults it seemed.

Bemused, Katarina sat back on her heels. According to just about everyone who worked here, people didn't go into the vaults these days. Rats and ghosts lived down there. *"On your life, Katarina, keep away...."*

But the vaults were Giovanni's world, the dark realm into which he'd taken his then-real Mignon. Maybe he'd gone mad when Mignon left, but madness was a human failing, it couldn't possibly apply to ghosts.

Once again Luther's words came into her head. *"Find the magic, Kati..."*

She eyed the pipe, letting that strange blend of excitement and fear build inside her. She knew she should fight this, put on her sneakers and join her friends at the local bistro. But why would anyone play music deep within the theater's vaults?

A smile touched her lips. It was foolish, but she had to know. And there was only one way to find out. She must go down into Giovanni Verrone's mysterious underground realm.

Chapter Three

If there was one thing Katarina didn't lack it was nerve. Common sense was another matter.

It wasn't wise, this foray into the unknown. There were dark shadows everywhere: on the worn stone staircase behind her, in the rafters above, between the cobwebs that fluttered and danced in the breeze she stirred up. They lurked on the water-stained walls and even among the rows of decrepit wooden shelves that her morbid side compared to medieval mortuary slabs.

She stood motionless at the top of a second staircase, a wooden one this time that descended into a black pit.

Her sneakers were silent on the aged wood. Her flashlight beam played on the stone floor bar below. She could still hear the music, now approaching its final crescendo. If it stopped, so would she. But for now her curiosity lured her downward.

She talked to herself as she descended. "You don't know what you're walking into, Kati. A woman died in this theater. Babette blames an architect, others blame a ghost. What if ghosts can kill?"

She kept going, down the stairs, through a large vacant chamber with rusty chains on the walls.

But maybe she should go back.

The sound of dripping water reached her, at odds with the beautiful music. She saw broken furniture, empty picture frames and finally the head of a porcelain doll. Chopped off by a miniature guillotine? She shuddered.

She felt moisture in the air, and a cool draft that could have come from a dozen different directions. Darkness stretched into infinity as did the passageways ahead. Taking a deep breath, Katarina moved on. One more chamber, then she'd turn around.

The magic had her in its spell. Somewhere in this Gothic labyrinth Giovanni had made his home. Maybe she'd find his puppets. The ones in the Museum were original creations but not the first, not the puppets Giovanni had made.

She sidestepped a gridwork of jointed beams and passed into a cramped room, cluttered with casks and crippled racks that might once have held wine. She went deeper into the room, paused, then lifted her head.

The music played on—but was there another sound beneath it? A soft scrape? A brush of cloth on stone? Or maybe a footstep.

She spun around too quickly. Her hand banged against a piece of rough timber, sending a stab of pain up her arm. She watched the flashlight tumble from her fingers and would have grabbed for it except that suddenly it was no longer there. And the hand that had caught it, though long and slender-boned, definitely belonged to a man.

"Giovanni!" She whispered the name out loud then tried to cover it with an accusing "Who are you?"

Whoever he was, the man stood wreathed in shadows, visible only in silhouette. He had a lean build and was maybe six feet tall compared to Katarina's own five feet six inches.

His shoulders moved in a dismissing gesture. "Not someone you want to know." His voice was low, faintly accented. Her blood chilled.

She hesitated. Please, don't be a killer. If anything, be a phantom.

Katarina stiffened her spine, telling herself not to be so accusing this time. "What are you doing here?"

There was a hint of ironic amusement in his tone when he said simply, "Surviving." He leaned back against one of the giant casks, aiming the flashlight at the floor. "For the moment, these vaults are my home. Why are you here?"

"I heard music." She chose her words carefully. "I thought it came from down here."

"You're not afraid of ghosts?"

Again that trace of humor, and Katarina relaxed the stranglehold on her muscles. "I like ghosts," she said, then something shuffled softly behind her, and she glanced nervously back. "I don't think that's what you are, though."

"We're alone," he said. "And no, I'm not."

Back away, her instincts warned. But how? He stood between her and the door!

Katarina's palms began to perspire. Who but a ghost would choose to live in these gloomy subchambers? Except maybe a murderer!

A shiver swept through her, but she had to stay calm. She could be wrong.

She summoned her courage, wishing she could see his face. "I should be going. My friends know I'm down here. They'll be worried."

He raised the flashlight a fraction, enough for her to glimpse the faded jeans and denim shirt he wore. Cuffs rolled back, a dusting of dark hair on his forearms, slender-boned as she'd first thought, but probably the possessor of deceptive strength. He didn't appear fragile, anyway. He also didn't seem concerned by her statement.

"Your friends are at Chez Marcel," he said softly. "There's no need for you to be frightened, *chérie,* I won't hurt you."

His English was impeccable. Masking her nervousness, Katarina took the light he gave her and tried to see him better without the bright glare in her eyes.

He had dark hair, very long, at least in the back where it curled over the collar of his shirt, narrow features and wonderful hands. She trembled slightly when his fingers brushed hers.

She momentarily forgot her fear. "Do you live down here?" she asked, then paused and said in a small voice, "How do you know my friends are at Chez Marcel?"

He came to stand in front of her. He didn't touch her, but she could feel the heat from his body as surely as if he had. "I listened to your conversation."

Babette's earlier comments returned. A fresh ripple of panic went through Katarina's body. This man's accent was Spanish.

She swallowed the sudden renewed surge of fear and fascination that rose in her throat. "What are you going to do to me?" she asked.

To her amazement, he lifted his hand and gently brushed his thumb across her cheek. "Nothing," he said so softly that she almost didn't hear him.

She trembled, but stayed put. "You mean I can leave?"

He shook his head, his features still obscured by the shadows. "Not just yet, Katarina."

It took every ounce of her self-possession not to panic and shove him out of the way. "How do you know my name?"

It seemed odd that his tone should contain a mixture of weariness and resignation. "I've seen you in the museum," he said. "And on the stage. You should be Mignon. Babette is a prima donna."

"I know. When will you let me leave?" she asked him, for no doubt remained in her mind as to this man's identity. He was the architect, Raul Sennett, the man accused of killing Claudia Clercy.

He didn't answer, and using her fear as a catapult Katarina attempted to duck past him. She stifled a cry when he caught her by the arms and brought her firmly up against him. Thankfully what she could see of his expression appeared patient, almost impassive. And his grip wasn't painful.

"There's no need to run, Katarina," he said when she'd ceased her struggles. "I told you before, I won't hurt you."

His voice was low, quietly reassuring, easy to believe. She twisted out of his grasp without difficulty, watching with an edge of mistrust as his hands dropped back to his sides.

His eyes were visible now, dark and hypnotic and long lashed. And his features were narrow, beautifully boned, his mouth full and sensual. And stamped over all of that was just a hint of arrogance. Something to do with the tilt of his dark brow as he stared at her. Or maybe it was the gleam in his deep brown eyes that gave him such a confident air. Handsome, yes, and sexy. And not a murderer...

That last thought sprang out of nowhere, flashing through her mind with a certainty that surprised her.

Katarina took a deep breath. "What exactly are you going to do to me, Raul Sennett?"

He smiled faintly, but beyond that didn't react to her use of his name. She felt his fingers close about her arm, heard the sigh in his tone when he murmured, "It looks like I'm going to tell you a story."

THIS WAS A FOOLISH act of self-indulgence. But then, Raul had understood that from the start. He'd known it when he decided to play the music, even though he did not want to believe that he would consciously try to lure Katarina down here. Maybe he was delirious.

He felt her behind him in the passageway. *Run from me,* the saner part of his mind willed. Enough damage has been done for one day. It's my fault and for my selfishness I've put you in danger, too.

"Where are we going?" she asked. A cautious question, but she wouldn't run.

"Not much farther," he promised. Yes, this was very foolish of him. She knew exactly who he was. He'd heard Babette's nasty remarks upstairs.

He tipped his head back as he walked, closing his eyes briefly. What was he doing to himself?

He glanced over his shoulder. He still felt like hell, but it would pass soon enough. His aching body had been begging for sleep all through the day, but of course he'd ignored it. Then he'd promptly turned around and made everything worse.

He saw Katarina push absently at the hair that had come loose from its braid and allowed himself a small smile. Not everything was worse. Seeing her this close was more than worth the risk he took.

She was a truly exquisite creature with her delicate features, elegant bones and legs that were longer than his brain had envisioned. Black lashes framed the soft green eyes that stared back at him when he looked around again. Suspicion lurked in those gorgeous eyes, but who could blame her? Babette told a one-sided story. And why not, since she was almost certainly mixed up in whatever schemes had made it necessary for someone in this theater to murder Claudia Clercy.

A wave of dizziness hit him suddenly, affecting both his thoughts and his balance, and he stopped in the passageway, bracing himself against the cool stone wall.

"Are you all right?" Katarina came up beside him. To his surprise, she took his face between her hands, lifting his head until she could see him in the dim light. "Are you sick?"

It was tempting to invite her to play nurse. But he wouldn't give in to that desire.

He should be creeping around upstairs looking for the proof he needed to clear himself of murder, not taking the lovely Katarina on a tour of the vaults.

The dizziness subsided. He forced a dispassionate smile, "It's nothing," he lied, pushing himself from the wall. "A dizzy spell. I'm fine."

"Are you?"

Her hands left his face, and he sighed a little inside. Catching her fingers in his, he brought them slowly up to his lips. "No," he agreed, his dark eyes on hers. "But I will be."

And pushing open a thick oak door ahead of them, he motioned her into his makeshift home.

LA RIVE GAUCHE—the Left Bank. Babette curled her lipsticked mouth in disgust. She hated it over here, especially the view. Ian had promised her dinner at Fouquet's and instead they walked along the Seine, right across from Notre Dame.

It was sacrilege to stare at such a magnificent cathedral and then to talk of robbery. But no, she must not think this way. Religion was her mother's burden, not hers.

She studied Ian now as they walked. Ian Renshaw, London born, manager of the Puppet Theater. He was a tall, stiff-looking man with brown hair like mud, boring features and a drab dresser as well. This was not a person to excite a passionate woman. However, to work with him and his small band of thieves these past eleven months had proved most profitable.

"You said we would go for dinner." She pouted, tired of the silence that stretched between them. How could she be seen by important theater people if they didn't go where the people gathered? "I am hungry."

Ian kept his flat brown gaze focused on the carved facings of the cathedral. "Your stomach doesn't concern me, Babette," he said without emotion. "There are matters we must discuss privately, and this cannot be done over a plate of escargots."

"I hate escargots," she retorted angrily. "And I hate all this caution we must now take." She made an impatient gesture. "Ever since Raul Sennett murdered Claudia, it has been this way. Why don't the police find him?"

"Possibly because they don't know where to look." Ian's eyes gave nothing away when he looked at her, but Babette knew a moment of fear and liked that even less than the architect who had murdered her friend.

But there was no reason for fear. Claudia had been one of Ian's thieves, so her death had had nothing to do with their stealing. Raul Sennett had killed her. Babette would not permit herself to think otherwise.

Although the sun had set, the river beside her still shimmered. Chestnut trees grew to her left. The scent of blossoms floated in the warm air. She saw the flower wagon ahead of them. A white-haired woman in a peasant blouse busied herself arranging colorful pots. Just like Mama. Poor, humming while she slaved to put a loaf of bread on the table. Babette hunched her round shoulders. For her, things would be very different.

Ian had lapsed into silence again. He did that often, and it irritated her. But he would talk more when he was ready.

In the distance she heard weak strains of American music. Her pout grew more pronounced. Katarina Lacroix was an American.

Cool, tragic Katarina. "She is nothing," Babette had said to Ian when this woman appeared.

And yet the owners of the Puppet Theater, Pierre Fousard and Francois Lupier, had thought to cast Katarina in the role of Mignon. "To give you a rest," the elegant Monsieur Lupier had assured her, but Babette had not been born yesterday.

"A fresh face is all they desire," she'd raged at Ian. "Someone new at whom they can leer from their private boxes."

That's when Ian had stepped in.

"Let Katarina be Vignette," he'd suggested, and in the end they had capitulated, although Babette had never really understood why.

Again that frisson of fear passed through her. Ignore it, she thought. Other things matter here. It wasn't merely because of the play that she hated Katarina. No, she had a stronger reason than that, and his name was Philip Gordon Hambleton.

This was the man Babette might have won had it not been for Katarina's arrival at the theater one month ago. Beautiful Philip, with his long golden hair, his eyes blue like the sky, his face so handsome and perfect, his parents so very, very rich....

"I have discussed the situation with the person in charge," Ian announced unexpectedly, breaking into Babette's thoughts and unsettling her in the process. She had never met this mysterious "person in charge". It made for less stress on her nerves to forget his existence whenever possible. But then Ian would remind her, and she would have that uneasy cross to bear along with everything else.

Babette looked hopefully to her companion. "Will we do another robbery? It has been many weeks since our last one, Ian. I am growing quite poor."

"Then this will be to your liking." He smiled but there was no emotion in it.

"Who do we rob this time?" she demanded.

He pursed his thin lips. She glanced around. There was no one but the old woman selling her flowers to hear them. He was too careful.

Suppressing her annoyance, she lowered her voice and tried again. "Please tell me, Ian. I do not like the suspense."

"There will be a backstage party next week, for our wealthiest patrons. The person in charge, the puppet master, will decide then upon our next move. This is all I can tell you."

"But why? Surely you know more. Why can I not know as well? Am I not one of your very best people?"

Ian's bland eyes met hers. "You get angry too easily, Babette."

"That is not true!" she protested in a shrill voice, then immediately clamped her mouth shut. "That is not true," she repeated quietly. "I am most discreet."

He merely stared at her. "Sometimes you say things you should not. The puppet master finds this rather distressing. He wanted me to tell you that he has noticed it and that he is not pleased."

"Then why does he not tell me so himself? We call him the puppet master, Ian, but I am not a puppet. I do not wish to be treated as one."

A smile crossed Ian's tight mouth. He didn't say a word, but quite suddenly Babette saw the irony of her position. She was indeed a puppet, a thing to be controlled. She turned away from the fear taking root in her heart. But she could not so easily hide from the truth.

Chapter Four

"It's positively feudal," Katarina said, staring at the room before her. "It looks like a monk's cell."

Raul nodded downward over a low half wall. "There is a much larger area below. It's austere but livable."

Maybe, Kati conceded. The walls were stone as was the floor. The air was murky and surprisingly fresh considering there were no windows or vents to be seen.

She took stock of the surroundings: army cot, canvas chair, rumpled sleeping bag, battery-powered tape deck, suitcase, cartons filled with files and nonperishable food. There were even lights rigged up, naked bulbs swinging on cords from the ceiling. And behind them, several deep niches in two of the three walls.

Intrigued, Katarina moved closer. Her eyes lit up. "Puppets!" she exclaimed. On several of the shelves sat marionettes with porcelain heads and faded features. "They look ancient and yet they've still got their strings."

Old feelings of magic and make-believe stirred inside her. She heard Luther's gentle voice again as she stared at the puppets, haunting portraitures of the human condition. "I wonder what made Mignon choose to go live in the harshness of the real world?" she said aloud.

Something brushed against her thoughts, a movement near the timbered railing. But she couldn't look away from the puppets.

She touched one, transfixed. Paint still clung to their tiny fingernails and lips. Even with their clothing split by the ravages of time and dampness, they were works of art. The silk and satin costumes were handmade and intricately embroidered, the once bright shades faded now to the softest pastels.

"These are very old," she noted, then asked, "Do you know them? This one is Silvain, the winged nymph. He's guardian of the twins, Vignette and Verona—but you don't have them here. You have Renato, though. We call him the yellow-haired prince. Jo-Jo's here too, he's the jester gnome, Renato's constant companion. The other ones you're missing are Mignon and Giovanni's alter ego, Nicoli."

"Life imitates art," the dark-haired man behind her murmured in vague amusement. It seemed a strange statement. "Is there nothing more pertinent you want to ask me, Katarina?"

She fingered one of the silver bells attached to Jo-Jo's jester costume. "Where did you find these?" It was an automatic response, ridiculous under the circumstances, but then that was her problem. She didn't think. She surely wouldn't be here if she did.

Raul lounged against the low wall, once more engulfed by shadows. "I'm an architect," he said in his low, unhurried voice. "I have the designs to both the theater and the vaults. Many of the passageways down here could not be found without such tools. I discovered these puppets in one of the lower passages."

Why didn't she believe that?

He moved slightly, and Katarina glimpsed the dark hair that curled over his neck. "Isn't there anything else you would like to know?" he asked.

The word *no* almost slipped past Katarina's lips. Maybe she did want to believe that he was a ghost. Maybe it was preferable to the truth.

She turned from the distraction of the puppets to concentrate on the shadow within the shadows. "Did you do it?" she asked with acceptable frankness. "Did you kill Claudia Clercy?"

"No."

Not a trace of rancor in the denial. No bitterness, or even anger.

She pressed her fingers to her temples, pushing gently. "If you didn't kill her, then why are you hiding down here?"

"Because the police are convinced that I did kill her."

"Why here? Paris is a very large city. You could go anywhere."

His shrug dismissed the idea. "This was convenient," he said, combing the fingers of one hand through his hair. "No one, not even the police would think to look for me in these old vaults. And if by chance they did, they would only wind up lost in such a great labyrinth."

Reasonable but not entirely true, Katarina's instincts cautioned.

"Babette said you were caught over the body. Were you?"

Another shrug. "Claudia was dead when I arrived," he said. The words seemed to come from a vast distance. "I was checking for a pulse."

"Your fingerprints were on the knife that killed her."

"It was my knife. If I had wanted to murder her, I could have found a less incriminating weapon with which to do it."

Katarina conceded the point with a slight shiver. She hated the topic of death. "Don't the police find this knife business a bit convenient?" she asked.

A measure of weariness crept into his response. "No, *chérie*, they don't. They think I was caught in the act, that

I would have taken the knife with me if I had managed to elude them."

"How do you know all this?" she asked. Her eyes were on Renato's yellow hair. He looked like Philip. She wondered if Nicoli looked like Raul.

"I read the newspapers."

She played with the Silvain's tangled hair, aware that Raul watched her from the darkness. "So you leave this place sometimes?"

"Sometimes," he agreed. "Not often."

"If you never found the murderer, would you stay down here forever?"

There was no mistaking the absolute certainty in Raul's quiet response. "Not forever, Katarina. And I will prove my innocence."

She left the puppets, moving closer to the wall where he stood. "You expect to do that from the vaults?" She bit the inside of her lip as another thought crept in. "Do you know who did it?"

"I know some things, *chérie.* Nothing I will tell, so please don't ask me. What I do know isn't enough."

With a single easy movement, he left the wall and the shadows and it was all Katarina could do not to gasp. Handsome, sexy, hypnotic. The words raced through her mind, through her body.

She stared at him. His eyes roamed over her face, her cheeks, her mouth, even the strands of hair that had loosened themselves from their braid. Lifting his hand, he smoothed those stray strands back into place.

"*Si belle,*" he murmured, then smiled just a little. "You think I should want to stay here, don't you? Here, where Giovanni hid himself away. Maybe you even think I killed Claudia, but I promise you I did not. We went out for dinner twice and one other time to a cabaret. We did argue before she died, but it was over an unimportant matter. If you had known Claudia, you would also have known that for her this was nothing new. She liked to argue, and I was in a bad mood. From these positions it required very little effort for us to disagree.'' He moved one shoulder in a typically Gallic fashion that Katarina found charming. ''Now you know my side of the story. I didn't kill her, but I can't prove it. And so I live down here until the day when I can find that proof.''

There were probably a dozen things Katarina could have done or said or asked, but right then she couldn't think of a single one. She couldn't seem to stop staring, either, at the way his mouth moved when he spoke, the flashes of light in his dark eyes, the way his brown-black hair curled down over the back of his neck, and of course the touch of his cool fingers on her cheek.

''Why did you let me find you?'' she asked softly, knowing that music or not, she wouldn't have gotten this far if he hadn't wanted her to.

The smile that curved the corners of his mouth was ironic. ''Because I'm human. Sometimes I do things without considering the consequences.''

The heat coming from him was incredible. It was cool in the vaults, and for one rash moment Katarina wanted to press her chilled body against his, to feel the warmth and hardness of his muscles, maybe feel his mouth on hers.

He continued to stroke her cheek, which didn't help at all. With difficulty she took a deep breath and forced her thoughts back into line. ''Will you let me leave here?'' she asked in a hesitant voice.

He seemed surprised. Something flickered deep within his eyes, then vanished. ''I wouldn't hold you against your will. I think you know that much already.''

''But I don't understand. I could tell them about you.''

''Yes, you could. But I don't think you will.'' With a faintly regretful smile, he took her hand in his. ''It's getting late, Kati. I'll walk you back to the stairs.''

She didn't say a word as he guided her through the maze of shadowy passageways until they reached the wooden staircase and he handed her the flashlight once more.

On impulse she put her hand on his arm, forestalling his departure. She felt his warm skin, and beneath it the firm strength of sinewy muscle. "I believe you," she said. "I won't tell them anything."

Again that somewhat sad smile. But this time she felt rather than saw it as his mouth brushed lightly over hers. "I know you won't," he said. And he vanished without a sound into the darkness.

KATARINA SPENT the next four hours trying to rationalize the bizarre encounter. By the time she came offstage at ten o'clock, pulling severed strings from her fingers, she could almost believe that none of it ever happened. Almost.

Behind her, gliding back and forth across the stage with its dark screens, its medieval murals and eerie lighting was Morden, nighttime narrator of Giovanni's legend. He told the story, the puppets acted it out. He was the specter in the shadows, the link between players and audience. But Morden couldn't begin to compare with the shadowy man in the vaults.

"Bourgeoisie, pah! These people are peasants." Babette stomped from the stage in a temper. "What do they know of symbolism? They appreciate nothing. Go away from me," she snarled in the same breath to one of the young pages who, in the tradition of eighteenth-century French theater, drew the red velvet curtains across the stage. Lifting her head, Babette appealed to Ian Renshaw, an ever-present figure in the wings. "I cannot go back out there before these stupid people. You must not make me."

Calm as always, Ian lit one of the Gauloises cigarettes that invariably made Katarina choke. He sent Babette a heavy-lidded look, then watched without reaction as she spun angrily around to do her performing duty.

When she was gone, he blew on the cigarette's glowing tip and arched a brow at Katarina. "You're enjoying your work here, I presume? No problems to report?"

Katarina forced a smile. "It's very satisfying," she said.

"And Babette? You get along with her?"

Tact was one thing, but lying... "No. Did you expect I would?"

"I have no expectations, Katarina." A thin stream of smoke spiraled into the deep mauve spotlight. "I merely hoped that Babette would make a new friend. She needs a confidante, someone to whom she can complain."

"A replacement for the late Claudia Clercy?"

Ian's eyes slid to her face. "You've heard about Claudia, then. From whom, I wonder? Few people in this theater are willing to talk about her."

"Babette is," Katarina told him. "She says that Claudia was murdered by the architect who was hired to restore the theater."

"But you disagree."

"It isn't a question of disagreement, Ian. It just seems to me that the evidence against this man is awfully convenient. A public argument, being found over the body, his fingerprints on the knife." She almost said "his" knife, but caught herself in time. Babette hadn't mentioned that detail. "What I'm saying is that maybe the police shouldn't be so single-minded in their search."

"I see." Ian's smile was tight-lipped. "And you drew all these conclusions from the information Babette gave you?"

Now she lied. "Yes."

Drawing deeply on his cigarette, Ian faced the stage and the unearthly blue illumination that signaled the end of the play. "If I were you, Katarina, I wouldn't listen to anything Babette might say. She talks a great deal, but she's not the most reliable source. Raul Sennett did murder our Claudia. Soon enough, the police will find him and he'll be sent to prison, which is no less than he deserves."

"Doesn't he deserve a trial first?" Katarina began, but cut herself off when she caught sight of long, golden blond hair in her peripheral vision. In his customarily cheerful fashion, Philip Hambleton bounded down the winding wooden staircase from the rafters where he gave his performance as a puppeteer.

"Good crowd tonight, wouldn't you say?" He unrolled the sleeves of his white silk shirt. Even in full stage makeup he was a spectacular looking man, flawless to the last detail. One china blue eye winked at Katarina. "What do you say? Dinner tonight since you missed out at Chez Marcel?"

Katarina started to nod, then hesitated. In her mind she saw a male figure. But his hair wasn't the color of spun gold, and his eyes, though beautiful, were definitely not blue.

She touched her fingers to her lips. Strange that she could still feel the imprint of his mouth where it had brushed across hers...

And then it hit her what Raul had said. "Kati." She hadn't noticed that earlier, which was truly amazing. Maybe she should find him again, make sure he was real, that she hadn't brought Giovanni Verrone to life in some twilight fantasy.

Philip's arm encircled her waist. "Auberge des Deux Signes." He whispered the name of her favorite restaurant in her ear. "Picture it, love. We'll dine in the age of our medieval ancestors, talk of music and Muses and anything else you wish. And then over cake and champagne we'll gaze at the Notre Dame and wonder about the ghosts that haunt the sacristy." He pulled her with gentle insistence against his taut body. "Say you'll come."

A symphony of light and sound swirled around her, like the smoke from Ian's cigarette, a great shimmering cloud that seemed to draw Katarina into its vortex. How easy it would be to get lost in all of this, immersed in the escape Philip offered.

And maybe for tonight, Katarina needed to be lost. So many questions haunted her, a thousand nebulous thoughts. And it was mid-May—the month she'd married Davide. She tried very hard at this time of year to forget that tragic mistake. She never quite could.

Katarina squeezed her eyes closed. Yes, she craved a diversion, the enchanting kind that only Philip could supply. Besides, she enjoyed his company.

Ian was watching her, she realized suddenly. Without really appearing to, he waited for her decision. Philip Hambleton had a great deal of money to toss around. The more he chose to throw in the direction of the Puppet Theater, the better Ian and the two owners liked it. Mercenary manipulators. And they called Philip a performance puppeteer.

"Katarina?" Philip pressed again, completely ingenuous.

Shaking her dark thoughts away, Katarina smiled and nodded. "Of course," she said, ignoring the satisfaction in Ian's expression—and the oddest feeling that someone very close by was not at all pleased with her decision.

Chapter Five

He wasn't alone in the vaults tonight.

Raul knew that long before he reached his temporary living quarters. Six months of stealth, of prowling around in gloomy passageways and theater shadows had given him this sixth sense or at least honed his instincts to a fine edge. Someone was waiting for him in the darkness ahead.

He moved on in silence, his hair damp, his denim shirt replaced by a navy blue cotton T-shirt. He was cleaned up, but in a foul mood and still troubled by an elevated temperature. Maybe he should turn himself over to the Paris police and be done with this mess. What was the difference between these vaults and a French jail cell?

His mind offered a few answers but none more poignant than the name that would probably haunt him forever. Katarina. His beautiful love, never to be truly his unless he could figure out who had killed Claudia—then find evidence to prove it.

The thick oak door stood open a notch. From behind he caught soft strains of music. No one else would hear—the speakers had to be positioned in a certain way beneath the theater's old air vents for that to happen—but the selection didn't improve his mood one bit.

He slipped soundlessly into the room. As expected, his secret ally was seated in the sling-backed chair, a glass of wine in one hand, a half-eaten cream pastry in the other.

"All the comforts of a hotel," Louise noted dryly, turning off the music with her foot. "Right down to a private shower."

Raul tossed his wet towel onto the end of the cot and scooped up a bottle of water. "Why are you here?"

"I came for your laundry."

"At midnight?"

She shrugged her angular shoulders. "I thought you might want to talk."

"I'd rather sleep."

"Which you should. But you won't, and I know why."

"Do you?" He dropped onto the cot.

Louise propped her feet up, sipping her brandied wine. "You're asking for trouble, love. I like Katarina very much, but she's out of your reach right now. Solve the big problems first, worry about your love life later. And don't go dragging her into this debacle."

"I wouldn't do that, Louise." Raul tipped his head back, easing the tension in his neck. "I don't want to hurt her."

"I know that. I also know you. You want this woman. And what you want you go after. A fine quality, I'll agree, except that you happen to be wanted for murder. You're living in the vaults under the Puppet Theater, searching for proof that someone upstairs did what you've been accused of doing. You've no time to be infatuated. Besides, your prowling tonight was all for nothing. She's having dinner with Philip."

Raul slouched against the stones, swallowing a mouthful of the bottled water and masking a grimace. "I know."

"I know you know. And you shouldn't. Why do you think I'm screaming at you?" She rose gracefully from her chair and came to sit beside him. "Katarina's had enough pain in her life, Raul. And Lord knows you've had more than your share lately. Be smart for once. Leave things be until after this murder business is resolved. She's not going anywhere."

The wall felt like a block of ice through Raul's shirt. It cooled his skin and his irritation. It didn't alter his problems. Neither did belated advice, and Louise should know that by now.

"All right," she said, pressing a bite of gooey pastry to his lips. "At least eat something, then. You'll feel better."

He gave her a dark look and took a reluctant bite. She was worse than his sister.

Wincing, Raul pushed the pastry away and with it all thoughts of the people he missed in his native Spain. He couldn't see them, couldn't even communicate with them beyond the message he'd sent five months ago to his brother, Riccardo. He was alive and in a safe place. He'd come home when the truth came out.

And he would bring Katarina with him!

Louise finished the pastry then picked up her wine and polished that off, too. "Have you learned anything more since we talked last week?"

"Nothing, except that I'm convinced Renshaw's in charge of the lackeys."

"Like Babette?"

"Among others, including Claudia."

"Cozy up to the theater's wealthy patrons, learn all their secrets, then turn around and rob them blind." There was no humor in Louise's chuckle. "All done with absolute discretion and no one suspects a thing—except us, of course." She frowned. "You know, being the unoriginal creature he is, I'm amazed that Ian could mastermind such a plan let alone organize it."

"He didn't."

"Hardly surprising. So who really runs the show? And please don't say Babette."

Raul smiled faintly. "When I figure it out, I'll let you know."

Louise handed him her glass. "Maybe you'll get lucky and it'll be Philip. Katarina's not the marry-a-murderer type."

Something twisted in Raul's stomach, but he kept his expression bland. "I thought you wanted me to stay away from Katarina."

"Fat lot of good my warnings ever do. I've known you far too long to be fooled. Your family and my family—friends for three generations, remember? You say you don't want to hurt Katarina and I believe you. But I don't want to see you hurt, either. And that you'd bloody well better remember." She kissed his hair. "End of lecture. Now, do you need anything besides the impossible?"

He moved a shoulder. "If the night watchman's not there, you could change a few puppets around in the museum."

She laughed. "What for?"

"To make them wonder."

"About ghosts? I don't think so, love. Whoever's pulling the strings here isn't likely to be spooked easily."

"I had someone else in mind," Raul said.

Louise's eyes darkened, then cleared. She grinned. "Very cruel, Raul. Babette will be pulling her hair out by month's end if she thinks Giovanni's on the wander."

Raul looked at the tattered puppets in their niche. Several were missing, but they could turn up any time.

Louise lifted her head. "Did you hear something?"

Raul smiled to himself. Sofia was slipping. "No," he lied. He allowed a trace of weariness to enter his voice.

Louise took his face in her hands as Katarina had done earlier and kissed his lips as he wished Katarina had done earlier. "Be careful," she warned. "You're playing a very dangerous game here. Try not to forget it."

Raul sent her a smile. "Dangerous," he agreed. "But worth it."

THEY NEVER MET in Passy, Ian noticed. That was where the person in charge lived, the most elegant district in Paris. It was always some other place, away from home. Today's selection was the Café Blanc across from a dingy little market in a section of the city no tourist would ever visit.

A heavyset woman in black stockings shuffled over to glare at him. "Coffee," he said, quietly. "And a croissant. Hot." She surveyed his brown suit with something akin to contempt, sniffed, then shuffled off.

Ian had long ago become accustomed to such rude treatment. He'd decided that he must be one of those individuals who, no matter how hard they tried, simply rubbed people the wrong way, including the man to whom he reported.

"Good morning, Renshaw." The person in charge materialized at Ian's sidewalk table. "You're early."

No, he wasn't. Ian stared blank-faced at the cobbled street and all the grubby photographers who were tacking up their pictures. No point hoping for respect he would never get. "You told me to watch Babette," he said.

"Yes."

"She's been talking to the new American actress, Katarina Lacroix."

The puppet master smiled charmingly at the black-stockinged woman then picked up Ian's coffee and took a long sip. "By talking, I assume you mean discussing matters that she should not. What has she said?"

"Nothing damaging, but she seems rather stuck on the subject of Claudia's death." Ian paused as the man took a bite of croissant. "I trust you're enjoying my breakfast."

He shouldn't have said that. The person in charge disliked polite sarcasm. And he could be quite dangerous, as Ian well knew.

"You push our relationship, my friend," the puppet master warned silkily. "Tell me what I wish to know, or remove yourself from my sight."

Ian sighed and made his tone appropriately servile. "Babette's becoming suspicious of the circumstances surrounding Claudia's death. She talks in fear and anger to Katarina. And I need hardly add that the police have been entirely unsuccessful in their search for Raul Sennett. If I might make a suggestion, I think it's time we took matters into our own hands, hired our own detectives to flush the man out."

"Imbecile," his companion muttered, sending him a cold look. "Do you honestly believe I have not already done this?"

Ian's lips thinned, but he hid the reaction. "In that case, perhaps you'll allow me to make another suggestion."

"What is it?" The man sounded annoyed now.

Ian proceeded carefully. "Perhaps we shouldn't use Babette for awhile."

As expected, the person in charge waved this idea away. "She is part of our operation. She will remain active until I decide otherwise. Now to business. Our wealthiest patrons will attend a performance at the theater this next Thursday evening. I've invited them to our backstage party where, at my instruction, you will do your usual job of ferreting out whatever information we still need from them. Do you understand, Ian?"

Words spoken as if to a child. Ian set his somewhat pointed jaw. "I understand," he said. And wished he dared throw the remains of his coffee in the other man's face.

"GOOD AFTERNOON, Katarina." Pierre Fousard and Francois Lupier, owners of the Puppet Theater, both greeted her when she walked across the deserted stage. They sat in the audience seats, Pierre, with his long brown hair that he usually wore in a ponytail hanging loose for a change, and Francois the more dignified figure, several rows back, a mere silhouette in the shadows.

"How are you today?" Pierre asked absently.

His head was bent over papers and files, his white shirt sleeves were rolled back, his linen vest was open and one booted leg was hooked over the chair arm. Before she could answer, he flung the file he was studying to the floor.

"What is this nonsense?" he demanded, presumably of Francois. "I will not have a man from Venezuela restoring this theater. It is sacrilege. Speak to Ian, Francois. Raul Sennett surely cannot be the only capable architect in all of Europe."

Katarina saw Francois's elegant shoulders move. "What can I say to Ian that he does not know? You hired Raul Sennett, my friend. I was not consulted. True, Ian is no judge of these matters, but there is luck to consider. Perhaps this person from Venezuela is very good."

"And how many Gothic châteaux will he have restored?" Pierre scowled. "Talk to Ian, Francois, before I do, because *if* I do I will surely say things his ears will not wish to hear."

The shadow that was Francois stood with a kind of fluid grace that made Katarina think of an old-world vampire. Smooth, almost boneless. "As you wish," he said. He sounded amused. "Perhaps this time we will find an architect who does not murder young women in his spare time?"

"Enough." Pierre's dark eyes smoldered. "I am not the only one in this theater who has made errors in judgment."

If there was an underlying significance to that remark, it escaped Katarina. Without a word, Francois dissolved into the darkness while Pierre dumped the remaining papers he held on the floor and strode off in the opposite direction.

Katarina turned toward the Puppet Museum, her peasant skirt and petticoats catching at her ankles. Her mind was a jumble of thoughts, things that shouldn't be bothering her, but were.

Raul Sennett. Had he really been as handsome as she remembered, or did he just remind her of Giovanni, of the way she pictured the medieval puppet master? Maybe she'd built this mysterious man in shadows into something he wasn't.

She let the thought go as she entered the hushed environs of the Puppet Museum. It was so peaceful in here, so quiet. She loved it.

It was empty now. The last tour group had been ushered out the doors fifteen minutes ago.

It was 4:45 p.m., another glorious Paris-in-the-springtime day. The sun that shone through the cracked stained glass window had a soothing quality about it. Katarina was tempted to grab all the puppets from their locked cases and start playing with them on the stone floor. Or maybe she could go down to the vaults and play with an entirely different set of puppets...

"No," she whispered out loud. She'd gone through this at dinner last night. She would think of Philip, not Raul.

Philip was a very sweet man. Maybe too sweet?

The clang of an iron gate far ahead broke the silence in the museum. She heard voices, a man's and a woman's and then another sound, something closer that followed the approaching footsteps by only a few short seconds.

Katarina halted beside one of the massive stone columns. The female voice was Babette's. Naturally she sounded upset.

"I tell you I saw this thing with my own eyes," Babette was insisting loudly. "I do not have hallucinations. The puppets, they are wrong."

Puppets, wrong? Katarina glanced at the case behind her. Or rather she started to. Before she could bring the display into full focus someone's hand came down over her mouth. At the same time a strong arm hooked itself around her waist, snatching her back into a warm, hard body.

Her reaction was automatic, an elbow in the ribs, a kick with her heel. She would have bitten the hand next, but a low voice in her ear stopped her.

"Kati, it's me. I'm not going to hurt you, but you must be quiet."

It was difficult to be otherwise with his hand covering her mouth. She stopped struggling, then felt herself being drawn deeper into the shadows.

He held her tightly against him, his body pressed into hers. The close, intimate contact made her dizzy. She didn't move a muscle or fight him in any way.

"Look there," Babette announced in triumph. "Vignette and Verona, the twins, they sit facing the glass walls instead of each other." Katarina heard a swish of skirts on the other side of the column, and the tiny quaver of fear in Babette's voice. "You see, Ian? I did not make this up. Renato, he is not right, either. I tell you, someone has moved them. Someone—or something."

Katarina couldn't see Ian's face, but she could imagine his expression. Right then, however, she had her hands full just standing still. Oh, she wanted to move, all right, but not away from Raul as her brain instructed.

His breath came into her ear. "Don't squirm, *chérie,*" he whispered softly. "They're very close."

So was he. Katarina wriggled despite the warning. He was close and frighteningly seductive. She must not relax against this man. At least she shouldn't enjoy it.

"You think this something is a ghost?" Ian addressed Babette's fears. "That's nonsense. There are no ghosts, and if there were they wouldn't waste time moving puppets."

"Explain it to me then," Babette insisted. Her voice grew shrill. "How does this happen if not through Giovanni?"

"You're acting like a child, Babette," Ian snapped. "There are no ghosts. And these outbursts of yours don't sit well."

"With *him?*" Babette challenged, and Katarina felt Raul's body stiffen slightly.

Babette spun away in anger, stomped her foot and made a rude remark in French, something about how different it would all be if she was the puppet master. An odd comment, Katarina thought.

"Please, Ian," Babette implored, whirling back to face him. "You must look into this for me. How can I work under such conditions? How can I think?"

She made a good point, Katarina decided. A tremor ran through her as Raul shifted position. She felt on the edge of some emotion she couldn't pin down. Then Raul's mouth brushed lightly over her cheek and the elusive feelings gave way to a more urgent sensation.

Who cared about Babette or Ian? She was plastered against Raul's hard chest, his hair was like silk on her face and his mouth, his beautiful sexy mouth was touching her skin, making her feel things she couldn't begin to describe.

But what if he'd lied to her? A murderer would be good at that. She believed in his innocence, but then she believed in Giovanni, too. A smart person would push his arm from her waist, his warm mouth and hair from her face.

"They're leaving, *chérie,*" Raul murmured, and this time his lips moved against her ear. She felt the warmth of his breath, the heat from his slender body. She closed her eyes and melted into him.

For a moment Katarina had the strangest sensation of drifting through darkness. To the vaults and Giovanni's shadowy world?

The iron gate clanged again, and reluctantly Katarina forced her eyes open. An ancient mural towered over her. Sunlight poured through the stained glass windows, heating the stone floor and brightening the shadows.

Turning, she saw Raul's face, his handsome features still slightly tanned despite his underground confinement. Dark brows, dark hair, just a little curly, and those incredible dark eyes....

A smile she couldn't quite read touched his lips. His eyes were unfathomable, beautiful, as he placed his hands on either side of her face and slid his thumbs lightly across her cheekbones.

"You should have run, Kati," he said softly. And drawing her firmly against him, he covered her mouth with his.

Chapter Six

One small kiss shouldn't take her breath away. But it did, it left her startled and speechless when Raul lifted his head and the heat from his mouth was suddenly no longer there. She wanted to pull him back, but even that simple act was beyond her.

She stared, shocked, then saw a rueful smile curve his lips. With his knuckle he stroked her cheek. "Another mistake, I think," he murmured obscurely. And then he was gone. Like a ghost....

There was no sign of him in the shadows. Where had he gone? To the vaults through a secret passageway?

Katarina leaned against the column. She needed to regain her composure before she faced anyone.

She raised her eyes to the puppet display. Yes, the puppets were wrong. But who would change them around? For what reason?

Maybe Raul had moved them. It seemed a plausible explanation considering that he'd been here when she arrived—but all it really did was lead to more questions.

She didn't waste time making a list. That was pointless. She would talk to Raul, get to the truth that way.

Katarina pushed off from the massive column, determined. She was going to help Raul prove his innocence. There was no valid reason to do it, of course, but to help him seemed important somehow. She preferred not to let her thoughts go deeper than that.

She headed for the theater and her dressing room. Her slippers made no sound on the stone floor.

The dressing room door stood open slightly. To her surprise, Katarina caught a tiny noise from inside. It sounded like a rusty giggle.

It couldn't be Babette or Louise. And no one else had any business being in that room, not even the cleaning crew.

A ripple of alarm passed through Katarina's body. She paused, her hand pressed to the wall. There were no allies in the vicinity, no sound to be heard anywhere, except in her dressing room five feet ahead.

"Pretty," an unfamiliar voice said, a crackly, old, female voice. A door creaked. The closet?

Katarina inched forward, breath held. Still there was no one in sight, and no sound beyond the rattle of hangers in the closet. She was an impertinent intruder, whoever she was.

Katarina crept into the room. It should be safe. The crazy person was in the closet, the open door was behind her. She'd be able to escape, especially if the woman was as old as she sounded.

From behind a rack of Babette's clothes Katarina caught a flash of motion. A pair of black tights landed on the floor at her feet.

"Ugly," the voice declared.

Babette's black gym bag flew out. Katarina had to duck to avoid it. Then more clothes sailed passed. That did it!

"For heaven's sake, stop that! Who are you?" Annoyed now, Katarina shoved the closet door open wide.

All movement ceased instantly. Katarina narrowed her eyes. "Look, I know you're in there, so you might as well come out and save us both a lot of—"

She broke off as a face suddenly appeared from between two dresses. And what a face it was. Beyond old, this creature looked positively ancient. And tiny. She couldn't have been more than four feet, eight inches tall and no heavier than eighty pounds.

The word pixie sprang to mind as Katarina stared at her—and was stared back at, she realized. Her gaze fastened on a pair of brightly curious eyes, blue and uncommonly alert for someone who must surely be more than one hundred years old.

Katarina found her tongue as the woman who'd crept out from behind the dress rack hesitated. In the end a bewildered "Who are you?" was the best she could manage. How could she yell at an elf in rough peasant's clothes who beamed at her with chipped teeth and dancing eyes and skin that looked like wrinkled tissue?

"You are Katarina." Definite blend of accents, but nothing Katarina could place.

She nodded warily. "Have we met?"

"No." The woman took a step forward. She wore a pair of tiny, black lace-up boots and thick brown stockings with holes. There was no hint of a wobble in her walk. "Katarina." She blinked but kept staring. "Were your parents Russian?"

"I beg your pardon?"

"Russian, you know, from the old Soviet Union."

"I know where Russia is."

"Of course you do. All young people do. It was not the same in my day. We were not so aware. But I knew a Katarina once, she came from Moscow, and that's why I ask you this question."

"I see."

The woman cackled. "No, you don't, but it is—how do you people from America put it—okay? I went over there once, on a boat, to a city called Boston. I liked this city. But Salem, I didn't like so much. I heard they burned witches there. Always it was women they would burn, as if men cannot be evil. I don't think a real witch would let herself be burned, do you? But that is a man for you. They pretend to know everything, at least the men in my day did.

"I know one young man who is very nice, very sweet and sexy. I know many old ones who are not so sexy. There is a place by the river, an old basement under a barn, where we meet. I get to this place from the vaults. I don't know if my sexy young friend could do this. He's very smart, but there is only one other who knows the vaults as I do. He does not come up here much. I think he's not so curious as me."

Katarina was lost. "Who doesn't come—?" she began, then she interrupted herself. "Wait a minute, what are you doing?"

The woman was going through Babette's makeup drawer. "Pretty," she exclaimed, holding up a gold compact. "Can I have it?"

"Well, it isn't really mine to give."

"Does it belong to the woman with the black curls?"

"Babette? Yes."

"Then I will take it." The compact disappeared into the pocket of a ratty gray cardigan, the front of which bagged almost to the woman's knees. "Tell her Sofia stole it if she asks."

"Sofia. Is that your name?"

"It's the one I use." She picked up a perfume bottle and sniffed. "I have many names. Don't you?"

"Two." Katarina ignored the minor theft, but warned, "If Babette finds you going through her things, she's liable to call the police."

Sofia's laugh was gleeful. "She would have an old woman arrested? What a monster she is."

Katarina watched as Sofia picked up a cosmetic brush and began applying powder to her lined face. She wore a paisley kerchief tied under her chin. Her hair was a steel gray, thick and braided. The tail hung past the bottom of her sweater. Katarina was fascinated. What a strange woman.

Sofia looked around, located a new item of interest and darted over to the small refrigerator in the corner. "You have food, here? Can I have some?"

"Help yourself."

Immediately, Sofia unwrapped a package of cheese and started to chew.

"Do you think I am a starving person?" she asked suddenly, surprising Katarina. "Is that why you stare at me so strangely?"

Katarina blushed. "I'm sorry. Was I staring?"

"Yes, but I understand."

"Are you a street person?" Katarina asked.

"No."

"Do you live in the vaults?"

Sofia grinned and broke apart a puffed pastry. "I do not like to tell where I live."

Katarina smiled. "Do you want me to tell Babette about the compact?"

The pastry muffled Sofia's feisty "I like you. Yes, I live in the vaults, but no, I will not tell you where. If that worries you, it shouldn't. I am sixty-four years old, you know."

"Really?"

"No." Sofia licked whipped cream from her fingers. She laughed. "I am also a terrible liar. You like ghosts?" she asked.

"Love them."

"I thought so. You make good stories when you walk with people in the museum. I know parts of the legend that you do not, but who would pay to hear an old woman talk about dead creatures? Have you seen Giovanni?"

"Excuse me?"

Sofia broke open a loaf of coarse French bread. "Giovanni's ghost. Have you seen him? You went to the vaults yesterday to meet my sexy young friend, didn't you?"

Katarina tipped her head to one side. "How do you know I went there? For that matter, how do you know Raul?"

"I saw you. And I know about him because he lives in the vaults. I like him. His eyes tell me that he is no killer. He has beautiful eyes. Have you ever looked into them? They are not cold like the snake."

"Any specific snake?" Katarina asked carefully.

But Sofia merely shook her head.

"I do not know who killed the creature with the yellow hair. You did not answer me before. Have you seen Giovanni?"

"No," Katarina said. "Have you?"

An unreadable smile, sly in a way, split the woman's face. "Yes and no."

That was a nice ambiguous answer. "So it's true what they say about his ghost wandering around down there?"

"I believe it is true. My friend with the beautiful dark eyes does not. Maybe when he is old he will. I think he looks as Giovanni did in his youth, but he has very different ideas about how he would live his life. He doesn't wish to be confined under the ground. I understand this. I wasn't always old myself. How can forever darkness be to the liking of any young person? For me, it is different. I've seen many things. Perhaps I am today as Giovanni was when he was alive. Tired of ugliness, ready for the mysteries of the dark."

"That sounds clever." Katarina thought about it. "What does it mean?"

"I don't know."

"But you just said..."

Sofia swallowed her bread and leapt nimbly to her feet. "I must go," she announced. "The bells say six o'clock, and I hear someone far away down the hall."

Katarina glanced at the open door. She didn't hear anything.

On the threshold, Sofia glanced left then right then back at Katarina. "You think about what I have said," she instructed. "I am old, yes, but I'm not blind. My eyes have seen much."

More clever remarks. Katarina had no idea what any of them meant. "I'll think about it, Sofia," she promised anyway. But when she looked up, she realized she was talking to the air. Just as Raul had done earlier, the old woman had vanished.

Katarina looked absently about the messed up room. It took a moment to register, and even when it did it was only another mysterious item to be put on the ever-growing list.

Sofia was gone, but she hadn't left empty-handed. Not only had she taken the gold compact, she'd taken Babette's black gym bag and leotard, too.

RAUL CROUCHED at the top of the stone staircase, hidden behind an oak armoire in Ian's office. Renshaw was involved in Claudia's murder, Raul knew that. But to whom did the puppet report?

Dislodging the back panels carefully, he stepped inside, waited, but sensed no movement beyond the doors. Good.

He slipped out of the wardrobe. It was advantageous that the pattern of Ian's life was so predictable.

He doubted there would be anything to find; there never was. But who could say what small item might prove important? He didn't expect diaries with confessions of murder, but then Raul couldn't see Ian being the one to actually have stabbed Claudia. That would have been the puppet master's deed.

He glanced briefly out the window, then let his eyes fall closed. Bloodthirsty ghoul. Claudia had not died pleasantly, or quickly. He could still picture her corpse, the work of a butcher. She had been stabbed at least a dozen times.

Raul opened his eyes to the splendor of the city. He didn't want to think these things, but the more pleasing danger was no less disturbing. To get Katarina involved was to risk having her wind up like Claudia, and then nothing he could do, not even killing the person responsible with his bare hands, would be able to alter that.

Shuddering, he turned to the desk and began opening drawers that were laid out with scrupulous care. There were scripts and documents and strategically dog-eared paperback novels inside, all things he had found in his three previous searches. The books were for show only. Ian didn't read classics. His tastes ran to the porno magazines tucked far in the back of the bottom drawer.

Raul flipped through one of them, pausing in the center. This wasn't art.

He jammed the magazines back and moved on to a high corner cabinet. He found nothing there except theater posters, a puppet and finally the wall safe combination mixed up in a folder with many other papers. Ian was so unoriginal. Unfortunately, today as always the only item of note in the safe was a brown leather address book. Many prominent names were listed there, but that discovery was an old one for Raul.

The Puppet Theater had a number of rich patrons. Someone had decided to capitalize on that fact. Discreetly of course. The police had no idea who was behind the recent rash of robberies, but then, why should they? The security secrets wormed out of the unsuspecting patrons would surely be done in a clever fashion or this arrangement would have collapsed long ago.

How was it done, though? Raul could imagine a few inventive ways. But proof was a thing he didn't have.

"*Santa Maria,*" he murmured in a weary half prayer. He believed in God and justice; he also believed that the truth would come out. But when?

He set his jaw as he shut the safe, leaving the address book inside. No point in taking that, and the money Ian stashed there meant nothing to him. Raul had money. He did not have freedom.

The tap of flat leather soles in the corridor broke into his thoughts. Someone approached! He shoved the concealing portrait back over the safe and ducked swiftly into the wardrobe.

The person outside slowed, then stopped. The door handle turned. It must be Ian.

Raul considered a new tack—choke a confession from Renshaw's throat. Tempting, but he preferred not to be so violent. Yet.

The door opened with a bang and a man strolled in. Raul glanced through the slats in the armoire, eyes narrowed. Not Ian. Philip Hambleton, the spoiled prince with the moneyed father.

Chuckling, Philip sauntered over to the desk and tossed a piece of paper on the top, "It means so much to you, doesn't it, Ian?" he said. "You want to feel important. Well, here's a bit of importance for you." Another chuckle. He flipped open Ian's silver cigarette case and helped himself. "Thanks, old man." He gave the empty chair a mock salute. "I know how you love to share with your friends."

The humorous gleam in Philip's eyes reached Raul across the room. There was something behind it, but he would consider that another time. The note on the desk, this was more immediately important.

He waited in the armoire, impatient, while Philip smoked the cigarette and then lifted a bottle of Bordeaux from Ian's private stock. "More thanks, old chap. This will be put to good use, I promise." The door clicked shut behind him.

Raul felt himself snarling with frustration and pent-up anger. With the heel of his hand he shoved the armoire open, unconcerned about the resounding crash of wood. Let Philip hear it and come back. It would give Raul the chance to wipe that grin from his face. "You won't get Katarina," he vowed.

He shook himself. Forget those things. Go back to the desk. What does Philip's note say?

Raul flipped the paper open. Café Faustine, it read. Jean and Jeanne Duperay, owners. Boulevard Saint-Michel.

He recognized the address in the Latin Quarter, but not the names or the café. Perhaps this meant nothing, but Raul committed the words to memory anyway, and returned the note to Ian's desk.

He heard the soft scrape behind him too late. Someone was at the door, about to enter the office. Raul tensed. There was no time to reach the wardrobe. He swore silently and ran for the office door that opened inward.

It was no good. He was trapped. He would be seen. He had to think fast. How could he get out of here unnoticed?

The room was stuffy with the early evening sun pouring full force through the windows. Raul's hair clung to his neck and forehead. The orange rays blinded. Would they blind the person who came in?

The door swung back. Raul's head came up. He smelled Drakkar Noir cologne, saw a flash of brown suit. Ian!

Damn this man to hell. Raul swore under his breath. Renshaw closed the door, then locked it. The trap was sealed.

Chapter Seven

The door was closed, bolted. No chance now of escaping undetected. That left only one option.

"Bloody hell," Raul muttered to himself, his muscles tightening instinctively.

Five strides carried him to the desk. Ian was there already and about to turn. Raul couldn't allow that to happen.

He launched himself from the wall. Ian's head came up. He looked sharply right but couldn't have seen clearly the man who wrenched one arm up high on his back. He cried out, but only for an instant. Then Raul's hand was on his neck, slamming his head with force into the nearest wall.

Ian's body slumped to the floor.

Raul looked down. Frankly, he found the sight of Ian lying there unconscious strangely pleasurable. Raul wasn't cruel, but perhaps he had become a little colder, a little harder, since his confinement to the vaults.

He gave himself another shake. No time for dark thoughts. This had to look like a burglary. Rifle the desk and the cabinet, he told himself. Force the safe. Take the money and of course Ian's watch and wallet. Leave the address book and Philip's note. Wipe away all fingerprints.

Then go back to the vaults?

Raul debated for a moment, glancing sideways at Ian's body. He saw no sign of consciousness returning soon and two other offices were close by, those of the theater's owners, Francois Lupier and Pierre Fousard. Only a very stupid thief would rob Ian and overlook two more lucrative targets.

Letting his head fall back to ease the tension in his neck muscles, Raul regarded the high plaster ceiling. Then he closed his eyes and sighed. There was no choice. He must ransack the other two offices.

HOW QUIET IT WAS up on the fifth floor of the theater, Katarina thought. This was the private level, an unearthly sanctuary from city noise. Cool stone corridors branched off in a dozen directions to rooms that had been boarded up more than two centuries ago. And inside them, what? Dusty furniture? Cobwebbed puppets? Or silent secrets only.

"Riddles like Sofia," she murmured as she passed Ian's office.

Actually she tiptoed past, praying he wouldn't slither out. There was something about him she didn't like. Besides, it was really Francois Lupier she'd come to see. Or at least she'd come to deliver three letters of his that had been left with her theater mail by mistake.

Some of the people around here called him Count Francois.

"He never comes out of the shadows," Genevieve in wardrobe insisted. "When he goes out of the theater he always wears a hat, and a long black coat. And white gloves. Maybe they are not gloves at all, but his skin. Bloodless skin of the undead."

Count Francois. Well, it was a theory. But then, Genevieve came from a small town in central France, a region steeped in folklore. Francois was a spooky man, Katarina didn't deny it, but surely not an undead thing. He was more like the Italian merchant, a figure of mystery from a legend born right here in the Puppet Theater.

Francois had a cat, a black one. She saw it now, twenty feet in front of her, sitting calmly outside his office like a feline sentry.

The animal stared into the room, no doubt at its master.

Not an undead thing, Katarina thought again. But she slowed anyway. A tremor ran through her body. Her skin felt suddenly chilled. Silent footsteps brought her to the open doorway. Someone was inside. Of course, Francois. She heard a drawer being closed and shivered again.

She squared her shoulders, took a deep breath and marched across the threshold. And came to a dead stop not two feet inside.

"My God, what are you doing?" she gasped.

Raul snatched his dark head up. For an instant Katarina thought she saw a flicker of guilt in his eyes—a child caught with his hand in the cookie jar—but that vanished swiftly. A second later he had her by the wrist and was setting her firmly back against the office wall.

The cat didn't move. Katarina didn't breathe. It was a ridiculous time to notice, but Sofia was right, Raul did have beautiful riveting eyes.

"You shouldn't be here, Kati," he said in a low voice. "And please," he closed his beautiful eyes for a second, "don't ask me to explain this."

"Explain what?" she whispered. "You're robbing Francois."

He shook his head, running his thumb across her lips. "You have to trust me. This isn't what it seems."

She should pull away. She didn't move. "But why steal from Francois?" An idea came to her suddenly. "Is he involved in Claudia Clercy's death?"

"No." Raul's denial was too swift. But he was also standing very close, and that made thinking clearly difficult for Katarina.

One thing she did know. She believed him, and that was dangerous. Raul might be murderer, thief and liar for all she really knew about him.

She swallowed her doubts. "Talk to me," she said. "Please. I won't turn you in, Raul. You know I won't."

He let out a deep breath, pressing his forehead for a moment against hers. "You believe me, and I don't even know why. I'm grateful for that, but you're missing something important here. Every question I answer will only put you in greater danger. I started this, but it can't go any further."

She refrained from pushing the dark hair from his face when he lifted his head to look down at her. "I saw what you were doing," she reminded. "All I want to know now is why you were doing it. How much more dangerous can my knowing your motives be?"

"Probably the damage is done," Raul agreed. Katarina accepted the disappointment that swept through her when he stepped away to run a weary hand through his hair. "It was my mistake to get you involved in the first place. Now I compound it." He moved a tired shoulder, then indicated the safe. "This theft was necessary, to cover up a similar one in Renshaw's office."

"You robbed Ian, too?" That probably shouldn't shock her, but it did. "Why?"

"Because he came in unexpectedly when I was searching."

"Then he saw you—" She stopped as Raul gave his head a slow shake "—he didn't see you," she finished. Her momentary confusion cleared suddenly. "You mean you...?"

"Knocked him out? Yes. And then to make it look like a burglary I went through his office and Pierre Fousard's and now this one."

It made sense. It wasn't ethical, but ethics didn't concern Katarina right then. As strange as it seemed, nothing mattered except proving Raul's innocence....

The sound of footsteps echoed far away in the hall.

The cat meowed loudly, then took off down the corridor to the right. Katarina's head snapped up. Someone was coming! She grabbed Raul's arm, but he'd already heard.

"Go!" He mouthed the word at her and gave her a firm push toward the door.

He didn't want her to be caught in here, she understood that.

He went to retrieve the bag with the money while she ran to the door. "There's a short hallway and then a corner to the right," she said. "To the left the corridor runs in a long straight line. I don't know where it leads, but maybe you can get out that way. I'll stall whoever's coming."

Before he could stop her, Katarina slipped into the hall. Fragments of thought raced through her head. She would intercept whoever came. It couldn't be Ian. It might be Francois.

She made it to the corner, stopped, then held her breath and risked a quick look around. Long dark hair, white shirt, boots—Pierre.

She pulled herself upright, leaning back against the wall. Think! In a minute Raul would come and haul her away—and get caught.

She couldn't let that happen. She had to step out, confront Pierre, make up a clever story. Luther always said she was good at that.

Stay calm now, Kati, she thought.

She tossed her hair—and slipped into the right-angled passageway. But then a noise erupted from one of the branch corridors, and she froze. Who else was up here?

Pierre obviously wondered the same thing. He stopped walking.

Katarina didn't move. She did not want to attract his attention prematurely. Her fingers curled into a fist where they rested on the wall. "Do something," she willed him. "See who's making the noise. Raul needs time to get away."

Her eyes closed. Thank heaven, Pierre was turning, pivoting to peer into the shadows at the source of the sound.

"Francois? Is that you?" Impatience took over from inquiry in his tone. "What is it you do there?"

Francois? Katarina didn't know whether to be relieved or not.

She glanced back at Raul as Pierre marched out of sight to confront his partner. "It's all right," she said. "They've gone down another corridor. I can get past them without being seen. Go on," she added at his dark expression. "I'll be fine, I promise."

She stole silently along the corridor, past Ian's office. She hoped he was okay. The early evening sun broke apart the shadows, but the coolness remained. The smell of dust and a hush that seemed at once appropriate and eerie hung in the air.

A chill slid down her spine. Fear. Not for all the horrors she knew, but for the ones she didn't. This theater was a magic place, and yet a woman had been murdered here, killed by someone who still wandered about freely, someone who might decide or even need to kill again.

"Stop hitting the doors!" Pierre's irritated voice broke apart Katarina's thoughts. "Do you wish to renovate this floor as well? I remind you, Francois, that we have no architect for the work we have agreed upon, and where will we get the money necessary to restore the many rooms along here? I have no tree that bears such fruit in my cellar."

"You have money, my friend," Francois replied.

There was a mocking edge to his voice. There always was, though Katarina never really understood it. Truthfully, she didn't understand their whole partnership. If ever two people appeared not to like each other, these men were the ones. But what if it went even deeper than that? What if neither of them thought Raul killed Claudia? Maybe each one suspected the other....

"So where is your cat?" Pierre demanded as Katarina drew to within three feet of the hall where they stood. She wanted to get just a little closer.

"Amadeus?" Francois chuckled. "I have not seen him. Why?"

"Because I did see the wretched creature." Suspicion invaded Pierre's voice. "He ran in here. There is a wall in front of us, and he did not run past me to get out. Where did he go?"

Katarina's stomach tightened. Francois's soft laughter always sounded like silk, like darkness and danger and something that went deeper than both.

She stole a cautious look around the cornerstone, then promptly snatched her head back. Francois was staring directly at her. Had he seen?

"You ask about Amadeus," he said with marked humor. His eyes looked her way but obviously he hadn't seen her. "You do not care at all about a cat, Pierre. But where did the beast go? Ah, now this does interest you. Do you think perhaps I have found a secret passageway up here, and Amadeus has crept into it?"

"You make no sense," Pierre replied. "What is this talk of secret passageways? I wish only to ensure that there have been no shifts in the foundations of this very old building. If the structure is no longer intact, if there are gaps or cracks large enough to admit a feline, then I would like to know about it before I fall through one of them myself and wind up forever in a hole in the ground."

"You do not wish to die," Francois translated, and Katarina shivered despite the dusty beam of sunlight that spilled across her throat and shoulder. "I am glad to hear that, my friend. Most glad."

What a spooky conversation. Get out of here, Kati, now.

Summoning her courage, she looked again. Both men faced the end wall. Gathering her skirts, she murmured a silent prayer and ran swiftly past the opening.

Pierre must have heard the swish, but he couldn't have seen her. "Mice," he muttered. "Filthy rodents. And how many of these pests does your pampered feline ever bring to your office door?"

Francois's quiet amusement reached Katarina's ears. "Such a prosaic man you are. Always and forever you think in dimensions of utter simplicity." The words were very close. They made absolutely no sense, but then Francois's words seldom did.

With a sigh and a perplexed "You are so strange, Francois," Pierre emerged from the passage.

Katarina barely had time to whirl around and start walking toward them. There was no time to escape. She must go the other way, pretend she'd just come up here.

She couldn't read Francois's expression. He stood in a long black shadow, his narrow features invisible in the thickening gloom. A smile lit Pierre's handsome face. Oh, he could charm when he chose to. She looked but saw no suspicion in his eyes.

"Katarina," he exclaimed, while in the background Francois acknowledged her with a small nod. "You still wear your tour guide's costume. Should you not be downstairs dressing for tonight's performance?"

"I—" At the last second she recalled the letters in her pocket. "These were left for me by mistake." Digging them out she handed the envelopes to Francois.

Only his mouth was visible. It curved into an inscrutable smile.

Alarm rippled across her skin. She managed a thin smile of her own.

"Thank you, Katarina." Francois took the letters. His hands had olive skin, not white. She relaxed, then remembered Ian and stiffened again. How long would he stay unconscious?"

"Pierre is correct, however," the man in the shadows continued. "It grows late. You should change your costume. Babette will return from dinner soon, and then the mirror will be lost to both you and Louise.''

Please let Raul have gotten away. Katarina nodded. ''You're right, of course. I'll go now.''

''I hope you break a leg tonight,'' Pierre remarked in parting.

And as she turned away, Katarina prayed that was the worst thing that would happen to her.

Chapter Eight

"Enough of this, Ian," the puppet master warned. "Your complaints grow tiresome."

Possibly because you aren't suffering the aftereffects of a blow to the head, Ian thought with a spite he didn't dare display.

They walked in picturesque Montmartre today, Mountain of Martyrs. Was there a message in that? Ian sighed. There was sunshine on his face, and a cemetery at his side—the person in charge had a malicious sense of humor.

They walked briskly past a small cabaret, the Lapin Agile. Ian's feet hurt and his head ached, but he kept silent. Soon they approached the vineyard, and it was there that the puppet master stopped. His expression said, "You are a peasant," though his mouth didn't move except maybe to compress slightly.

"We verge on an important time," he remarked finally, gazing out at the unripened vines. Beneath that impassive surface beat a scorpion's heart. He hadn't even asked about Ian's injuries. "Many parties are held this month," he went on. "You received the note with the Duperay's name and address, I trust. Your thief did not steal this?"

Now he mocked the incident. Ian fumed but said calmly, "I have it."

"Good. Then we proceed as planned."

"You don't think this theft should be investigated?" Ian inquired politely and watched as the eyes across from him hardened.

"No, I do not. You will say nothing to anyone at the theater, and most assuredly not to the police. More attention from them we do not require. The authorities search for Raul, and that is sufficient to occupy their time. Need I remind you that these matters in which we involve ourselves are illegal? Excessive attention is not to our advantage." His lips formed a cruel line. "Do I make myself clear?"

Ian's shoulders screamed with unreleased tension. "Quite clear. When will our next 'illegal matter' take place?"

The person in charge chuckled. Ian's tension increased. "In three days. The Fontaines of Argentina have planned a fiesta to celebrate the engagement of their daughter. Officially we will not number among the guests, though this is a trivial point. In two weeks, however, the Louis-St. Desmonds will host their annual spring gala at their château in Versailles, and these festivities we shall attend. Perhaps I will bring a date this time, I have not yet decided. For the Fontaine affair, I will give you your instructions now. We will wait on the other. You will pass my orders along to our troop this evening. And, Ian," he added in a menacing tone that Ian quite believed. "You will watch Babette closely in this."

Ian followed the line of the man's gaze to the cemetery, sighed then dipped his head. There was much meaning in that small look. One mistake and Babette would die. And so might Ian Renshaw.

"OH, PRAY TELL ME, puppet Vignette, how did Giovanni bring his beloved Mignon to life? Were the golden threads given to him by the Italian merchant truly magic?"

Babette lit into Katarina immediately after the Thursday night performance, trailing her from stage to dressing room. In her hand she clutched the neck of a wine bottle, open and half-consumed. Good, with luck she'd trip on her gown and wind up an unconscious lump in the hallway—just like Ian.

Katarina banked her frustration. She hadn't meant to think about that. Thank heaven, though, the excitement over the office thefts had died quickly and with no mention of Raul Sennett as a possible suspect.

"Bad publicity," Philip had informed her wryly the morning after. "We'll have none of that in this theater." His smile dazzled. "So, what do you say, love? Dinner tonight? I have it all arranged. Dinner and stories of mysteries from another time. I know how much you enjoy that."

Yes, she did, and Giovanni's legend most of all. Philip did know how to tempt her.

For that selfish reason, plus a few more disturbing ones, she'd accepted his invitation last night. And as a result had to deal with Babette's jealous fury tonight.

"Did you tell Philip again how Giovanni took the gold threads from the merchant and braided them into Mignon's hair?" Babette demanded. "Did you go further and pretend to be Mignon for him?" With her free hand, she grabbed Katarina's arm, pulling her to a stop in the deserted corridor. Her black eyes glared. "I hate you, Katarina Lacroix."

Katarina yanked her arm free. "Feeling's mutual, Babette."

"Feelings, hah! What do you know of feelings? What do you know of anything?"

"Enough." Katarina started walking. "Don't touch me," she warned when Babette would have grabbed her again.

The woman's hand fell. There was a slosh of wine then a venomous "Where did you go for dinner? To Philip's apartment?"

"Go away, Babette," Katarina said over her shoulder. "What I do when I'm with Philip is my business, not yours."

She reached the dressing room at last, but there was no sign of Louise.

Babette marched to the center of the room, folded her arms and tapped her foot on the floor. She had a stranglehold on the wine bottle, and a snarl on her lips. "You think you are so clever," she said scornfully. "But you know nothing about life."

Katarina ignored her, opened the closet and found a long cotton print skirt in shades of ochre and copper. So far Babette hadn't missed her compact, leotard or gym bag, but it would come and that would be another scene to deal with.

"Monsieur Philip Hambleton." Babette made a dramatic gesture. Her voice was slurred now. "You believe he's so rich, but you are wrong." Uneven footsteps carried her to the nearest seat, an empty plant stand next to the minifridge. "It is Philip's father who makes the money. He depends upon Papa's good favor."

Katarina glanced over. "And you still want him?"

"I love him."

"It doesn't sound like you do."

Babette flapped an impatient arm. "What do you know of love, or anything?"

Katarina sent her a sullen look as she tugged on a sienna tank top and picked up her slouch socks and ankle boots. She managed, just barely, not to throw the boots at Babette's head.

"I do not need Philip's money," Babette went on with pride. The wine bottle dropped to the floor, empty, and rolled away. She tapped her chest with her fist. "I have my own wealth."

Bending over, Babette yanked open the refrigerator door and began rummaging around inside. "My mother is a peasant," she revealed unexpectedly.

Katarina began lacing up her boots.

"She's a pathetic person. Do you believe she is happy to be poor? I think she is stupid."

Katarina raised her head. "Why? You just said she was happy."

"I also said she was poor. Do you understand poor? All day she washes other people's dirt, and all night she prays and reads her Bible."

"So?"

Babette pulled out a turkey leg and scowled. "She has nothing else. No clothes, no jewels." She sat up, more or less, and swung her slippered feet. "Me, I have it all. I am going places. I dine at the in spots. Claudia and I would go after a performance to where the important people gather. But for this one needs money." She tore off a strip of turkey with her teeth. "Claudia, she was my friend. And now she is dead. And so I go to him and I ask, with whom will I work now?"

Him? Katarina studied Babette's face, wanted to ask a question but held off.

"It is not fair," Babette insisted, making an abrupt motion with the half-naked drumstick. "She did nothing wrong. Claudia did not make mistakes. So you see, it must have been the architect who killed her."

Who was she trying to convince? Katarina stayed silent.

"Raul Sennett," Babette continued. "He murdered Claudia. He wanted her. Besides, who else in this theater could commit murder? No one."

Was the quaver in her voice fear?

Katarina finished lacing her boots, pulled her skirt down and shoved back her hair. "What if he didn't do it, Babette?" she suggested. "I mean, are you absolutely sure that no one except Raul Sennett might have wanted Claudia dead?"

Babette's breathing rate increased. But her dark eyes were bleary now. "I tell you, she did nothing wrong. We worked together, I know this."

"Worked..." Katarina repeated. "Here at the theater?"

Babette chuckled. "How naive you are," she declared. She laughed again and would have stripped the last piece of meat, but something stopped her.

Her gaze focused on the door, open a crack to admit the cool night breezes. The bleariness vanished, and with it most of the color in her cheeks.

Katarina looked left, saw a face in the doorway with bland features, and then part of a brown jacket. Ian? He was gone now, but the smell of his French cigarette wafted in.

Babette slid from the stand, swayed and wiped her mouth with her open hand. "Naive," she said again. Her eyes were fixed on the door. "To think that anyone but Raul Sennett would murder Claudia. So maybe Claudia did do something wrong. She let this architect seduce her. Then when she tried to be free of him, he killed her. He is a beast, not like Giovanni who, for love, allowed his Mignon to go free, to leave him in the vaults where he wished to live and she did not."

Someone's knuckle rapped the door. "May I come in?" Ian's polite voice inquired.

Babette straightened her shoulders while Katarina hastily mapped out an escape route. It was too convenient, Ian's showing up just when Babette was running off at the mouth.

Katarina's fingers groped for her purse. The air felt very cold all of a sudden. Or did the chill come from inside her when she spied the swatch of tan bandage on Ian's forehead?

"I heard you talking," he said. He had a pleasant expression in his pale brown eyes.

When neither woman spoke, Ian raised a brow in Katarina's direction. "You're leaving, I see. Shall I drive you to your apartment? On the Left Bank, isn't it?"

Katarina's fingers tightened on the strap of her purse. "Yes. I mean, thank you, no, I don't need a ride."

It was no problem to slip past him at all. Actually, Katarina sensed that he wanted her gone. He and Babette were eyeing each other like wary cats.

The lights of the city settled Katarina's nerves as she exited the old château and hailed a passing taxi. She climbed in and collapsed against the worn leather seat. Too many thoughts in her head confused her. How on earth could she expect to sort through this?

She closed her eyes and let the panorama unfold. The sway of the taxi lulled, but it was no good.

She had to walk, to breathe the night air, let the babble of voices disturb her senses. She told the driver to let her off near the Place Saint-Michel. There were cafés and theaters and lots of people here. She needed humanity tonight. She needed Raul, too, but that was out of the question.

She should have gone down to the vaults before leaving the theater. She hadn't seen him since that day in Francois's office.

The Paris night glowed around her. Soft breezes blew off the Seine. She caught the scent of lilacs in the air.

In her mind she saw Raul's eyes, clear and dark and compelling. Then she saw Philip, a pale imitation. Wisdom told her to fall in love with Philip. He encouraged dreams, Raul did not. She shouldn't love a man wanted for murder.

I don't love him, she told herself firmly.

Katarina's head started to hurt. She needed to think of something else. What had Babette said? She and Claudia had worked together, and not just at the theater, either.

Then there was the alarm in Babette's black eyes when Ian came to the door. There had to be a connection there. Her mother was a peasant, Babette had money. Where did she get it?

Katarina looked up at the night sky. What a complicated world this was. She sighed. "If I were Mignon, I would have stayed with Giovanni in the vaults forever."

"But you aren't Mignon, chérie," a familiar voice murmured in her ear. "And forever is a very long time."

"ARE YOU CRAZY?" Katarina demanded in a strangled whisper. She didn't turn around to see Raul, kept her eyes fastened on a sidewalk café in front of her. "There are two policemen sitting at that table over there."

"I see them."

"I don't want to sound like an alarmist, Raul, but *what if they recognize you?*"

"I don't think they will. Besides, it's worth the risk. I wanted to see you, so when you left the theater I followed."

"Raul!" She spun to face him—and gasped at what she saw. She peered closely, at his features. "Raul?" This time it was a question.

His eyes answered for him. Dark, expressive, riveting, she'd recognize them anywhere. But the face she didn't recognize.

She stared, astonished, at a man with hair a mile long, a big thick mustache and tinted glasses. He wore black pants, a black shirt and a black jacket. This was not the Raul she knew.

"You look like Yanni," she said, staring at him.

"Is that good?"

"Very." They started walking toward the river. "Did you do this yourself?" she asked, tugging on his hair.

He smiled and his expression reached his eyes, warming them. "My sister Gina owns a salon. She says changed hairstyles change appearances."

"Your sister? Really?" Katarina rubbed her arms, though it was far from cold. "I'll bet you have a family, too, don't you?"

He pressed his hand to the small of her back, guiding her along the busy sidewalk. "Does that surprise you?"

"No. How big?"

"I have three sisters, Mara, Gina and Marti who is eleven, and a brother Riccardo, who is four years younger than me."

"And your parents?"

He regarded the clutter of tables and people, but didn't seem to see them. "They're alive. They can't be sure that I am, but I managed to send a note through Riccardo after the murder—to say that I was all right."

"They must be frantic."

"Probably." He shook away the darkness and arched a brow at her. "You have no family?"

"None. An aunt and an uncle in New Orleans, but they don't count."

He smiled. "You don't miss your home in America?"

Katarina let her gaze slide across an open café, down to the light that spilled in noisy smoke-filled pools onto the street. "I only miss Luther," she confided. "He took care of me when I was little. He was my friend. He died a month before I left." A knot formed in her stomach, but she went on. "I was married for four years, but my husband died, too." A blast of hot jazz reached her through the din, and then a closer Gershwin tune. "Davide was a musician, you know, a guitarist. Maybe he was good. I'm not sure if he really knew how far his talent went. He did drugs."

Raul stopped and stared down at her. "Then he was a fool."

It was difficult to look at this man's face and not lose her train of thought, but she understood. "No, he was lost," she said. "Searching for something, I think." With her fingers she lifted the thin gold braid in her hair. "Like Mignon."

Raul laughed. His palm on her back sent stinging points of heat through her body. It was impossible not to be aware of him. Disguised or not, Raul was strong and vital and so sensual that he made her feel on fire inside, hot from wanting something she knew could quite easily turn to pain.

She forced her gaze back to the street, her tension slowly beginning to subside. Everyone in Paris came here it seemed.

"I know something," she said, looking up at him now through her lashes. An unfair tactic, but she wanted to know everything, the truth from start to finish. "We could talk, maybe trade information."

His smile told her he wasn't deceived. "I'm going to regret this," he murmured. "But saying no to you doesn't seem to be possible for me." He looked left. "Where will we do this trade? By the river?"

"No. I want to see your face." She took his hand and tugged. "My apartment's near here. We can go there and be safe."

"Safe?" Again his dark eyes smiled at her. With his fingers he stroked the curve of her cheek. "No, Kati, I don't think that you will ever be entirely safe with me."

Chapter Nine

"The Café Faustine on the Boul' Mich, do you know the place?"

Raul sat on the counter in Katarina's small bathroom, watching as she removed the mustache from his face. Her hands touched his skin, and what sensation could be more exquisite than that? Except the one that burned much lower in his body.

Control. He must exercise this tonight. Explaining his situation, that was one thing; kissing her lightly, acceptable. But mistakes potentially more lethal than these he could not permit.

So far he'd learned that she had cause to suspect Ian and Babette, and perhaps Claudia Clercy of being involved in something other than the Puppet Theater. "I don't know what, though," she'd admitted.

God willing, she never would.

In return he'd said, "I disguised myself tonight, so I could visit the café named in the note that Philip left on Ian Renshaw's desk three days ago."

With a damp cloth, Katarina wiped a smudge from his cheek. "The Café Faustine," she repeated now. "Yes, I think I do know that place. I've never been there, though."

Raul continued to watch her face. The angles created by the pale light were haunting. "It seems that the Duperays, the owners, have been hired by Ian Renshaw to cater a reception at the Puppet Theater next week."

"The backstage party, I know. We have them sometimes. Our rich patrons come in all their glittering splendor to drink champagne and eat caviar."

She attached no importance to the note. So maybe it meant nothing that Philip had given the Duperays' name to Ian. Ah, but the party next Thursday, theater patrons with money and jewels and magnificent homes congregating backstage, this might be a completely different story.

Katarina touched his hair and he tightened down low. Thoughts of the party dissolved. Keep his hands off Kati, that was the command of his mind. Don't stare at the soft line of her mouth, the curves of her body and breasts. Ignore her smooth skin and the light Oriental scent she wears.

He stared anyway, but knew it wasn't fair to do so. People told him he conveyed things through his eyes, feelings he didn't always want expressed. Unless, of course, he was being deliberately cautious, and then he could push all emotion back and out.

He could push little back with Katarina. The bathroom and the night were warm, they strengthened his awareness of her. She lived in a garret of rooms with small connecting staircases. There were bookshelves everywhere, and comfortable furniture. The place had a certain old-world charm that came partly from the sixteenth-century building and partly from Katarina herself. This was a woman who adored things of mystery, from the delicate Italian screens in her bedroom to the elegant little puppet stage on her mantle where hand-painted marionettes dangled on strings, tiny dolls with faces so real he could almost believe in them himself.

Raul smiled at that thought. He liked Katarina's apartment too much. Paris loomed beyond the cut glass windows, the elegant French capital with its rooftops and coffee houses, its Eiffel Tower and Opéra, its phantoms and its tragic ghosts of legend. The smell of Greek cooking hung in the air here. He only loved Barcelona more. And the woman whose fingers gently brushed strands of damp, dark hair from his cheek.

His muscles ached from the strain of not moving. It had grown hot, and the lights flattered. How could he resist his body's demands and Katarina at the same time?

His eyes continued to stare deeply into hers. His hand found her fingers and brought them slowly to his mouth.

Don't do this, Raul!

But his mind shoved the thought away. Katarina touched him, swayed toward him. She moved between his legs, brushed his inner thigh with her hip. How could a small kiss put her in any greater jeopardy than she already was?

"Now you look right," she murmured as he drew his lips from her fingers.

He regarded her steadily. He couldn't seem to drag his eyes from her face. With a smile Katarina took his hand and pulled him from the counter.

"You want to dance with me, *chérie?*" Raul questioned, smiling just a little.

"If you do." She took the traditional pose for the waltz and waited for him to come.

This invitation he could not resist. He brushed the hair from her temple, then ran his thumb lightly down her cheek. He put his hands on her waist. And giving her just enough time to know what he would do, he bent his head and set his hungry mouth on hers.

SILENCE THICK AND HEAVY permeated the corridors of the Puppet Museum. Maybe it was warm outside, but never, even at the height of summer, did that warmth seep into this tomb.

The puppet master's heels clicked on the smooth stone floor. Marionettes inside glass cases seemed to leer at him. He despised the things. They were caricatures of humanity, grotesque bits of cloth and wood and paint. They looked as if they knew some black secret for their bright, beady eyes always stared.

Except for the puppet that was not one of Giovanni's creations. This puppet had no name. Dark and dangerous-looking, he stood alone, swathed in black robes and hood. Black sandals were strapped on his feet and there were only flashes of features visible. The tip of a nose, the point of a chin, the shadowy curve of a cheek—this creature was good. He looked as Death might if such an abstraction could assume human form.

The puppet master's eyes went cold. "How alike we are," he said to the image in his mind. "But there is one difference. You, merchant, are a puppet. I am not. I am the true essence of Death personified."

A smile curved the puppet master's lips as that night of blood came back to him.

"You see this knife in my gloved hand, Claudia?" he whispered softly. "It is for you. It is pointless to cry for help. No one can hear you."

Blackmail, it was an ugly word. The puppet master felt the coldness grow inside him.

"I know all that you do," Claudia had taunted. "I know how you do it. And now I know who you are. The man who pulls our strings. But you are not a man, not really. Like the rest of us, you are simply a puppet, a slave to your own greed. You stand above your lackeys and pretend that you are a dark lord."

She had shrugged and laughed, and it was the sound of her laughter that had sealed her fate.

"So be a dark lord," she'd continued. "Be the darkness itself, I do not care. Give me money, more than you give to the others. Do it, and no one shall know the truth. Do not, and I shall tell them all who you are. Maybe I will even talk to the police."

She had given him a hard look. And the simplest of choices.

"Goodbye, Claudia. . . ." he had whispered to her.

A concentrated hush fell now within the old walls. The puppet master stared at Nicoli, alter ego of Giovanni Verrone. This was a creature of slender build, dark hair and pale, narrow features, man of tragic sadness.

"No, Giovanni," he said. "You wounded yourself. You allowed Mignon to leave the vaults. You relinquished your control over her. You can never do that, ever. You should have pulled the gold threads from her hair, reduced her to the puppet she was once and would be again.

"I did not make such a mistake with Claudia," he went on. "One by one, I severed the threads of her life. I will do the same thing to Babette if it comes to that." And of course it would.

"Another death," he whispered to Jo-Jo, the jester gnome. "Another moment to savor."

Jo-Jo stared blankly. Bells gleamed on his hat and collar, and what a silly grin he wore on his mouth.

"You are a buffoon," the puppet master accused, "not unlike many humans I know. They are beings to be manipulated, nothing more."

He turned away.

A tiny sound broke the surrounding stillness. A tiny rupture in the fabric of silence, a brush stroke on the edge of his senses. Amadeus perhaps. He dismissed the intrusion and returned his gaze to the glass case.

Something not immediately evident to the puppet master's conscious mind glimmered deep within his brain. His skin began to prickle. Why this odd reaction?

His eyes narrowed. The glimmer began to take shape. Something was different now about Jo-Jo. Not about his constant lewd smile or clownish stance. But something brought the puppet master's eyes into sharp focus on this particular painted face.

Another death. Another moment to savor...

His dark thoughts seemed reborn. He twisted his head, let his gaze sweep over the shadowed museum. No one was here. He imagined this whispered haunting of his mind.

He looked back at Jo-Jo. And then, it did register on his consciousness. Yes, there was a difference!

A film of sweat broke out on his skin. He felt his composure drain away, his blood go cold.

Look again at the puppet, his brain commanded. The mouth is carved, it's made of wood. And yet the smile has become an open expression of laughter!

Another death. Another moment to savor...

Again his thoughts mocked him, resounded in his head. But they were not his thoughts now. They were a distorted echo. His own mind did not create these words.

Slowly he backed away from the case. He stared at it, could not look away. Jo-Jo's arm moved. It pointed at him. No one pulled the strings. Jo-Jo was moving. And now his mouth began to work, a jerky motion like that of a mechanical doll.

"I know what you do. I know who you are. You are the darkness...."

They were Claudia's words this time. The puppet master recalled them clearly. Her words, spoken by Jo-Jo, into his head. There was no disturbance in the museum's silence.

The puppet master allowed the thoughts to come. He let them feed his fear. Because deep inside, he did believe. He did not doubt what happened here. Forces existed in this world, dark powers that need not be understood to be accepted.

His face became a rigid mask. "Dark, you are," he whispered. "But not born of the darkness itself. If you are mortal, you are nothing. And if you are more than legend, then you are no longer of this earth. You cannot interfere. I wear no strings. I cannot be controlled."

A PRESENT WAITED FOR RAUL on his cot when he returned late to the vaults. It was a gold compact, a gift from Sofia, he assumed, and a note on the blanket beneath it.

He considered reading the note but his mind wouldn't oblige. His body was here; his thoughts were still with Katarina.

He thought of the elegant waltz. He'd deepened the kiss, fitted her more snugly against him. The taste of her, the contact with her warm body increased the pressure in his loins.

"Come to me, Kati." He'd murmured the words against her lips. "Touch me."

She'd slid her hands along his rib cage to his waist and then down to his hips. He had meant for her to touch him with her mouth, with her tongue, and she did that, but God help him, she also brushed her fingers across his zipper. He groaned way down in his throat.

She wasn't surprised, he realized with a start, only tentative. Her instincts held her back. She wasn't sure what might happen between them. Raul had squeezed his eyes closed, felt the pain intensify. She was right to be unsure.

Another sound had come from his throat, a burst of frustration and self-denial as he'd dragged his mouth from hers. "I can't do this, Kati. I'm accused of murder. In the vaults I walk a fine line between fantasy and reality, possibly between freedom and imprisonment forever. I have no direction. I'm wrong for you right now."

He'd managed to say all of this while setting her away from him. It was torture to force the words out, to see her lips damp from his kisses, her hair tangled and falling across her face. He did it, but not with any degree of serenity. And it was not enough.

He needed to be apart from her completely, at least for a time.

He'd tipped his head back, regarding the plaster ceiling. "Do you understand?"

"I understand." Her fingers were pressed to her mouth. Her eyes were dark and wide as she stood there in the middle of the floor. She'd watched him closely, her breathing as uneven as his, and a vague, unreadable expression on her face. "Maybe this isn't the time," she'd agreed.

It was this look Raul clung to now as he lay on his cot, his forearm resting over his closed eyes. What was it, 3:00 a.m.? And he'd been walking about undisguised for who knew how many hours. A reckless act, but to walk had been essential, and to be in a familiar place where not everything around him was buried within the shadows.

A tremor ran through him, and he shifted on the narrow cot. Something cold and hard dug into his side. The compact. With a tired sigh, Raul located the metal case and the note.

"To my friend with the beautiful dark eyes," the writing began. Amusement pulled on his lips. Sofia seldom called people by name, but her descriptions were usually clear. His eyes moved down the page.

> I am glad that you went up. I did not see you. I hope you wore a good disguise.
>
> Now, whatever you are doing at this moment, you must stop. Open the pretty case and see the initials inside: V.R. I do not know names but you told me that a viscount called Richelieu was robbed many months ago. If he has a wife I will bet you a bottle of wine that this is part of the loot.

Loot? Mild amusement became a smile and a shake of his head. Raul roused himself from the cot to scoop up a loaf of fresh Parisian bread and open a jar of raspberry jam. His eyes confirmed the initials inside the compact then returned to Sofia's note.

I took this object from the dressing room of the woman with the black curls. I took other objects, too. Then I put the money you gave me inside the sack I took and went to look for Giovanni's ghost.

I know you do not believe in him, but he is here. Maybe I found him, I cannot be sure. Anyway I felt something in the air, so I asked it to help you capture the butcher who likes to cut women with knives. I hope it was Giovanni I talked to.

The shadows change now. It is late. I must go to meet friends who seek shelter in the outer passageways, the ones near the river. I do not understand why they never come deeper inside. Maybe they believe in Giovanni's ghost, too. I took food from your box for them. Tomorrow I will come to see you. Good night, handsome friend.

Sofia

P.S. I think the pretty young one with the long hair and eyes like the sea should be Mignon.

S.

Raul chuckled as he finished the note. Setting it aside, he chewed his bread and regarded the inscribed compact. Part of the Richelieu booty? Probably. Babette must hold back certain items from her employers.

Was that important? Maybe. Claudia had not been killed on a whim. The puppet master was sadistic, but he didn't kill for no reason. At least that was Raul's belief. It might not be correct. And if it wasn't...

Black thoughts came to him now. A shudder swept through him. He should not think in these bleak terms. No harm would come to Katarina. He wouldn't allow it.

Standing, he paced the stone floor, raking his fingers through his hair. The backstage party—this was his opportunity to learn something of worth. Sofia had called upon a ghost; he would call upon his wits. And luck. He would get in unnoticed and out with the whole truth. He would strip away the mask of the puppet master.

IT WAS seven o'clock in the morning when Genevieve Capri let herself into the Puppet Theater and walked quietly to the wardrobe department where she worked.

"I do not care what anyone says, he is not human," she maintained with a quiver of revulsion. She flashed a nervous look at Francois who walked past in a corridor far ahead and shivered again.

She clamped her mouth shut as two young men with mops and pails came out of the wardrobe room.

"There was very little damage," one man said to her.

She frowned. Her mind still conjured coffins and demons with black wings. "What is damaged?" she demanded.

"The water pipe. It made a big puddle on the cabinet. Then the puddle made a river that ran inside. Perhaps some ribbons got wet, but these things can be replaced, *non?*"

Letting herself in, Genevieve surveyed the cabinet where all the ribbons and scarves and gold threads were stored. This wasn't damage? The doors and drawers stood wide open. Pools of water shone on the polished wood. All that had once been inside now lay scattered at her feet. And the floor was the wettest thing in the room.

"They empty drawers where the water can not possibly reach and throw the contents where there is enough of it to fill an alpine lake. Idiot men."

She rescued the less saturated items from the floor. A red bow, a yellow hair ribbon, a strand of silver beads, a white envelope . . .

Genevieve paused and looked again. In her hand she held a sealed white envelope with a folded paper inside, and only the start of a number on the outside. Should she look?

Her curiosity won. No name or address was marked on this thing. Who would ever know? Perhaps it was a love letter from her assistant to the handsome performance puppeteer, Philip Hambleton. Or to Pierre, with his long brown hair and sexy body. He was her favorite.

She eased back the flap and shook out the paper. Her eyes flew over the neatly written page, scanning the words only. It was Claudia Clercy's handwriting, she knew this from memos Claudia had given to her. But what did the words say?

"To the Chief Inspector," it started.

Genevieve felt a ripple of alarm go down her back. Claudia wrote to the police?

She rushed through the letter, her brain picking out words and phrases, frightening things.

A name followed, and still more words, sentences that made Genevieve shake with terror. This could not be! She was home in bed, dreaming. No man was so sick as this.

She caught a soft rustle of sound in the open doorway. Her head jerked up. A light of panic shone in her eyes. She could not hope to hide it from her unexpected visitor.

"What is it that you have there?" he asked, closing the door with his foot and advancing slowly.

Her throat muscles wouldn't work. She could not scream or even move. Eyes wide and unblinking with the kind of mind-numbing fear that she had never known before, she watched him come closer.

"You stare at me as though at a ghost," he said with a slow smile. "But I am no ghost."

He removed the letter from between her thumb and finger. His eyes skimmed it, then returned to her face.

"And so, Claudia reaches out from the grave to expose me." His free hand wrapped itself cruelly around Genevieve's wrist. "You will tell me all that you know."

She found her voice at last. "No," she whispered, then at a more hysterical pitch, "No! Please, monsieur, I beg you, do not kill me. I will say nothing, I promise." The volume increased as her panic unleashed itself.

His smile widened, the smirk of a cobra. His fingers on her wrist tightened. And then his hand let go. In one swift move it came up and sharply down between neck and shoulder. Blackness rushed in, a thick tingling curtain. Through it she saw the outline of a steel blade, and in her mind heard one final sound—the eerie chuckle of a madman.

Chapter Ten

A newspaper hit the table on the roof of the Puppet Theater, pulling Katarina out of her disordered thoughts. Actually it didn't land on her table but on Babette's right beside it.

"Latest edition," Louise said, dropping into an empty chair and squinting up at the lancet windows above them. "There's been another big robbery. I tell you, the risks some people won't take for money."

Babette ignored her, preferring to send sulky looks at Katarina who shared her outdoor table with Philip.

Philip winked at Katarina, she had no idea why. In fact she kept wishing he would go away, which was horrible of her because there was no reason in the world for her to feel like that.

Who was she kidding? There was a perfectly good reason, and he was probably prowling around in the vaults at this very moment.

"Among other things," Louise continued, "the thieves made off with an emerald necklace, an uncut diamond, plus two original paintings by Daumier. In and out on proverbial cat's feet, and not so much as a sooty fingerprint to be found at the scene."

"What do the police know?" Babette flapped a cranky hand. "They should question the guests. Surely one of them did it."

Guests? Katarina asked. "Was there a party?"

The atmosphere felt funny all of a sudden, like an old horror movie. Even Philip's chuckle didn't sound quite right, but then she might be imagining that.

"I thought everyone in Paris knew of the bash the Fontaines were throwing to celebrate their daughter's engagement," he said. "The columns were full of it."

The Fontaines. Katarina glanced at him. Louise hadn't mentioned that name. "Do you know these people, Philip?"

He lit a cigarette, leaning back in his chair. "Quite well, actually. Old Henry belongs to my father's club. Stuffy old codger. Personally, I don't much care for the son, either, but Lucy has her moments."

"Does she really?" Louise gave her hair a lazy ruffling. Was anything here relevant to the murder charge Raul faced?

Philip shrugged, ignoring Louise. "I didn't go to their party last night, even though Carmela, that's the wife, is said to be a smashing hostess."

"Who is a smashing hostess, Philip?" Pierre joined them, wearing jeans and dusty black boots. He also wore a black silk T-shirt and leather vest.

Eclectic taste in all things, Katarina reflected, sipping her coffee. Including partners. She wondered what those two might know that she didn't.

"Where's Francois?" she asked for no reason except that Babette's nasty looks were starting to irritate her. And the air felt so weird out here....

A snarl curled Pierre's lip. "Who cares? Hanging from a beam in the vaults perhaps." Katarina managed not to choke on her coffee. "I have not seen him today." He swung a heavy leather satchel from his shoulder and set it on the stones. "Right now I wish to find Ian Renshaw."

"Perhaps he's hanging in the vaults with Monsieur Lupier," Babette remarked sourly, still pouting and casting angry looks at Katarina.

"That is less than helpful, Babette." Pierre set his jaw. "Imbecile. He leaves the theater early yesterday with the promise that he will arrive early today. And now the one time that I want him, he doesn't keep his word. Then Francois disappears also. And so it happens that when a problem arises, I have only black cats and puppets to talk to. And who is a smashing hostess, Philip?" he demanded, switching topics midbreath. Pierre was very good at that. "Perhaps we could hire this person to help with our backstage party. I cannot seem to locate Genevieve from wardrobe, who was supposed to greet our guests for us. Not that I feel she was the best choice for this role, but Francois insisted. Genevieve was close with Claudia, but she does not have the same finesse. And do not blanch at the mention of her name, Babette. I know that Claudia was your good friend. But she is dead and that is the fact of it."

"Murdered," Louise corrected. "And I don't think Carmela Fontaine—" she emphasized the name, studied his unresponsive features, then went on "—puts her social skills on the block, so to speak."

It was a casual remark with a deliberate hesitation. But why try to get a rise out of Pierre? Katarina sighed. Raul was right to prowl. Something creepy was going on at this theater.

Louise stretched. "Did you know, Pierre, that the unfortunate woman and her husband were robbed blind last night? Of course, I imagine they were heavily insured."

"Rich people usually are," Babette snapped, then hunched her shoulders.

Pierre shook his head. "Everyone has become strange all of a sudden. I ask a question and bombs go off on the roof.

Do you people take funny pills while I fight with architectural firms to finish a job that must be done before this château collapses into the vaults?"

Philip inhaled on his cigarette. "A bit unstable around the ankles is she, old boy?"

"She, Philip?" Katarina raised a cool brow, although she couldn't for the life of her understand why she was being so cranky today. "All things old and decrepit are automatically feminine, are they?"

Philip was immediately contrite, which of course only made her feel worse. He leaned forward, his gold hair swinging about his face. "I'm sorry, love. Did I offend you?"

"Reality offends her," Babette stated before Katarina could assure him that he hadn't and apologize. Standing, she shoved her chair back. "You people know nothing of real life. You are all peasants."

Louise's measuring look was at odds with her teasing tone. "Spot a wrinkle in the mirror today, did you, Babette?"

Babette's only response was a crude word in French. She stalked off while Pierre shook his head. His gaze swept the tables. "If Ian or Francois appear, tell them that I will be down by the river, away from ringing telephones this afternoon. You might also say that I would like to know what is being done about our party."

Philip waved his cigarette. "All taken care of, Pierre, from soup to nuts."

Pierre frowned. "How do you know that when I do not?"

It was a fair question, Katarina thought.

"I spoke to Ian," Philip said. "He *is* in charge of this shindig, isn't he?"

"Someone is, that's for sure," Louise muttered. Then she raised her voice. "Don't step on the cat, Pierre. She's right behind you, sitting on your satchel."

"He," Katarina corrected as a very dusty black feline landed in her lap. "Where have you been, Amadeus? You're all covered with dirt and red paint."

The last word came uncertainly as her eyes strayed to the cat's paw. Something was wrong here. This "paint" was wet and sticky, and it had a coppery smell.

A thin streak rubbed off on her fingers. She looked at it once, then again more closely.

She felt her skin go suddenly cold. A lump of nausea climbed into her throat. Not red paint, her shocked senses whispered. Blood!

IT WAS LATE WHEN KATARINA was finally able to slip into the vaults. No one was left in the theater—she hoped. For although it had taken most of the day and then a distracted performance, she had been and still was figuring a lot of things out in her head.

Someone had murdered Claudia Clercy. Not Raul, but someone at the theater. And Claudia had been involved in something not in her usual line of work in wardrobe. The same went for Babette. She and Claudia had worked together, Babette had said. But what had they done?

Also, Louise had deliberately mentioned a robbery today at lunch and then she'd thrown a newspaper describing it down under Babette's nose. Did that mean Louise had knowledge of this work, or at least a suspicion?

"I'll bet you do, Louise," Katarina said softly. Then she took that line of reasoning a step further and concluded that Babette must also be connected to the rash of similar robberies that had been stumping the Paris police for months. Babette, the late Claudia Clercy—and Ian Renshaw.

Ian had been lurking outside their dressing room door the other night. He'd made Babette nervous. The connection made sense.

So now Katarina had several things linked together. Except the cat with blood on its paws.

Whose blood?

Katarina shuddered but couldn't get out of her head the thought that no one had seen or heard from Genevieve Capri in wardrobe today.

"There's no answer at her apartment," one of her associates said. "And only two cleaning men say they spoke with her at the theater early this morning."

Katarina lowered her lashes and stopped thinking as she approached the wooden staircase that would carry her deep into the vaults.

Which way to Raul?

Her flashlight beam was a strand of silver. It scarcely pierced the shadows. Would Raul be here?

She was considering this when her light caught a quick movement ahead. Something white flashed through the beam. A hand?

Katarina's heart gave a momentary lurch. She took a startled breath, jerking the light to the side.

The hand came down slowly to reveal a man's face. Raul? No. She squinted at his narrow features and long dark hair. "Who are you?"

A faint smile appeared on the man's lips. She sensed sadness in it. "No one to fear," he replied. He spoke English with a soft French accent.

She pointed the flashlight slightly away from him. She could see his features more clearly without the glare.

He was a stunning man, a lot like Raul actually, except that his skin was a bit paler. But the slender build, the dark hair with its lovely deep curls, and brown-black eyes surrounded by spiky lashes—the similarities astonished her. Even the age was about right.

A thought occurred to her. "Your name wouldn't be Riccardo, would it?"

His smile widened, although the wistfulness remained. "I sense you confuse me with another. My name is Jean."

Not Raul's brother. Katarina took quick stock of the man's clothing. His black pants were streaked with dirt, his tweed jacket frayed at the cuffs and collar. He wore worn-out boots and an old white T-shirt and had a long, gray silk scarf wrapped around his neck like an aviator. His clothes were ragged, he probably hadn't had a haircut for a year and he was too thin. Did he live down here?

"I'm Katarina Lacroix," she said cautiously. Why the sad expression on his face? "Are you a friend of Sofia's?"

"Sofia." His eyes took on a curious glint, sort of visionary, Katarina thought. "Yes, I think I know this woman. Spry, full of energy. Very old."

"If you call sixty-four old," Katarina agreed with a smile. "Are you looking for her?"

He shook his head. "Tonight I only pass through. I do not usually travel to this part of the vaults. We stand now directly under the Puppet Museum. We are not so far below the ground as it seems. If you listen hard you can hear the thunder of a coming storm. But go deeper inside, to the place that is all grottoes, and then it is the Puppet Theater that rises far, far above. The ornate stage with its velvet curtains, the seats, the balcony, the private boxes—it is a place of beauty and magic and exquisite facades. But there is evil within the beauty."

"Evil?" The word scraped across Katarina's senses. "What kind of evil?"

"Many passageways exist, avenues of sound if no longer of direct access. You must never go near them, of course. I think the ever-adventuresome Sofia would not even try it now. But I have learned things on recent walks past these many portals. It is a sickness, Katarina. Day by day it grows. The ugliness mutates in upon itself."

"Whose ugliness? I don't understand. Are you talking about someone at the theater?"

"The legend," Jean said. He moved a step closer and with a feather-light touch ran his fingers along the thin strands of gold that she always forgot to remove from her hair. "You know the story as correctly as is necessary. Think on it, Katarina. In this tragic tale resides your answer. Tell it to the young man you love. Perhaps there are things that he and you will see, conditions of relevance that will ultimately free him from this nightmare of darkness."

Katarina stared. "Are you sure about this?"

His nod was solemn, his eyes dark with something that went way beyond knowledge. Wisdom, perhaps.

"Who are you, Jean?" she whispered. She should be afraid, but right now she was more awestruck by the possibilities. "And how long have you been down here?"

He stroked her cheek, smiling sadly. "Not so long as you might believe. The legend, it fascinates you, but do not attempt to live it. It is not healthy. That much I have learned from experience."

His hand dropped. Yes, he was very much like Raul, but probably not the ghost she wished him to be. A spirit's touch wasn't likely to be felt, and Jean's cool fingers had definitely brushed her cheek.

"Go now, and find your Raul," he said.

"You know him?" she demanded in astonishment.

Jean's smile lost its tragic edge and became a small tease. "As you say, intimately. No, wait." He held up a hand at her shocked expression. "That sounds bad. I mean to say that Raul Sennett's is a soul I feel I can know and understand as surely as if it were my own." He made a circle in front of his face with his open palm. "Perhaps I feel this way because of the resemblance. You have noticed it, yes?"

Katarina didn't fully trust this conversation. "Have you met him?"

His expression was sorrowful as he shook his head. "I keep to myself most of the time. Only when it's necessary do I mingle with others. I wished to advise you, though I do not claim to possess an abundance of wisdom. I am what you call a stateless individual. Today I am here, tomorrow who can know?" He caught her eyes with his. "Know this, however, Katarina. The evil I speak of, the malignant sickness, is real. It kills. It enjoys killing, and this is far more dangerous than one who brings death and then feels remorse. Remember what I said about the legend. Tell it to your young man. Think on it, both of you, find the evil. Then turn away from the darkness and go toward the light. There is magic in that world as well. But do not look to handsome young princes with golden hair for happiness. I promise you, you will not find it there."

"What are you talking about?" Katarina asked.

But there was no answer. Jean had stepped back into a large sooty shadow. And when she shone her flashlight beam through it she saw nothing. The man with the dark, tragic eyes had quite simply vanished.

SHE CAME TO HIM sometime after midnight. Raul didn't know why she did, only that he felt elated and hungry for her and horrified and guilty all at the same time.

She wore a khaki green vest, snug fitting and buttoned up, with a white ribbed tank top under it, matching khaki pants and lace-up ankle boots of tan leather. Her hair was thick and loose and curling from the high humidity, a perfect frame for her delicate features. She ate the apple beignet he gave her and they shared a litre of white wine. She sat cross-legged on his cot, and between bites and sips, said the most alarming things to him.

"I met Sofia, Raul. I also met a man tonight, a young man, very handsome. He said his name was Jean. He knows about you. He even looks like you. He told me that someone at the Puppet Theater is evil and sick, and getting sicker each day. He says this person actually enjoys killing. He also says the legend is the key, but I don't know what he meant by that, do you?"

Raul shook his head and she continued. "Well anyway, Babette's a thief, I'm sure of that. Ian, too. And Claudia

Clercy before she died. But then, you already knew those things, didn't you? You, and I'll bet Louise, too." Her expression was accusing. "You let Louise help, but you won't let me. And don't say it's too dangerous. I've heard that before and I still don't buy it."

Guilt gnawed at him. He should tie her up and carry her into the grottoes, far away from this place and the Puppet Theater and all the people who might threaten her life. He should, but he couldn't. This Jean, whoever he was—and Raul had an eerie feeling that he maybe did know this man—was correct when he said go to the light. In their place fantasies were acceptable, but they were no substitute for life. Raul wanted desperately for Katarina to see that.

Other matters unsettled him, too. "How can an ancient legend contain the solution to my problem?" he asked her. "That doesn't make any sense."

"I know, but Jean said it did."

Feeling caged, though not unpleasantly so at this moment, Raul folded his legs beneath him as Katarina had done and faced her on the cot. It was torture to keep his hands off her but he managed. He even forced himself to confront her still critical eyes.

"Amadeus, Francois's cat, had blood on his paws today."

Her statement hit hard, and Raul almost choked. "Are you sure?"

"Yes." She set her beignet down, wiping the powdered sugar from her fingers with a napkin. He watched her wad the tissue in her fist. "Maybe he just caught a bird or something, but did you know that one of the women in wardrobe is missing?"

Raul's already strained muscles tightened further. "Who?"

"Her name is Genevieve, and although I say she's missing, she *was* seen early this morning. No one's really worried about her disappearance yet, but then nobody else saw the blood on the cat's paw."

Blood...

Raul's stomach turned over. "This is going from bad to worse."

He let his head drop forward, scrunching his eyes closed. He wanted to be home with his family and friends, with Katarina most of all. He wanted sunshine on his face and a bed with sheets and no more talk of murder and death and sickness and blood. No more cutting of women by evil butchers with long sharp knives.

He felt a movement on the cot, then Katarina's fingers linked themselves around his neck. Her mouth came to rest against his hair. "I'm only guessing, Raul," she whispered, but she sounded scared. "Maybe Genevieve had a family emergency or something."

"Maybe." Raul went silent, letting her kiss his hair while he fought the shudder that gripped his body.

Accused of murder, trapped in the vaults or in prison, what could he offer her? At best, the promise of life in hell.

With a tired sigh, he moved closer, set his forehead on her shoulder and slid his arms about her waist. "Tell me the legend, Kati," he said softly. "If the answers are there, then I want to hear the story from beginning to end."

And then he would pray that the answers didn't reside within it. Because if they did, then the person he sought to expose was not only brutally homicidal, but insane.

Chapter Eleven

The Legend

"This tale was born in a dark age many centuries ago. It was a time when people believed strongly in witches and demons and evil spirits.

"Giovanni Verrone came from a family of wealth. His father was Italian, his mother French. There was no tragedy in Giovanni's early life, but he was a lonely child even so. When he was twelve years old, his parents died and he was given into the care of an old and eccentric uncle who lived in central France, in the Berry region. This was a highly superstitious area even for the time, and stories of witchcraft and sorcery ran wild. Evil forces did exist, and Giovanni's uncle didn't dispute this. Although he himself didn't possess a warlock's power, he communed with the spirits every night. With their help he brewed potions for sale, concoctions to ward off blight and the Black Death, and others that weren't so wholesome. He also made poppets and he would often chant over these and perform unholy rituals in his kitchen. Sometimes he would do this for days, and when he did Giovanni would become frightened and hide in the cellar where no one could find him.

"But the poppets, the little rag and button figures, these Giovanni liked. They were his friends. And so when it happened that he was finally able to leave his uncle's house and travel to Paris, where his mother had been born, he took several of the little dolls with him.

"In the Opera Quarter he purchased a grand château and immediately hired workers to convert it into the Puppet Theater. For puppets, though, not for the poppets he'd brought with him and that he ultimately put on display in the theater lobby. Now Giovanni hadn't inherited his uncle's sinister tendencies, but the fanaticism and the loneliness, those qualities he did possess, and in abundance.

"He discovered the ancient vaults below the château before he even bought it. He would often go into them. The darkness was his friend, a place where he could feel safe. Soon after the construction started he built an elaborate workshop deep inside the maze, and it was there that he began to create his wonderful puppets.

"Mignon was the first, the love he'd never had. And she was beautiful, dark-haired, blue-eyed and delicate. He dressed her in a gown of deep rose pink and tied a matching ribbon in her hair. She was his most precious creation, but she wasn't real. And so, because he couldn't give her life, he made a puppet of himself instead and called it Nicoli, which was one of his own names.

"He made other puppets after that. Silvain, a creature of the forest, a winged nymph who was faithful to Mignon and Nicoli and whose duty was to watch the twins, Vignette and Verona. The twins were identical in every respect, except that one was good and one was evil and nobody knew which was which.

"Giovanni loved dichotomies. His mind didn't recognize normal human limitations. He saw no lines of division between fantasy and reality. Anything was possible, and he swore he would prove it. He believed that his love would bring Mignon to life. But then, if fate, in which he also believed, didn't intend for this to be, then he would become a puppet himself. His soul would enter Nicoli's wooden body, and he'd be with Mignon that way.

"Before either dream could be realized, though, he wanted to make more puppets. The next was Renato, a beautiful male aristocrat with hair like sunshine and eyes the color of a summer sky. Where Nicoli was handsome, Renato was stunning, a definite rival for Mignon's affections. Together with Jo-Jo, the jester gnome who was Renato's constant companion, he would attempt to steal Mignon's heart away from Nicoli.

"Soon Giovanni became thoroughly involved with his puppets. Performances were staged nightly in the jam-packed theater, but his assistants did the work, he no longer wanted to participate. His first puppets never even saw the stage. They lived with him in the vaults, and that was pretty much a literal truth, because in Giovanni's mind these puppets actually did live. But they didn't breathe, and without his help they couldn't move or talk. They were still made of wood and cloth and he wanted desperately for them to be flesh and bone, especially Mignon.

"In time, he gave his other puppets their own world and problems to deal with in it. Renato no longer pursued Mignon. He got involved with the twins instead. Jo-Jo and Silvain, too. Nicoli and Mignon were separate puppets now.

"He took these two with him, deep into the vaults, into what the puppeteers above considered to be an area approaching hell. From his uncle, Giovanni had learned a number of rituals that he now refined for his own purposes. Life for Mignon or his soul transferred into Nicoli's little puppet body, he didn't care which, but one of those things must happen.

"Night after night he chanted in the vaults. But then there came a night far into the fall when all the leaves were dead and the skies were threatening the first great storm of winter. Giovanni and his puppets were alone. They'd come up to the theater for food. The hour approached midnight when a man emerged from the darkness and the driving wind. He wore a thick black robe with a hood that covered his head and only allowed for glimpses of his pale features. He seemed an angular man, monklike in both manner and dress, stiff in the joints, Giovanni noticed, and not French born. He was Italian, Giovanni decided, and touched with the fever of madness. He wore sandals on his feet in this horrible weather. A person couldn't be sane and do that.

"The man was a merchant, he said. He had wares to sell. And he'd heard Giovanni's pleas through the spirits. 'What you desire most is the wish I can grant for you. But be careful, monsieur. Is it life you truly want for Mignon? Alive, she cannot be controlled. Humans have wills of their own, puppets do not.'

"Giovanni ignored him. Possibly he never even heard the merchant's warning. 'Give her life,' he said. 'Do it now.'

"The merchant offered no further cautions. Payment, though—that he did require. Such a gift as life would not come for a small price. Giovanni would have to relinquish the title to his famous Puppet Theater. He could keep the vaults below, but he could never set foot in the theater again.

"Giovanni agreed instantly, and from the folds of his robes, the merchant produced three long golden threads. 'Braid these into Mignon's hair,' he said, 'and she shall have life. Forever life—although perhaps not a manner of immortality you would understand.'

"His words were ambiguous, Giovanni discarded them. He took the threads, he took Mignon and he even took Nicoli, and then he descended deeper than ever into the subterranean passageways, down to the very heart of the vaults. There he constructed a fantastical world for himself and Mignon. There would be no need for them ever to go above again.

"He waited only until his magical kingdom was complete, then he braided the golden threads into Mignon's hair and watched in awe as she came to life. She was real, human at last. His Mignon was alive.

"It was wonderful at first. Giovanni loved Mignon and she loved him. Days became months and finally years. Human now, Mignon became curious about the world above. What was it like, she would ask him. And he told her the truth as he saw it. Evil thrived beyond the dimensions of the old vaults. Sunlight, too, but its rays were tarnished by corruption and sin and all kinds of other horrors. 'There is pain and suffering and witchery out there,' he said. 'Murders in alleys and madness and cruelty and monstrous creatures who feed on human fear. I will not take you to this world, and you must never go there yourself. To do so will destroy your innocent nature completely.'

"But Mignon wasn't satisfied with that. She didn't believe him. How bad could a world of humans be? Giovanni was human—and now so was she.

"She waited only until he fell asleep one night, then she sneaked away. She vanished into the world above and although Giovanni searched all of Paris for her he found no trace. She was gone from the vaults and from his life.

"In despair he left the filth of the city streets. Maybe he would come out again and look for her at night when he wouldn't be forced to see the squalor and the death. But even in his grief Giovanni came to realize that this wouldn't be fair. He couldn't deny Mignon the chance to see life and be a part of it. He had to let her go, return to the vaults and pray that she would come back to him.

"He was about to descend when the Italian merchant came to him. 'I see that she has left you, after all,' he said with such coldness that Giovanni felt immediately angry toward him. He said nothing, however, until he heard the merchant laugh, a sound even colder than his voice. 'I told you this would happen, monsieur. It is rich, is it not, that I should predict the outcome of your actions so accurately?'

"With that he disappeared into the theater, *his* theater now, and Giovanni knew an even greater despair to think of that loss.

"But then the merchant's gloating remarks repeated themselves in his head, and he became enraged. Maybe it was his pain that drove him to break his word, but he burst into the theater in a fury and confronted the merchant, whose manner remained unchanged.

"'Leave my theater, monsieur,' he commanded, but Giovanni refused and so the merchant approached him. 'I warned you, and you did not listen. Nothing can be done to bring your precious Mignon back. She is human now and free to make her own decisions. So it should be for all puppets.'

"He stopped and the light hit him in such a way that Giovanni could finally see his eyes gleaming deep inside his black hood. His voice had no warmth or sympathy in it. He faced Giovanni. 'If I could but make it so, monsieur, all puppets would be as Mignon—free—and all humans would be puppets. More of both than you will ever know have already undergone this transformation. So what then can we truly say is real?'

"Furious, Giovanni lunged at the Italian merchant. He saw nothing except the face of the woman he'd lost and the unfeeling smile of the man around whose throat his fingers were now wrapped.

"Of course, the merchant fought back and the two men struggled for several long minutes. Then in a final burst of rage, Giovanni ripped away the hood and began clawing at the merchant's hair.

"Something changed in that moment, some horrible thing happened, the truth of which Giovanni's brain would never fully absorb.

"In a trance he stood up, staring at the hair he clutched in his hands. And then he stared at the body that lay before him on the floor, a lifeless being, no longer with breath in its lungs. Two gleaming eyes stared back at him. Eyes of marble, set in a body of wood. And threads of gold caught in Giovanni's fingers.

"The Italian merchant who'd given Giovanni Verrone the magic that could bring Mignon to life was a puppet. He wasn't real. The world wasn't real.

"Giovanni dropped the threads and ran to the vaults, ran deep down into the darkness. He was shocked and horrified—and quite mad."

HUMAN PUPPETS; gold threads that gave life to wooden limbs, darkness and rituals in the night. Mad ghosts...

With his face still buried in Katarina's neck, Raul rolled his eyes. How could he hope to find answers in such a jumble of nonsense? It was a good story, but only Katarina was real to him at this moment.

He pushed temptation aside. "I think your friend is wrong about the value of this story," he said into her shoulder. "It's fascinating, but only because it's you who tells it."

Placing her hands on either side of his face, Katarina lifted his head and stared solemnly into his eyes. "You're a cynic, Raul Sennett. These vaults are as much a fascination as the legend. They exist and yet they don't. They shut out the world because the world doesn't know they're here. It's like a two-way mirror. You can see out, but no one can see in."

Raul sighed. "Kati, do you really want to live behind a mirror, forever looking out?" He took her hands in his and kissed the tips of her fingers. "What a horrible fate to be a ghost who wanders in a black void, trapped between worlds, unable to affect either. Is that what you want?"

She didn't answer, but slid from the cot, her expression troubled. Raul closed his eyes. He'd made her sad. He hadn't meant to do that.

"I just don't want to hurt anymore," she said quietly, picking up one of the puppets from the shelf. "I'm so tired of people dying," she went on. "Some that I love, others I only hear about, but the injustice still bothers me. And then sometimes I look around at all the bad things and think how nice it would be if I didn't have to be a part of it anymore. Luther used to say I had the eyes to see the magic and he was right. But now I think maybe you're right, too. Maybe I see too much magic and that's as unhealthy as not seeing any."

Raul left the cot. She was playing with Renato's long golden hair. He took the puppet from her and set it back on the shelf. He looked down at her. "One day, Kati, I'll show you a better place than this. Not a perfect place, but not one of darkness either."

She said nothing, so he slid his fingers to the sides of her neck and set his mouth on hers. A light kiss only, a reinforcement of his promise. Further than that he wouldn't go, not until the darkness was a thing of the past. He would not make love to her within the confines of a mirror.

THE NIGHT SWELTERED. A clap of thunder beyond Katarina's bedroom window made its presence known in her sleeping mind.

Strange dreams swam in her head tonight, contrasting images. She saw wisps of things in the gloom, painted ceilings with puppets in them.

Her mind shivered. A sudden chill of awareness made her look down. She couldn't believe it. The puppets walked!

The Italian merchant glided past, eerily silent, then Nicoli, who looked very much like Raul. Sorrow darkened his beautiful eyes. Katarina wanted to rip the threads from the merchant's hair for him.

"You are an American peasant," Babette screamed from inside a glass case. "You know nothing!"

"Yes, I do," Katarina told her. "I know that you're a thief!"

Music distracted her then, drew her down to the vaults. But this Pied Piper didn't lead her to doom.

People floated through the maze. Sofia in a black kerchief, mourning for something—her lost youth perhaps?

"It is a sickness, Katarina." Jean's voice pierced the shadows. "The legend... Tell it to the young man you love."

Katarina twisted around in the sheets. Her mind went in circles. What was this dream saying?

The young man she loved—Raul! But how could Jean know what she didn't know herself? Who was this man with the dark tragic eyes who reminded her so strongly of Raul?

More thunder crashed outside. It came in violent bursts now. The air was hot and sticky, unbreathable.

Raul's mouth touched hers. Katarina's body jerked in response. This felt very real, dangerously so. Her senses wanted him, longed to touch every part of him.

Lightning flashed against her eyelids. Rain pelted on the roof, the street. Thunder shook the bedroom windows and with a startled gasp Katarina awoke, sitting up swiftly, the sheets and her cotton nightgown tangled around her legs. She breathed hard for several seconds. What a garbled nightmare.

She fell back against her pillows, listening to the lulling rain. What truth did the legend hide?

"Jean..." She sighed his name, then sat up again with a gasp. "Jean is French for John. And John is English for..." Katarina pressed her fingers to her temples, staring at the bedclothes through astounded eyes. "John is English for Giovanni."

She let her gaze travel to the window and the night sky beyond. "Dear God, is it possible?"

IAN HAD AN APARTMENT in the Île de la Cité. Babette didn't like it. But anxiety outweighed aversion tonight and so she'd come here after a disastrous dinner at Lucas-Carton, for a nightcap she did not want.

How was it her fault that a piece of food had gotten stuck in her throat? She could have choked to death, and what had Ian done? Continued to warn her that her mouth should say lines from the play and nothing else.

But Babette's indignation dissolved as she thought again of Ian's words. Had Claudia's mouth said too much? A shiver crawled down her spine, and greedily she took the wineglass Ian handed her.

Her fingers choked the stem. "Please, Ian, tell me what you meant at the restaurant tonight. You said our puppet master watches me closely now."

"No, I said he wants me to watch you," Ian corrected. He lit a cigarette. "He thinks you tend to be indiscreet."

"You have said this before," she snapped, then softened her tone. "I ask you plainly now. What does this man of mystery do to one with whom he is dissatisfied?"

Ian stared out the window at the rain that melted the bright lights of the city. "I think the puppet master can be rather unkind, Babette," he said finally. "I wouldn't cross him if I were you."

Fear and suspicion crowded into her head. You are frightened of him, she wanted to charge, but that would be a fool's victory. "He frightens me," she admitted instead. "I don't know why, but I am afraid of this man who controls my life yet whose face I have never seen. I do not think he trusts those who work for him. But why not, Ian? You know his identity. Why can you be told and the rest of us cannot?"

But she knew the answer before she even asked the question. Ian was a man who followed orders, always.

Again Babette shivered. Ian said nothing to her, merely shrugged and blew a thin stream of smoke toward the ceiling light.

Setting her glass down, Babette took a deep breath. "Ian, tell me," she pleaded, then grimaced because begging was so beneath her. "Did he kill Claudia? I must know this."

Still no expression touched his face, but he didn't look at her and that was very bad. He evaded best when he didn't look.

"There's nothing I can say to you, Babette. Nothing I will say. I've spoken to the puppet master in your defense. That's all I can do."

"Did he kill Claudia?" Something close to panic infected her voice now.

Ian crushed out his cigarette, stood and recovered her raincoat from the rack beside the door. "I think it's time you went home," he said. There was no inflection in his tone.

A peculiar numbness took over Babette's limbs. She felt lifeless, wooden. Like a puppet, she thought, and almost laughed hysterically.

Perhaps the overbright gleam in her eyes betrayed her, she couldn't say. But Ian regarded her now in a most mindful way, and he was not a man noted for his shrewdness.

"I will speak no more on this subject," she promised, fighting the panic that invaded her mind and body. "I will do as the puppet master wills."

Ian's nod was dispassionate. He opened the door for her, motioning her into the hallway. He did not follow. But then, it wasn't Ian who posed a threat to her life, of that she was certain.

Her legs felt like sticks of marble. The door shut behind her with a click. Had Claudia heard a different click before she died? Claudia, who had not possessed Babette's loose tongue, who did not make mistakes? Her friend who now resided in a graveyard?

Babette signaled for the elevator, steadying herself against the wall with her hand. To breathe was next to impossible. A giant rubber band wrapped itself around her chest. This was the worst fear she had ever known.

The architect had not killed Claudia, she understood that now. She knew. The puppet master had done it. And he could do it again.

IAN WAITED ONLY until his apartment door closed. Then he let his shoulders slump in dejection. He hated what he had to do, but it was her life or his, and he had no desire to become the puppet master's next victim.

Turning slowly he picked up the telephone and dialed. He got only a busy signal on the other end. When he was busy the person in charge took the receiver off the hook. And he was busy now, wasn't he, plotting their next big theft and the theater party that would precede it.

With a sigh, Ian reached for his raincoat and umbrella. He must go to the puppet master's home in Passy. The puppet master wouldn't appreciate that, but it must be done. Babette was a danger, verging on hysteria. She'd have to be—handled. With luck, he might be able to buy her one last chance. But for the present he could only do his duty. He wanted no knives carving up his body.

Chapter Twelve

Rain like a tinseled curtain poured from the blackened skies on the evening of the backstage party. Katarina scarcely noticed it. She'd cornered Louise, at their usual preperformance restaurant, Chez Marcel, and she wasn't going to let her go until she got some answers.

There was no time now to ponder ghosts in the vaults. She'd been doing that for days with no results. She believed in the possibility but she had no proof. On the other hand, Louise had been avoiding her, that was a fact. And Katarina had no trouble guessing why.

She caught up with her friend near the kitchen door. "You know about him, don't you?" she said, coming up behind her.

Louise studied her face consideringly. She didn't pretend to misunderstand, which was good because Katarina hadn't had an especially pleasant day. And trust Babette to make it worse. She'd come into the theater late that afternoon, screaming about misbehaving puppets in the museum.

Katarina let her mind go back. She'd been sitting on the edge of the stage, thinking about Raul and not really listening to Philip describe what it felt like to "work" the performance puppets each night.

"Human beings on a string, old girl," he was saying. "I twitch a finger and they dance. Heady thought, that. Of course, my old father's been at it for years, I'll be damned."

"At what?" Katarina came out of her abstraction long enough to catch the last sentence. Then she spotted a figure deep within the shadows. Francois. And gesturing to him quite passionately was Pierre. That's when Babette had swooped onstage.

"Silvain moved," she shouted. "He flapped his wings, I saw this with my own two eyes." Moaning, she lifted her eyes to the ceiling. "It is an omen. Oh, Heavenly Father, forgive my sins."

Philip grinned. "Feeling a bit queer, are you, Babette?"

"What sins, Babette?" Katarina asked.

By now everyone in the vicinity was staring at the trio on the stage, including Ian who stood on the puppeteer's podium overhead.

"Babette," he said softly. Was it a warning?

Babette glanced up, lowered her voice a trifle then grabbed Katarina's arm and shook it. "Silvain's wings," she said again in an urgent hiss. "They went up and down, like a vulture's. You believe such things are possible. So explain to me how does *this* thing happen?"

"I don't know—" Katarina began, but Babette cut her off.

"I said to you that there are ghosts in this world when you first asked me to tell you about Claudia's death. You remember this?"

"Yes, but—"

"I also said that they could kill." Her fingers became claws on Katarina's arm. The shimmer in her eyes was scary. "I didn't really believe that a ghost killed Claudia, but what if I am wrong and one did? Could a spirit that is doomed to walk forever upon the earth be made to perform monstrous deeds? And were this so, could such a spirit then also be made to commit murder?"

"Specter puppets?" Philip gave a disbelieving laugh. "Are you mad, Babette?" He patted Katarina's knee apologetically. "No offence, love. I believe in the afterworld as you do, but ghosts being jerked about on strings? Not a chance. I think you need a rest, Babette, old thing. Your powers of reasoning are a bit off today."

Her grip wasn't, Katarina thought with a grimace.

She pried Babette's fingers loose, then jumped when a voice close by offered a subdued, "Philip is right, Babette. You are overwrought." Francois, in black pants and a black turtleneck sweater, now stood before the stage, his features still concealed by the shadows. How did he do that? "You must be fresh and charming for the performance this evening and the party that will follow. Many of our valued patrons will wish to meet the puppet Mignon. I do not think they will also care to discuss the movement of Silvain's wings, do you?"

He stared at them with hidden eyes. It unnerved even Katarina, and she wasn't the object of his scrutiny.

Babette's hand fell away from her arm. She looked so terrified that Katarina actually felt sorry for her. So what on earth gave her the nerve to lean closer to Katarina and whisper, "Genevieve is missing. Did you know that?"

"Off on a bender, I should think," Philip remarked without concern.

Babette stiffened. "Genevieve does not drink."

Pierre strolled over. Unlike Francois, he didn't keep to the shadows but rested his arms on the rim of the stage. "It is true, Babette, that no one has seen Genevieve for many days now. But what would you have us read into this? That she was carried off by Silvain the puppet?" His tone dismissed the matter. His dark eyes did anything but. "Go to your dressing room and lie down. Francois is correct in this one matter, at least. For tonight you must be fresh."

"Do it, Babette," Ian said quietly from above. "Practice your lines for the last act. It will keep your—mind—fully occupied."

Her mind or her mouth, Katarina wondered, wishing distantly that Philip would remove his hand from her knee, yet not really sure why such a trivial thing should matter.

"I'll take her," she offered, pushing Babette forward.

"There's no need, Katarina," Ian said. "I'll escort her. You go on to Chez Marcel and relax. We've an important night ahead of us."

The memory of this afternoon broke apart as a waiter exited the kitchen, smacking the door against Katarina's backside. She was in the present again and still waiting for Louise to admit that she knew about Raul.

Her friend said nothing for a long moment. Then giving her head a shake, which looked like surrender, she exhaled heavily. "Yes, I know. And now you want to know how, don't you?" Her eyes traveled upward. "Raul, you lovesick idiot. What have you done?"

She glanced at the tables. The chatter of eighty or more human magpies spilled into the corridor. "We can't talk here," she said and indicated the rain-soaked street. "We'll go outside, under the arch of the Pont au Change. No one will hear us there. We'll make up some clever lie and grab a quick cab. God help me, I'll tell you what you want to know. But let me warn you, you're not going to like what you'll hear. It's a deadly trap Raul's gotten himself into, Kati. And if the puppet master has his way, it's one he'll never get out of."

"HE STABBED CLAUDIA how many times?" Katarina asked in a small voice.

"Upward of a dozen, Raul says." There was a shudder of revulsion in Louise's response. "Not a pretty sight, I suspect. For my money, this person Raul calls the puppet master is a raving lunatic, rotten to the core."

She was perched on a low bench under the arch of the Money Changers' Bridge, but Katarina's nerves were too finely stretched to sit. She paced, palms together, fingers raised to her lips.

"Whoever he is, he's been taking lessons from the Marquis de Sade," Louise went on. Her eyes roamed back and forth, from seed shop to rain-washed quay to swollen, gray Seine. "But that's it, really. There's nothing more to know about this animal."

"Nothing except his identity," Katarina said softly.

She surveyed the massing clouds above. Night hadn't quite fallen, but the city was lit, a blurred glow huddled beneath an eerie gray veil. Layers of purple mist tinged the edges of the clouds, spooky colors. A chill crawled over her skin. She could almost taste the menace in the air.

This wasn't the Paris of painters and poets. Lovers didn't stroll here. For tonight puppets moved their wings and the clouds looked bruised. To Katarina, seeing them brought to mind thoughts of butchers and thieves and death, of a missing woman and a black cat with blood on its paw.

Katarina trembled inside. Then she was struck with a terrifying thought. She swung to face Louise. "He's going to try to sneak into the party tonight, isn't he?"

Louise frowned. "Raul? Not as far as I know. Why?"

"Because he's looking for the puppet master, and very likely that's where he figures he'll find him." Katarina pressed her fingers to her temples. *Put it in order,* she instructed her mixed-up brain. "He already knows about Babette and Ian and the other people whose names you mentioned a minute ago. But they're only puppets, human tools being used by the person who's in charge of this—" She groped for a suitable word, which Louise deftly supplied.

"Bloodbath. And I agree. Raul's after the top puppet, so to speak. But he wouldn't crash the party. Actually, I'm not even sure he knows about it."

Katarina bit her lip, feeling guilty. "He knows."

"How?"

"I told him."

"Oh. Well, so much for blessed ignorance." There was no recrimination in Louise's voice, but her eyes continued to dart about the quay. "What'll we do, then? There's no disguise that'll work tonight. This shindig's strictly by owner invitation."

"The owners being Francois and Pierre." Katarina stared at the river, sidetracked. "I wonder..."

"Oh God, please don't," Louise begged. "At least not about Pierre. He's asked me to go with him to the Louis-St. Desmond party next week in Versailles. I refuse to believe that I've accepted a date with a fiend. Wonder all you want about Francois, but for my sake stop there."

Katarina managed a weak smile. "I'll stop there for both our sakes." She rubbed her hands up and down her arms. Even covered by a leather jacket, her skin felt like ice. "We've got to get a message to Raul, tell him that he can't come, that at this particular party we can do all the things he couldn't possibly do." She glanced at her watch. "Oh, but it's already six forty-five. We barely have time to make it back to the theater and into wardrobe and makeup. We'll never have enough time to get into the vaults. Unless—" She cocked her head to one side. "Could we get him a message?"

"Smart lady," Louise said with a grin. "Yes, we do have a drop spot, as a matter of fact. Raul always checks it before he goes out of the vaults. I'll leave a note. My cue's fifteen minutes after yours. I can get down there and back again, no problem."

Katarina started to nod, but stopped. The skin on the back of her neck was prickling, as if it had been brushed by the tips of a thousand pins. She raised her head. "Do you feel something?" she whispered tentatively.

"Like we're being watched?" Louise sounded grim. "I've been feeling it ever since you told me about Francois's cat and your suspicions about Genevieve." She stood, wiping the palm of one hand on the leg of her pants and motioning for a taxi with the other. "Blood on a cat's paw, death in the air, and now paranoia on the brain. This feels exceptionally bad to me."

Bad, yes. But what Katarina felt in her bones at this moment wasn't paranoia, it was unqualified terror. It was the evil of a sick mind, and it was out there in the rain, waiting.

THE PUPPET MASTER stood on the Pont au Change beside Ian, watching as the two women climbed into a taxi.

"They know more than they should, I think," he said to Ian, who pulled his sopping raincoat tighter and nodded. "You must watch them now, too. Katarina most of all. It is to her that Babette talks most freely."

Ian hunched his shoulders. He would make one more attempt. "She hasn't said anything of importance," he said with great caution. He dare not sound impertinent tonight. The puppet master was in a foul mood, no doubt a result of Babette's outburst in the auditorium this afternoon.

"You think it is not important that she speaks of Claudia and a puppet ghost and now of Genevieve?"

The last thing wasn't a subject Ian wanted to discuss. He didn't know where Genevieve was. He didn't want to know. "Babette was overwrought today," he maintained. "I'll speak to her again before the Louis-St. Desmond gala."

"I will surely cut her up long before that," the person in charge declared. His voice sounded cold and brutal for an instant, but then he smiled as a viper might. "At least, I will if she makes even one more small slip. I can wait for that moment, I think. It will come soon enough."

Ian's stomach turned, the blood draining from his face. But the puppet master wasn't finished yet.

"Claudia was a disappointment," he said, as if reliving a poignant moment. "I could not do her properly. Ah, but Genevieve, I was able to take my time. And what is best is that she knew who did it to her. Do you know what it is like, Ian, to hold in your hand the power of life and death? You, who are afraid even of your mother? Tell me, does she still telephone to criticize you every day? Poor Ian."

Ian sighed. This was an old taunt, but not half as uncomfortable as what had come before. Until...

"Have you ever slept with Babette, Ian? I think you like her a little. I prefer the ones with hair of gold. Katarina, she is pretty, but I like the wildcats. I am also drawn to the women with fire in their blood, and in their hair. Louise is such a woman. Ah, but then, the fire is not for one like you."

His laughter was low and coarse, and for an instant Ian was tempted to shove him from the bridge. But he buried the urge as he invariably did. "I'll watch Katarina," he agreed tonelessly.

He didn't move even though the puppet master's umbrella dripped on him. What did such minor things matter? He took orders from a man who committed bloody acts of barbarism as a mere sideline to robbery. Yes, the puppet master was brilliant. But he was also dangerously insane.

THERE WAS SOMETHING in the legend. There was a monster in the Puppet Theater. And there was Jean in the vaults.

Katarina shivered. The air felt cold, the magic level practically nonexistent. Was it gone forever? she wondered sadly.

She entered the château through the Puppet Museum. Louise had gone straight to the underground passageways. Dead silence reigned in the museum. Light from the chandeliers made eerie patterns on the floor.

"Don't come to the party," she murmured out loud, then noticed a displaced shadow and snatched her head around.

Her eyes probed the darkness, but there was nothing. Then she heard a whisper.

"Katarina."

Not a puppet, but Raul, sexy, dark-eyed dweller of the vaults.

He wore black pants, boots, belt and shirt. His long, dark hair fell over his collar, with more curls than usual in it thanks to the rain. He stood in front of Nicoli's display case, staring at her as the puppet did, and for a moment Katarina was struck by the resemblance.

Nicoli, the beautiful, sad puppet fashioned in Giovanni's likeness, yet it could have been Raul upon whom his face had been modeled.

He reached her in three long strides. But there was nothing ghostly in the hands that encircled her waist. The man who pulled her with him behind a large stone column was warm and solid and entirely real. So was the mouth that came down urgently on hers.

"Raul," she protested when she could manage a breath. "You shouldn't—" He kissed her again, but she finished with determination that was in no small part fear "—be here. This is very dangerous."

"I know."

His hands moved to her face. His thumbs caressed her cheekbones and again he set his mouth on hers. His tongue probed deep inside, sliding over her lips and teeth with deliberate slowness. He knew how to quiet her questions, but did he also know that she wanted to pull him down with her onto the floor? To forget stages and parties and make love to him right here in the Puppet Museum? A hundred little puppet eyes would watch as a better form of magic than her imagination could ever conjure unfolded before them.

"Raul, I really don't think we should be—" His teeth caught her lower lip, drawing it into his mouth. He changed the position of his head, deepening the kiss. "—doing this," were the last words she could get out.

It was a token protest. She let it go, moaning slightly as his hands shifted to her hips, pulling her lower body forward to meet his very hard one.

She wore white denim jeans, damp from the rain and humidity. Every sensation seemed infinitely more intense. She absorbed it all, the heat from Raul's body, the demands of his mouth and tongue, even her fingers that were tangled in his hair and would keep his lips on hers should his reason suddenly reassert itself.

But it wasn't Raul's reason or hers that had any part in the start of surprise that ran through her when a voice somewhere very close by said softly:

"There is danger in this action. You must stop."

She sensed the immediate change in Raul's body, in his touch. He stopped all right, as the voice instructed, and so did she, although she was reluctant to move too far away just yet.

His head came up. "Did you hear something?" he asked, and if the lie tempted, it was only for a second.

She nodded. "Someone's here."

He put her away from him carefully, saying nothing, just making a thorough sweep of the cases with his eyes. Katarina did the same.

But there was no one in sight, and not a sound to be heard except the soft splash of rain on the stained glass windows.

And then she heard it, a quiet click.

Katarina's breath caught. Someone was entering the museum. She peered into the shadows, at the man who emerged. It was Francois in a great black cape with a hood. He shook the moisture from a dripping umbrella as he crossed the floor. Or rather, as he glided across, Katarina thought in amazement. His movements were fluid, as if none of the bones in his body had joints.

Raul watched with interest, and with suspicion, too. Or was that more speculation in his dark eyes?

When she was sure Francois was gone and she could breathe normally again, Katarina leaned against the pillar, raising her eyes to Raul's unreadable ones. "Louise told me everything," she said bluntly. Before he could respond, she pushed away from the column and took his face between her hands. "She's in the vaults now, leaving a message for you. Raul, you can't sneak into the party tonight. Francois and Pierre and Ian, they know all the guests by name and face."

Bringing her right hand to his lips, he smiled in a sad, mysterious way that made her want to pull his mouth back onto hers. "Did I say I would come to this party?"

"Well no, but you tend to omit a lot of details when we talk."

"I do that for your own good, *chérie*—and don't yell at me with your beautiful eyes. I knew you would learn the truth in time. I simply didn't want to be the one to tell it to you."

"Why?"

"Because I'm guilty of getting you involved in this to begin with. I hoped I would get my answers before you got to Louise—which I should tell you isn't an easy thing to do. Louise and I have been good friends for many, many years. She doesn't betray secrets."

Katarina studied him. "How good is good?" she asked with mild distrust, and wasn't especially pleased when his smile widened.

His thumb brushed lightly across her chin. "Very good. When we were young and her family came to Barcelona for summer vacations, we used to catch sand crabs together."

Katarina wasn't convinced. "Only sand crabs, Raul?"

Now his mouth stroked hers. "Measles once. I gave them to her because I wouldn't stay in bed as I was told."

He slid his lips to the side of her neck. His breath came into her ear, his teeth pulled gently on the lobe. Heat poured through Katarina's body and she let her eyes close, let herself enjoy the exquisite pleasure in her limbs.

"Don't be jealous, Kati," Raul murmured. "Louise didn't enjoy the gift of red spots and fever that I gave her. She let her cat loose in my room when she was better."

"You don't like cats?" she managed to ask.

"I like them very much, but I'm allergic to them." His lips curved against her neck. "It wasn't much of a punishment, but I never told her that." He stopped the banter there, gave Katarina one final kiss beneath her ear, then stepped reluctantly back. "You should go now, before I do more that I'll regret."

Yes, she should go. That didn't mean she wanted to.

"What about the party?" she pressed, sighing. "Please Raul, promise me you won't come. It's no big deal, really, except to Francois and Pierre. Anyway, Louise and I can watch everyone there without attracting any attention at all." She pushed at her unruly hair, thick and wavy from the rain. "Consider it as a night off. Listen to *Bolero,* drink wine with Sofia and Jean." A thought occurred to her and she stopped. She sent him a curious look. "Raul, do you believe in reincarnation?"

His dark eyes seemed puzzled. "I haven't given it much thought. Why?"

"No reason," she said, sliding her gaze to Nicoli in the puppet case. "Just a crazy idea I had."

Chapter Thirteen

"There is danger in this action. You must stop..."

The warning plagued Raul even after he returned to the vaults. Sofia was waiting for him there. She had no answers, either.

"I didn't do it," she said, then pulled two more puppets from her sweater pocket. "Vignette and Verona."

Raul smiled as he unbuttoned his shirt. "Where do you find these, Sofia?"

"Far away from here, in a deeper place." Her deft little hands arranged the twins on the shelf. "I do not know if I will find any more."

"The legend contains so many puppets," Raul murmured. "And secrets."

A smile lit her wrinkled face. "You listen to the pretty young thing with the long dark hair. She enjoys telling the legend. She does not quite know the correct story, but she is closer to what I was told than most people are."

Raul tugged a black T-shirt over his head. "And what is it that you were told?"

"I do not know much that is different about the legend than the pretty young one. But mostly I do not believe that Giovanni was mad. I'm a romantic, yes? I tell myself that Giovanni waits for his Mignon. But I do not know if she will ever come back to him."

"You believe in Mignon?"

Sofia poked around in his food box. "Certainly. She is a real puppet person. Katarina believes in her. Why are you always so skeptical? More is possible than what you can see and touch. But I think I waste my time with this talk. Do you have any new food? Ah yes, here is something."

She opened a box of cherry donuts and began to munch. Then she kicked up the hem of her long skirt and grinned. "See my new stretchy black things? Babette screeched when she discovered they were missing."

Raul took a donut for himself, holding it in his mouth while he tucked in his shirt. Then he bit half of it off and bent to kiss her cheek. "You're a character, Sofia. I'll miss you when I leave this place."

"Maybe I will come and live with you in Barcelona." She adjusted her cockeyed kerchief and went back to searching his food box. "Or maybe I will stay here with my friends who live near the river. I will never understand why they insist on doing this when I tell them every day that I who have roamed all through the vaults for many months now have never once seen a ghost."

Amused, Raul finished his donut, then he sneezed.

"There is a draft in this place," Sofia said.

"There's a cat in this place," Raul corrected, combing his fingers through his hair and looking about the small chamber.

It sat on the half wall that separated this level from those below. Typical feline pose, tail wrapped around its paws. Its amber eyes on his face didn't blink.

"What a pretty bundle of black fur." Sofia located a bottle of soda. She gave it to Raul to twist off the top. "You did not bring such a pretty bundle down here with you. Who does this creature own?"

The corners of Raul's mouth lifted in a smile. "Francois Lupier. The cat's name is Amadeus."

"What is that?" Sofia tipped her bottle back, pointing at the animal's front paws. "Amadeus brings you a present, I think. A skinny rat, or a fat minnow from the Seine."

Raul spared the thing a quick glance. In his mind he was planning ahead. He wouldn't go to the party. He would trust Katarina and Louise to watch and listen for him. He would search other areas of the theater instead, places he hadn't yet been.

Beside him Amadeus let out an insistent meow and again Raul looked over. With its paw, the cat took a swipe at its catch.

"It is a grasshopper," Sofia announced with certainty, but she was absorbed in breaking open a fresh *baguette*. She didn't see what Raul suddenly did.

His muscles tightened in revulsion. This couldn't be. His eyes were playing tricks on him.

He moved cautiously closer. The cat's stare was unflinching. Its paw rested on the thing.

Raul's stomach gave a violent lurch, the breath hissed out of him. He felt dizzy, disbelieving. It wasn't possible that he could be seeing this ghastly thing!

"What is it? What do you stare at?" Sofia demanded.

But Raul didn't answer. He couldn't think, did not want to consider the macabre implications of this or look at the cat who stared at his ashen face.

This was no slimy object from the river. This thing was perhaps six centimeters in length, jointed and with a neatly manicured nail at one end. It was part of a woman's hand.

"THIS IS REALLY BORING," Louise whispered to Katarina through a plastered-on smile. "Much more of this eat, drink and be merry nonsense and Madame Louis-St. Desmond is either going to blow up or slither gracefully under the nearest table. What on earth do the Duperays of the Café Faustine put in the food they cater to these affairs?"

"Plenty of liquor," Katarina remarked behind her glass of tonic. "Philip's father's starting to look wobbly, that's for sure."

"Bag of wind," Louise declared. "Why don't you sneak over and charm the wallet from his pocket, save poor Philip the trouble of having to kiss his..."

"Louise..."

Sipping her soda Louise moved off.

"Ah, there you are, love."

Philip appeared at Katarina's side, his blue eyes shining. He looked like an angel and Katarina sighed. It was her misfortune that she preferred a dark-eyed devil.

"Come and say hello to the folks." Philip nodded through the backstage crush at his mother in her gown of green silk and lace. Her emeralds shimmered in the dusky light. The puppet master must be drooling.

"Good evening, my dear," Francine Hambleton greeted. She was a lovely woman, nothing like her husband. "You were charming tonight on the stage. Do you wish to play Mignon someday?"

"Only if I choose to leave!"

No one could mistake Babette's superior tones, though it wasn't quite so easy to see her. Did everyone in Paris smoke? And it was hot, too. Katarina eased the bodice of her peasant blouse away from her heated skin and wished someone would open a window.

"It is a good party." Babette glued herself to Francine's side, smiling at Philip.

Katarina's gaze left Babette to travel about the room. Philip said something beside her. He was talking to Monsieur Louis-St. Desmond and Pierre, but it was a dull conversation. She found it far more interesting to watch the gaggle of patrons that were huddled next to the buffet table. Madame Louis-St. Desmond was there, she noticed, and standing a discreet distance behind her, Ian, making quick entries in a small brown notebook.

Katarina tried to attract Louise's attention, to edge closer to Ian, but just then Babette offered a loud remark about "security systems that a trained monkey could penetrate" and Ian immediately snapped the book shut, tucked it away, and headed toward their group.

"Of course we'll be there, Armand," Philip was saying in Katarina's ear. "Delighted to attend your annual gala."

Who was Armand? A gentle press of Philip's hand on Katarina's waist got her attention, and she turned.

Armand Louis-St. Desmond was a toothy little man who reminded Katarina of a weasel. She must have nodded or something, in answer to what she wasn't sure, but she sensed she'd just agreed to accompany Philip to the Louis-St. Desmond spring ball in Versailles.

Now there was a daunting prospect. Despite the heat and smoke that made her eyes sting, she shuddered. The Louis-St. Desmonds were famous for their outlandish parties.

Ian slunk in without a fuss, standing close beside Babette and whispering something in her ear. Katarina strained to hear, but someone else's hand touched her arm.

"You are coming to our ball?" Francine Hambleton asked. "We hold it on the Saturday following the Louis-St. Desmond gala. It is a splendid masquerade ball. Say you will come. I know Philip will be devastated if you do not."

There was no graceful way out of this. Katarina smiled. "Of course I'll be there, Francine. Is it period?"

"Puppet, old girl, puppet," Harold Hambleton put in. "In honor of Philip's fascination, you know."

He didn't stop, merely passed by with two other men trailing along in his wake. They looked like business associates.

Directly behind the trio she saw Louise, who pointed at Ian. He'd left their circle and once again had his little brown book out. He was up to something.

He followed Harold Hambleton across the floor to a high velvet curtain. Katarina half expected him to duck behind it, but he didn't. He just stood and listened to the three men talk.

"They were discussing a new security beam," Louise told her later when she and Katarina escaped to the wings. "Some new contraption for the home and business. In Harold's case, I suspect he's talking home."

Katarina motioned at Babette. "She was talking about security a while ago, too."

"I heard her."

Katarina frowned. "Do you suppose that's how it's done?"

"What?"

She looked at Ian. "He's been making notes all evening. Wandering around, not getting involved in any deep discussions, just strolling from circle to circle listening, jotting things down. Sometimes he starts a conversation, then he steps back and starts making notes again. Maybe he's responsible for all this security system talk. I mean, it isn't your normal party chatter."

"Not as a rule." Louise twisted her head around. "Have you seen Francois tonight?"

"He was here earlier. I noticed him over by the flower cart."

"And since then?"

"I haven't seen him for about an hour."

"I'll wager you didn't even see him when you saw him."

"You never do," Pierre commented dryly, coming up behind Katarina.

He looked like a wealthy poet tonight. His rich brown hair was pulled back in a ponytail and he wore an exquisitely cut tuxedo. Half the women there flirted with him. Funny she hadn't noticed that until now.

Pierre sighed. "It is night, Francois should be out. But possibly he required sustenance that he cannot get from the Duperays' menu."

Louise grinned. "Like Dracula?"

"For certain he is close." An unexpectedly charming smile crossed Pierre's lips, and he held out his arm to her. "Come, lovely Verona, I will find you a glass of our finest champagne."

Katarina watched them go, then turned back to Ian. Instead, she found herself looking directly into Babette's malicious black eyes.

It was a thin layer of malice, however. Beneath it lurked the unmistakable traces of fear.

"So," Babette said, "you will go to the Louis-St. Desmond gala and to the Hambleton ball. On Philip's arm, I presume."

"Why are you so scared, Babette?" Katarina asked point-blank.

Babette's wineglass splintered as it hit the polished wood floor. No one appeared to notice, so Katarina continued. "Are you afraid someone's going to kill you, the way *he* did Claudia?"

Babette's cheeks went white, her voice was nothing short of a hiss. "What are you saying?" She leaned closer. There was pure terror in her eyes. "What do you know? Do you talk to Giovanni's ghost?"

"Ghosts don't kill people," Katarina said, with no knowledge of whether they did or not. "Anyway, you told me the architect did it. Now suddenly you're blaming a ghost. Next you'll say it was a puppet."

"A puppet?"

Francois's voice came from the shadow of a walnut post, and Katarina controlled a start of surprise.

"It is nothing," Babette denied quickly. She looked a little green now. "We're playing a game, that's all."

"I see."

Katarina wished she could—see Francois's face, that is. His hair looked nice, thick and quite long. He also had a widow's peak, which wasn't terribly pronounced. A lot like Dracula's...

"What is it that you guess about, Babette?" he inquired. His voice had a silky texture to it. "Giovanni's legend? Or maybe matters more bloody than this?"

Katarina took a step back. She had to. Babette, immediately in front of her, would have knocked her over otherwise.

"I do not understand what you are saying," Babette insisted. Her heel came down hard on Katarina's foot. "I know nothing of ghosts or blood or robbery."

Had Francois mentioned robbery? Pain shot up Katarina's leg. Catching Babette's arm, she drew the woman away. "Excuse us," she said with a smile that was more to conceal her sore foot than anything, although she did sense something very weird in the air now. Was Francois the cause of it?

"He is following us." Babette whispered, trembling.

"No, he isn't." Banking down her own uneasiness, Katarina led Babette to an empty wall, then spun her around. "What do you mean you know nothing of robbery?"

Babette's breathing slowed. "I don't understand."

"Francois never used the word 'robbery,' Babette."

"You are mistaken. I heard him."

"Should I ask him?"

"No!" Babette's hand shot out. Her fingers gripped Katarina's wrist. "Please. I know that we do not get along, but you must not ask him questions. And you must not ask me."

"Why not?"

"Because."

"Because what?" Katarina leaned forward. "Are you in trouble?"

"She will be if she does not begin to mingle with the guests," Pierre remarked serenely in passing.

He carried on to where Francois stood watching and undoubtedly listening to every word Babette spoke. A small shock went through Katarina's body. She hadn't seen him move so close to them.

"I must mingle," Babette said lamely. The knuckles of her fists were white. "Where is Ian? Do you see him?"

Ian was about five feet away, hiding behind a fat man with a cigar. Eavesdropping, no doubt. Katarina shook her head. "Sorry, no," she lied. "Come on." She pushed a napkin and a chocolate strawberry between Babette's fingers. "We'll mingle together, maybe rescue Philip from his father."

And then they could pray to God that this party would end before the eerie sensations Katarina was feeling took on human form and came at both of them. With a knife.

"SOFIA, what are you doing here?" In a swish of petticoats Katarina raced into Raul's underground living quarters. "No, never mind," she said in the same breath. She went down on her knees in front of the tiny woman who lounged on Raul's cot, eating crackers and rummaging through his shaving kit. "Where's Raul? Have you seen him? I have to talk to him."

Tucking her spindly legs beneath her, Sofia sat up. "He took the bundle of black fur and left. I do not know where he went."

"Bundle of—oh, the cat."

"He called it Amadeus. The bundle brought him a present, but he wouldn't show it to me."

"Why not?"

"I thought it was a big grasshopper, but now I think it wasn't such a nice present. He took it with him when he went."

Katarina accepted the cracker Sofia pushed into her hand. An unknown present, a cat, and Raul off prowling heaven knew where at midnight. These were not good signs.

"I don't suppose he told you when he'd be back?"

"He said nothing. Would you like some soda?"

"No thanks." Katarina stood and walked over to the puppet display. "You found Vignette and Verona," she exclaimed in delight. "They're lovely."

"I brought them here today." Sofia chuckled. "Shall I tell you which one is evil?"

"You know?"

"Of course. I am old. I know many things." Her brow wrinkled. "I do not know how to find Giovanni, though. My friends who live by the river are too frightened to help me look, and my friend with the dark sexy eyes will not admit that ghosts even exist. You believe, but you do not live in the vaults. Your life is above, yes?"

Katarina saw the shrewd light in her blue eyes. "I suppose so," she agreed. "Sometimes I think living down here would be easier."

Sofia cocked her head. "Easier how? Don't you like people?"

"Of course I do. But people die, Sofia. Even in the Puppet Theater, they're dying. First Claudia and now, I think a second woman." She sighed. "And if the answers to all of this really do lie in the legend, I certainly don't see them."

"Answers in the legend?" Sofia pursed her lips. "What does that mean?"

"It's nothing." Katarina dismissed the matter and returned to the cot. "Tell me, do you know any men named Jean?"

"I know fourteen Jeans. Specify."

"Well," Katarina thought for a moment. "I think he lives down here."

"In the vaults? Six. Go on."

"This particular Jean is young, thirty maybe. He has dark hair, long and beautiful dark eyes."

Sofia cackled. "He sounds like another young man I know."

"Yes, well, actually he does sort of resemble Raul. And he knows you, or about you anyway. Does that sound like one of your six?"

"It sounds like two of them. The name you give is very common in France. Why do you ask me these questions?"

"I met a Jean down here several nights ago. He told me he lived in another part of the vaults, but he knew about Raul. Doesn't that seem strange to you?"

Sofia propped her chin up on her hands. "I know nothing of strange," she admitted. "I know only that I have not been able to contact Giovanni so that I might ask him to torment Babette. Frighten her into making a loud confession of her crimes. But," she brightened, "I will keep working on this problem. If Giovanni resides in these old vaults still, I will find him. And he will help both you and my sexy young friend with the dark eyes."

"You think so?" Katarina felt a surge of hope. Of course, it was totally irrational. "So you think he's a benevolent spirit?"

"He is a gentle soul," Sofia stated with confidence. "And surely not so mad as the legend tells. Kind souls with power from beyond might be deceived by evil once, but never two times. The butcher who likes to carve up women with knives must be caught. This creature is all evil. He and his wicked knife must be put in a cage of pads and steel. And never must he leave this cage."

Chapter Fourteen

Raul wandered deep into the black heart of the vaults, guided by an instinct he neither understood nor much cared about right now. The cat came partway with him, then disappeared. It had brought the horrible thing to him, and it didn't seem to mind relinquishing possession.

A shudder ran through Raul's body. He felt cold, lifeless, like a puppet on invisible strings. There was no thought behind his actions now, he simply walked.

Earlier his mind had functioned at a slightly higher level. He'd put the ghastly thing aside, gone into the theater and searched the back rooms.

But he hadn't quite been prepared for the memories in the prop room.

It had come to him in a rush, thoughts of Claudia before she died, the affronted expression on her face....

"What is this? You think you can take advantage of me and then just dust me off, Raul Sennett?"

Her shouts could have been heard in Spain. But Raul had come to understand her temperament well after two dinners and several weeks spent working at the Puppet Theater. He ignored her and went about his business.

Claudia, however, didn't want to be dismissed. She'd ranted for another twenty minutes, screaming things like, "I will not be used by a man, not ever."

Fury made her incoherent, and Raul irritated. How could something be over that had never started? He'd been hot and tired and frustrated by delays in the reconstruction. He was in no mood for a confrontation rooted in absurdity.

"Go away, Claudia," he'd snapped finally. "I don't have the patience for this. We ate dinner together. I didn't lead you on, and I didn't pretend to want you."

"Liar," she'd yelled. "You want me, you know you do."

Raul had rolled his eyes and turned away. But Claudia would not stop, and eventually he'd wound up shouting back at her.

Two hours later, he'd found her body....

His head throbbed with the memory of that sight. Blood everywhere, and her eyes dull, empty. They would haunt his nightmares forever.

And he also had this other horror to deal with, this thing he had temporarily hidden while he searched the theater and now had to bury far down in the deepest tunnel. Maybe he would get lost there. He ground his teeth together, hating his confinement and all the things he might never have. And all for no greater reason than that this was the way the puppet master wished it to be.

He might never have Katarina....

Raul's mind and body reacted fiercely at that thought. Enough of this self-pity! He would hide the thing and be done with it. This world of darkness was not going to become his. Katarina didn't belong with Philip, and if that was jealousy talking, fine. For Katarina and for himself, he was going to get out of here.

When he'd descended as far as he could, into some sort of a cave, Raul crouched down and buried the object beneath a good-size rock.

His first reaction had been to send it with an anonymous letter to the police. But that would only make things worse for him. He'd be suspected of committing another murder, assuming the woman from which this finger had been severed was dead. And God help her, she'd be better off that way if the puppet master had indeed done this to her.

The burial complete, Raul stood and raked his fingers through his hair. He had no idea where he was. So why did this damp and musty place seem vaguely familiar to him, a flicker on the edge of his consciousness? He hesitated, then dismissed the sensation and started back.

Again he gave no thought to direction, he simply knew how to unscramble himself. A mental compass in his head, perhaps? It didn't matter. Only Katarina mattered, her safety. What if the puppet master turned his knife on her?

There was an edge of panic in the tremor that jarred Raul's senses. He was still shaking when he reached a more habitable area, far above the caverns. Centuries of mold had clung to those ancient walls, seeded itself into the earth where he had dug. He could never live in mold. If only he could make Katarina understand the truth of this underground world.

He let the idea go as he approached his living quarters. For a moment he thought he was seeing things. Past one o'clock in the morning, and she was here. Katarina, dressed in her cotton layers of puppet costume, pretty peasant pastels with ribbons crisscrossed Tyrolean-style on the front.

She ran to him like an eager lover—his wish only, he thought wearily—flinging her arms around his neck and hugging him tightly.

"Thank God, you're back. Sofia was here but she left twenty minutes ago. I was getting worried." She pulled away to look at him, her eyes inspecting every inch of his face.

She touched his cheeks, his eyelids, his hair. He saw the tenderness in her expression. "What's the matter?" she asked. "Raul, are you all right?"

A glimmer of black humor slid through him and he shook his head. "No," he said. And he dropped his needful mouth onto hers.

"OKAY, MAYBE HE DIDN'T put his brown book in his safe, but it can't hurt to look," Katarina insisted, and for the tenth time since he'd agreed to this late-night search of Ian's office, Raul swore himself a fool.

But here they were even so, at the hidden staircase that led to the armoire.

"Kati," he began, almost too tired to think, but she shook her head.

"No, I'm coming with you. I left the party at midnight. That's early by the standards of these particular guests. Especially the Louis-St. Desmonds, who are hosting a huge gala next week, and about whose security system Ian was making all sorts of notes." She gave Raul a push. "Armand's a braggart. Has the best heat beams and pressure sensors in the country and he's going to let the world know it. He's practically begging to be robbed."

"And he'll surely get his wish." Raul led the way up the narrow staircase. "What makes you think this book will now be in Ian's safe?"

"Because he made an excuse and left the party right after Count Fernaud saw him with it and demanded to know if it was like his own little black book. Ian probably felt he'd better ditch the thing before Fernaud got his sleazy hands on it. The Count is a dirty old man."

"How old?"

"Eighty-three."

"And he has a little black book?" Raul remarked in abstracted amusement. This search wasn't a good idea. His instincts still objected loudly.

He heard Katarina muttering behind him. Something about his being the typical mentality of a European male. It brought a faint smile to his lips.

"Is Ian there?" she asked when he dislodged the rear panels.

"I don't hear him." Raul took her hand. "Come on, let's get this over with."

He stepped from the wardrobe into a room bathed in the wet glow of the city. Beyond the windows splashes of water-color light streamed one into the other. A painter's palette, but they hadn't come here to marvel at the view.

Katarina was already going through the walnut cabinet, shoving the merchant puppet, folded posters and files aside. "Nothing here," she said. "Where's the safe?"

"Behind this portrait." Raul pulled the frame from the wall. "Marie Antoinette on the guillotine."

"Let them eat cake," Katarina quoted softly. "Do you know the combination?"

For an answer Raul gave the dial three quick turns and twisted the handle. He located the brown address book and held it up for her.

"Is this it?"

"No. Too big." She flipped through it anyway. "Nothing else?"

"No jewels. Not even money this time."

"Can't blame Ian for that. What did you do with it, anyway?"

Raul stuck the address book back, closed the safe and returned the picture to its original position. "I gave Ian's money to Sofia. I still have Pierre's and Francois's. If neither of them turns out to be the puppet master they'll get it back."

"Generous of you." Katarina started to say, but then she stopped and grabbed Raul's arm as voices in the corridor alerted them to another presence up here, a man's and a woman's. Raul couldn't identify them with the door closed.

But would it stay that way? Something told him no. Katarina was tugging on his arm, heading toward the armoire. That was the correct thing to do. But who were the people outside? The man's voice was loudest, and it didn't sound like Ian's.

"Raul," Katarina whispered in desperation. "They're coming in. I hear keys rattling."

He relented to logic, crossing to the armoire.

"It's stuck." He snatched his head up as Kati tugged on the knob. "It won't open."

A kick would make it open, but it would also give them away.

"It's the dampness," he murmured, turning Katarina and pushing her toward the office door. "Go there," he said, "to the side where the hinges are. When they come in, you get out." He pressed a quick kiss to her hair. "I'll hide behind the desk."

Because if Katarina was spotted that would be the best possible position from which to stop dead any harmful pursuit. Assuming these people were dangerous...

The door was flung back with abandon. Katarina stopped it from hitting her, but let it open enough to conceal her, and that was good.

No lights were turned on, and only a man's silhouette filled the frame. It was Pierre, with Louise behind him.

Raul clenched his teeth. The little fool, what was she doing! Pierre Fousard couldn't be trusted, not yet. And still Louise walked into a darkened office with him in the middle of the night.

Pierre strode in with purpose, Louise idled by the edge of the open door, languishing on the rim, swaying as if to an unheard waltz. Then suddenly, her shoulders stiffened and her eyes went wide. She glanced sharply at Pierre then away. Her mouth moved in a silent whisper.

She didn't turn around, which was fortunate because just at that moment Pierre did. "Are you speaking to me?" he inquired.

Even in the feeble light Raul saw Louise's throat muscles constrict. "Er, yes," she replied, then firmed up her voice. "I said, are you sure Ian won't mind you taking his umbrella?"

"Why should he mind? I take it often." Pierre shrugged and extracted a large brown umbrella from the stand. He turned toward Louise, but a sudden frown marred his expression.

Raul's skin went cold, perspiration trickled down his spine. Did Pierre see Katarina? Automatically, he positioned himself to strike.

"What is that?" Pierre demanded, and Raul saw Louise jump slightly.

"What's what? I don't hear anything."

"With this one, you never do." Pierre motioned at the floor. "Villainous little beast. Francois's familiar, I think."

Raul lowered his gaze, and felt his entire body sag in relief. Amadeus stood on the threshold. For an instant Raul pressed his pounding forehead against the desk.

"A warlock or a creature of the night is my partner," Pierre remarked in a cynical tone. "Perhaps one day I will know the truth of his dark magic. Always he tells me things and I think to myself, how does he know this? But he will not say."

"Yes, well, he is unusual, I must admit." Nervously Louise gripped the doorknob. "So, shall we go then, before Ian comes?"

Shouldering the umbrella, Pierre strolled across the floor. "Don't concern yourself with thoughts of Monsieur Ian Renshaw. Tonight, we drive with my friends to a coffee house where the French crepes are lighter than air. Crowded, but always there is a price to be paid for perfection."

"I love crowds," Louise lied. "Let's go."

She would have closed the door, except that for some reason the cat refused to move. And it didn't wish to be moved as Pierre discovered when he bent to shoo the animal away. One swipe of claws and the attempt died.

"And so, Ian's office remains open," he said, not sounding as if he cared. "Come, Louise. My friends are waiting in the lobby."

She hooked her hand through his arm, glanced back then hastily down at the watchful feline. "Good night—Amadeus. Hope you catch a big rat."

They left, and Raul released a breath heavy with relief. His nerves, his muscles, his slamming heart, all screamed at him. Go to the police! Believe in God and justice.

Then he recalled what he'd buried earlier tonight and a lump of resistance formed in his stomach.

Where the puppet master was concerned there was no justice.

THE CAT MEOWED LOUDLY when Katarina bent to stroke its silky ears. Pierre and Louise were long gone. But what should she make of them together?

She called softly to Raul, then turned and literally collided with him. Her hands came up to his hard chest. Wrong time, she thought with a pang of regret. But what could one small kiss hurt? Not giving him a chance to react, Katarina wrapped her arms around his neck and pulled his mouth onto hers.

She sensed the urgency in his touch, in the thrust of his tongue between her lips and the way he pushed his hips against hers. Nothing subtle in any of it. He wanted her, and she wanted him.

"But this is an even worse place to make love than the vaults," he murmured into her mouth. "You make me do risky things, *chérie.* I think you should be ten meters away from me all the time."

Katarina grinned, but she had the good sense to step away. One kiss, that was all. "One thing about the vaults, though," she said. "They're private."

"They're gloomy." He tapped her chin, kissed the tip of her nose and then her lips one last hard time. "Come on. We're standing in an open office. This is like asking to be caught."

At her feet Amadeus meowed again, demanding attention. Too bad for him. Raul's mouth fascinated her, and his eyes . . . Katarina could stare into those beautiful, dark eyes forever. And maybe she would have if the cat hadn't begun batting her ankles with its forepaw.

"What is it?" she asked, not looking down.

Unblinking, he stared up, meowing at both of them now.

Raul's lips curved in amusement. With his head he motioned to the wall behind Katarina. "Maybe he's telling us that we didn't close the cabinet properly."

Katarina swung around guiltily. "That's my fault. I hope Pierre didn't notice it."

Raul's amusement became a full-fledged smile. "I don't think Pierre would care if he had found Ian's safe open."

"I suppose not. What *is* it, Amadeus?" Katarina demanded as the cat continued to swat her legs and meow. "Are you hungry? Did Francois forget to feed you?"

She could have sworn she felt a shudder pass through Raul's body, but he was gone from her before she could question it, shoving his fingers through his hair and double-checking the portrait.

Amadeus left her to rub against his legs. That produced a sneeze and a murmured, "You know I'm allergic to you."

Katarina smiled. "That's a cat for you."

Another meow.

Raul reached over to close the cabinet. Before he could, however, the cat sprang, landed neatly on the shelf and emitted the loudest howl it could manage.

"Hungry," Katarina interpreted, then interrupted herself to say, "Amadeus, stop that. Put the puppet down. Ian's not supposed to know that anyone's been here. Raul, grab him."

But it was too late. With the merchant puppet's leg in his mouth the animal leapt from the shelf and raced for the door.

Did he pause there deliberately? It seemed to Katarina that was exactly what he did. But why? Cats were smart, yes, but smart enough to challenge a human to follow?

"Wait here," Raul said. "I'll get him."

And miss all the fun? Katarina gathered her skirts. Not a chance.

The corridors were poorly lit. To the right she ran, then down a stretch of hall and left—into the very same dead-end passage where Francois and Pierre had talked last week.

Since he couldn't meow with a puppet in his mouth, Amadeus growled softly, paused again—this time Katarina was sure of it—then squeezed his agile little body through some kind of opening in the boards. Once inside he yowled loudly.

"He wants us to come in." Raul surveyed the heavy boards. "This is a very smart animal." He glanced at Kati. "Shouldn't you be in Ian's office?"

She smiled. "Raul, Amadeus did everything but crook his paw at us to follow. You expect me to ignore that?"

He tugged on the planks. "These are very old. Sturdy enough, but here at the bottom they've gotten damp somehow. The wood's starting to rot."

"So can we get inside?"

"Probably." He pounded the boards with the heel of his hand. "But I can only break maybe three of the panels. We'll have to slide along the floor."

Katarina's smile widened. "What fun."

Knocking loose three long strips of wood, Raul pulled them free then sat back on his heels and raised his eyes to the ceiling. "I don't believe I'm doing this at two in the morning."

"It wouldn't make much more sense at two in the afternoon." Katarina went down on her stomach. "Can I go first?"

Raul kissed the top of her head. "No."

Setting her aside, he worked his body through the hole.

"Anything?" Katarina asked when she saw his flashlight beam.

"Yes and no. Amadeus is here, but I don't think he wants to be caught just yet."

Typical feline. Katarina wriggled through the opening on her stomach, dusting off as Raul played the beam down a long, narrow passage. Amadeus sat about three-quarters of the way along, the puppet in his mouth, his amber eyes staring. The second the light fell on him he turned and trotted through an unblocked archway.

"Weird," Katarina muttered. "I hope he's playing."

She caught the note of humor in Raul's tone. "You hope, but you're too curious to leave here without knowing for sure."

She didn't deny the truth. "I guess that makes me catlike in my own right, doesn't it?"

She felt his fingers slide along the curve of her cheek and trembled a little inside. "Better for one so beautiful to be curious, I think. Hiding in the darkness and shutting out the mysteries of the world, that would be the real tragedy."

Shut out mysteries, and death. And love as well?

Katarina shook herself and let Raul draw her through the darkness. The silence seemed to echo inside her head. It was an eerie stillness, unbroken and yet infused with a quality she couldn't begin to describe. Something unfolded within it, whispers buried too deep for her ears to hear.

Song of the dead, her uneasy mind termed it. Which was not a good thing to think.

Shivering, she pressed closer to Raul. How could darkness feel wicked? She didn't like it, and if that made no sense, Katarina didn't really care. Something evil had happened here.

They'd reached the archway. Another corridor branched off, and three more after that before the cat finally stopped disappearing and planted himself outside a closed door.

He was a spooky little creature, clever to a near human degree. Did he play cat games with them? Katarina's instincts said no, but if not that, then where was Amadeus leading them?

"It's not locked," Raul said, testing the handle. Before turning it all the way, he played the flashlight over the stone floor. "There's no dust here like there was in the other passageways. There must be another entrance to this place, one that is used."

"By the puppet master?" A mixture of fear and awe made Katarina's question a whisper. "Maybe he stores his stolen merchandise here."

"Maybe," Raul said, and again Katarina felt a tremor of fear crawl down her spine, through her limbs.

But that was ridiculous. There was no reason to be afraid here, although to fear the puppet master could hardly be deemed silly. Still, he wasn't around now. He couldn't be or they'd have heard him.

"We've come this far," she reminded Raul when he hesitated. "The worst we'll probably find is an empty room."

"No," he corrected, tightening his grip on the handle. "That's the best we'll find."

And giving the door a shove he opened it to the blackened room beyond.

Chapter Fifteen

Katarina peered into the shadows. Empty. There wasn't a jewel or painting in sight, only a clean, swept floor and a cat with a puppet trotting over to sit beside a large water stain.

"So you're playing games with us after all," Raul remarked, but it was relief in his tone not annoyance.

A shudder passed through him when he considered what he had been expecting. Something far more gruesome than what he'd buried tonight in the vaults.

Katarina pressed her head against his arm. "I think I'm glad for the letdown," she confided. "I don't like the feeling here, Raul. Maybe it's a case of belated nerves, but I think we should go now and let the disappearing puppet remain a mystery to Ian. He probably won't even notice."

"Probably not," Raul agreed. His lips moved against her silky hair. "If he does, Pierre can explain it away along with the missing umbrella."

He regarded the cat as he spoke. For no reason, he simply stared at a fixed point, thinking about what Katarina had said a moment ago. She was right. Something evil lived in this room. He sensed it, too, and he didn't even believe in such things.

"Let's go," he said. "It's getting—"

Quite suddenly and with no forewarning he started, his heart banging hard against his ribs. He caught back a tight breath that he prayed Katarina wouldn't notice and struggled to keep his body from betraying him.

Katarina lifted her face from his arm. "Raul, what's wrong?"

She sounded puzzled. He'd lost the struggle to control his body. "Nothing," he lied, and pulled her head back onto his shoulder. "It's getting late, that's all. It's time we left."

She twisted free of his hand to stare at him. "Why the sudden urgency?"

He heard suspicion in her voice, saw it in her eyes. He had to ignore it, he couldn't let her see the mark. Snap off the light.

Unfortunately, his abused muscles didn't respond fast enough to the commands of his brain. She saw the pallor of his cheeks and spun around, following the line of his gaze to the floor and the cat. And then to the stain that resembled a splotch of paint.

"My God!" she whispered, staring now in the same paralyzed manner that he did. He didn't prevent her from inching closer. "Raul, that's not water." She raised horrified eyes to his face. "It's blood!"

IAN SAW THE PUPPET first, and then the mark. Dried but unmistakably copper-colored. Blood.

He squatted down in the empty room. It was morning. Blessed sunshine poured over the city. But here were only dark shadows, memories of what had been.

Not that he hadn't already known. Ian prided himself on his ability to accept the truth no matter how repellent or brutal it might be. And hadn't the puppet master in a graphic fashion confided his acts of butchery last night on the Pont au Change?

Unsteady fingers reached for the little puppet. So many problems flooded his mind, not the least of which was a growing concern for his own life. But no, the person in charge needed him. Ian carried out all the bothersome little tasks that he refused to do.

"You deal with petty matters. That is your job," the puppet master told him endlessly, and always in that same derisive tone. "I think, you act. I am in control of this theater. And of you."

Ian closed his eyes. Amadeus had entered the room and now sat staring at him. A cat wasn't important. All that mattered was that someone had been here.

He stood, trying desperately not to look at the floor. "Monster," he accused through stiff lips. "Butcher. Fiend. How could you do something like this? Poor Genevieve."

"Oh bravo, Ian," a voice behind him applauded. "You show anger at last. Tell me, do you hate me?"

Slowly Ian turned toward the doorway. He saw the smug gleam in the puppet master's eyes. Yes, he did hate him. But he wasn't foolish enough to admit it. "I question the necessity of killing Genevieve," he said. "Nothing more."

Hard eyes grew harder still. "Claudia left a letter about me that I did not wish the authorities to see. Genevieve found it. She read it. I killed her. It was that simple."

Hardly simple. Ian swallowed the bile in his throat. "Did you come through the passageway?" he inquired.

"And why," the puppet master challenged, "should I take that roundabout route when the more direct one is now available to any and all who do not mind getting their clothes a little dusty?"

He'd seen the dislodged boards. Very bad. His dissatisfaction came out as sarcasm, but Ian wasn't stupid. The puppet master was worried and just maybe feeling around for a scapegoat, another Raul Sennett. For surely he'd never permit himself to be blamed for murder.

"Whoever broke in here," the person in charge maintained, "is either extremely smart, or uncommonly stupid."

Ian frowned. "I don't understand."

"Idiot," he snapped. "Of course, you would not. To leave the boards dislodged is not something that would be likely to go unnoticed for any length of time. Therefore, the person who removed them either saw the blood and ran in fear, or saw the blood and deliberately left the boards down, knowing that I would see this and become concerned, perhaps even panic. But I assure you, this last thing will never happen. I will find this troublesome person and I will kill him. Or her. And I promise you, it will not be a painless death. No, not painless at all."

On that ominous note, he took his leave. Ian felt his shoulders sag with relief. No point suggesting to his superior that whoever removed the boards might not have seen the stain. That wasn't true, and Ian held the proof in his hand.

"Very foolish," he said in a pitying tone. His fingers tightened about the puppet's wooden body. "You shouldn't have let him know you were here. You should have covered your tracks."

He turned from the blood. He hoped that pain was something last night's intruder enjoyed.

THE SILENT MYSTERY of the night wrapped itself around Katarina. She lay on her stomach on the floor of her apartment and looked out the living room windows at the glowing city. Then she looked at the painted puppet stage Luther had given her a million years ago when the things that mattered most in her life were hot beignets, stories about the bayou and Papa's promise that he would take her to Paris.

Holding a croissant in her mouth, she picked up one of Luther's soft-bodied puppets. She wished this dark-haired man was Raul. She wished he were here, but he wouldn't come. He thought coming to her would endanger her life. He wanted to be with her, but not in the vaults, and now not in her apartment, either.

Katarina rolled onto her back, munching her croissant, and sighed. The texture of her thoughts deepened, which was normal for the night. Heat from the open window flowed over her limbs. The air smelled like carnations. What could she do about Raul? What could she do about the other horrible things she'd learned recently?

She pictured dried blood on the floor of a hidden chamber. Genevieve's? Possibly, but her mind still shied away from the now five-day-old image.

So what, then, could she do with her uneasy knowledge? Call the police? And tell them what? That she'd been prowling around on the fifth floor of the Puppet Theater for no particular reason and she'd just happened to stumble across a boarded-up room with this suspicious-looking mark on the floor?

She didn't dare mention Raul, or the cat, or the search through Ian's office, but she could remind them about Genevieve's disappearance. Yes, she could do that, then sit back and watch them redouble their efforts to find Raul. Because if the architect had killed Claudia, why not kill Genevieve, too?

Katarina shuddered down to her bones. No, she wouldn't call the police, she'd decided even before they'd left the room. And an uncharacteristically withdrawn Raul had agreed. They should just go, leave the boards down and the puppet on the floor next to the bloodstain. Let the real killer know that someone was onto his sick games. Shake him up, and Ian as well.

And keep moving puppets in the museum, Katarina thought now. Babette was going crazy over that....

"I will do no more tours," she'd shouted to Ian yesterday. "The puppets will not stand in one spot. See for yourself! Jo-Jo sits always on Renato's left. But today he is on the right."

Ian sounded weary. "Someone's playing games, Babette, that's all."

"And just how," she'd demanded in a frightened whisper, "does this someone make Silvain's wings move even as I watch? No, Ian, it's the ghost, I tell you. He punishes me. He tries to make me lose my mind. And soon he will come for yours."

"Keep your voice down," Ian had snapped. Katarina, tucked in behind a stone column, had never heard such a sharp tone from him. "This is guilt talking, Babette, nothing more. And I would advise you to stop before the puppet master hears any more about it. This isn't the Middle Ages. Puppets don't move by themselves, and ghosts don't do it for them...."

The memory dissolved. On the floor of her apartment, Katarina flung her forearm over her eyes. Images swam in her head, thoughts of blood and puppets and moving wings, Philip's face and Raul's. A groan rose in her throat. There was no contest between these men. Philip's features were hazy, Raul's darker ones were entirely clear.

Why had he become so withdrawn the other night? Because of the bloodstain? According to Louise he'd seen worse things than that. Not that Katarina hadn't felt nauseous herself, but Raul seemed to handle the sight with as much equanimity as any decent human could. No, something else troubled him, some secret he refused to share.

Restless, Katarina sat up. Think, she told herself. There must be a way to help him.

What had Jean said to her in the vaults? The answers are in the legend. She should concentrate, then, on Giovanni's legend.

"Puppets of wood and cloth and string," she murmured. "Puppets of flesh and bone. Mignon was a puppet. So was the Italian merchant. In the strictest sense, Giovanni wasn't a puppet, and yet in another that's exactly what he was. Everything that happened he allowed to happen. So yes, he was a puppet of sorts.... God, this is confusing."

Katarina released a tired breath. "All right," she said to the room. "Giovanni was a puppet. So are Babette and Ian, and everybody else who's being controlled by the puppet master. And cruelty controls the puppet master, or madness, or both. But how does that tie into the legend?"

She laid back down on her stomach, her head resting on her folded arms, and regarded the colorful puppet stage. The beautiful dark-haired man-puppet watched her back. In her mind she made him Raul, the man she loved but could not have. Not now, maybe not ever.

Katarina's fists clenched, her muscles tightened. She wanted to strangle the monster who murdered women and destroyed lives.

THE POLICE HAD COME to the Puppet Theater earlier that day. Raul went over their visit late Wednesday night while he shifted the contents of the display case around. They were subtle switches this time, but Babette would notice.

The police appeared more and more often. But still Claudia's murder hadn't been solved, and now Genevieve Capri could not be located.

Unfortunately, Genevieve had no family to push the matter, and in a big city like Paris missing persons tended not to be high priority with the authorities. Almost two weeks had passed since this woman had last been seen. But finally it had occurred to one of the inspectors in charge that Claudia's fate and Genevieve's might in some way be connected.

Guilt weighed heavily on Raul's mind. But a hundred times he'd gone over it, and that many times he'd come to the same conclusion. Turning himself in would change nothing. The police would believe they had their killer, and nothing would be solved.

He lifted Vignette's tiny arm and for a moment thought of Katarina. His love, and look what he'd done. Lured her into the vaults. Now she sought to help him and in doing so she endangered her own life.

An icy chill invaded Raul's body. What if the puppet master knew about her?

He straightened from the case, staring at his reflection and the strain apparent on his features. *Act, Raul,* his mind told him. *Make it right. Damn the puppet master to a fate worse than hell!*

KATARINA EXPECTED eccentric at the Louis-St. Desmond party. She didn't expect bizarre to the point of lunacy. No costumes were required, yet a full one-third of the guests wore one. At least she hoped they did. Togas and black vampire capes, Cleopatra gowns, dramatic makeup and masks, they were all here and more.

"There is Armand's daughter, Anjolie," Philip said as they strolled through the great hall. "Fancies herself a matador, I'd say."

Sequined toreador pants and jacket, red cape, bow tie, no shirt. "She's a very seductive matador," Katarina observed.

She eased her elbow out of Philip's cupped hand. Festive lighting and a thirty degree Celsius temperature made the mansion hot; otherwise, she told herself, she wouldn't have moved away.

"Ah, Philip, you have arrived at last."

Katarina almost didn't recognize Babette's subdued voice, or the pale features that accompanied it. Babette wore a clingy silk gown the color of saffron. Her eyes darted back and forth nervously.

Katarina focused on Babette as Philip treated her to his usual charming smile. "Here we are indeed," he said. "But I must say, I'm rather surprised to see you at this shindig, old girl."

"I came with Ian."

"Ian's here?" Katarina asked. How interesting. But then the puppet master would have covered that, wouldn't he?

Her heart skipped a beat. Would the puppet master come tonight, too? Even more frightening, would Raul?

Katarina peered at the costumed people languishing by the walls. A strange-looking assortment, but all appeared to be in conversation. No lone wolves. And no sign yet of Louise and Pierre.

"I wonder if Francois will come?" she murmured.

Babette, whose fidgety fingers appeared to be tying themselves in knots, said, "He is inside, in the room with the velvet curtains and the brocade furniture."

"The candle room," Philip translated.

"What's a candle room?" Katarina asked.

"Stupid." Babette snarled. She was never too nervous for that. "It is a room lit with candles, what else would it be?"

"Maybe a room where candles come to life," Katarina said without offense. Her gaze constantly swept over the room, searching. If Raul came, he would surely do so in costume. "Puppets come to life, why not wax figures?"

Babette's tension increased visibly. Her voice quavered. "Because Giovanni's ghost does not concern himself with things made of wax. Only puppets move at his command."

Katarina saw Ian walking toward them. On him, a black tux looked brown. It was difficult to know if he'd heard Babette or not. His smile was distant, polite as he took her by the arm.

"Come along," he said in a firm but unruffled tone. "Our hosts are inside. I think Armand would like to have a few words with you."

"More than words, I'll wager," Philip put in discreetly as Ian led the stiff-limbed Babette away. "Armand will whisk her up to his private study with his much used, 'Permit me to show you my Rembrandt etchings,' line so fast that the poor girl won't know what hit her."

Katarina forced a smile, but her mind had become a tangle of questions. Was that how it would be done? Use Babette as a diversion to keep Armand Louis-St. Desmond occupied while someone else robbed him blind? Or would Babette surreptitiously make off with his Rembrandt etchings? It was hard to say, but one thing seemed certain: security or not, these people were on the puppet master's hit list.

Which was fortunate, really, Katarina acknowledged with a chill that reached into her bloodstream. Better to be a robbery victim than one who fell victim to the blade of his knife.

Chapter Sixteen

It was madness inside the château, a decorator's nightmare. Raul stood unobtrusively in the curtained corner of a room where candles provided the only light source. Splashes of the supernatural overlaid a strong sixties motif. Not elegant, but a perfect setting for the unconventional guests.

Perfect for him as well, he had to admit. His disguise had gotten him in without a single question being asked, though how long it would hold up, Raul couldn't say.

"You are the merchant puppet," Sofia had exclaimed as he'd donned black pants, cape and boots in the vaults. "A creature of mystery and deceit."

"Not the merchant, Sofia." Raul indicated the leather mask on his cot. "Tonight I'm the Phantom."

"Another creature of darkness. They will only see your eyes. I think many women will fall in love at this party."

If only one did it would be enough, but so far he hadn't seen her in the crowd. She didn't talk of air and existentialism with the outlandish people nearest to him. She didn't stand with Francois, a phantom in his own right, who watched the proceedings as Raul did from the solitude of a shadowed corner. Nor was she with Louise and Pierre who had passed through ten minutes ago on their way to the verandah with its tropical flowers and singing birds.

A waiter offered him champagne from a silver tray, but Raul declined.

Louise and Pierre strolled past from the opposite direction. Pierre brushed at drops of water on his shoulders. So it rained, did it? That would bring the guests indoors. The puppet master, too, if he was here—which Raul suspected he was.

Louise ignored Raul's presence, but she'd probably recognized him. This black cap and leather mask was not the best disguise. Too much of his face could be seen. And if his dark hair was very long now, that was a minor difference. He took a chance coming here, a big one, but necessary if his instincts were to be believed.

Matters moved inexorably to a head. He felt it. He couldn't say why or even understand the feeling, but it was there and it spoke urgently to him.

He sensed, also, that the puppet master watched his robber puppets closely now. Maybe he watched everyone, Raul couldn't say, but Katarina was part of everyone and she shared a dressing room with Babette, who tended to blurt out her fears. And so this nightmare must end before it worsened. Before Babette endangered Katarina any further.

"Push her out a window," was Sofia's ready solution to this problem. But then tolerance wasn't one of Sofia's strong points. Ghost-hunting was her preference and that she still did with a vengeance.

She'd cackled with delight earlier tonight. "Babette sees the puppets move, and yet without the gold threads we know this cannot happen. And do not tell me that it is you who makes this movement happen. I speak of Silvain's flapping wings, a thing you could not possibly bring about, my sexy young friend."

Raul smiled to himself. Let her dream; he couldn't wait for a ghost to make things right. He must unmask the puppet master as soon as possible.

"An interesting party, do you not agree?"

Francois's low voice behind Raul made his entire body stiffen. He didn't turn. "Very interesting," he agreed, affecting a soft Italian accent and leaning one shoulder against the wall.

"You are a friend of Armand's, monsieur?"

"Of his wife's."

"Ah, I see."

It was a knowing tone. Raul refused the bait and shrugged. His eyes continued to scan the candlelit room. A sham, but Francois knew his face well enough to recognize him, mask or no. Of Francois's face, however, Raul knew very little, and that had long been a curious point with him. Francois wore a mask of shadows. Certainly he possessed an air of mystery. And what more fitting disguise for the puppet master?

"You own the Puppet Theater," Raul observed slowly. "An intriguing venture, monsieur."

"We will say unique." Francois chuckled. "For myself, I am not a fan of puppets. Like you, I prefer phantoms. The little puppet faces, they unsettle me—miniature creatures that evince human awareness where none, in fact, exists."

"I take it, then, that you do not believe in the legend of Giovanni Verrone."

"Ah, *oui*," Francois said, surprising him. "Now in this, I most certainly do believe."

Was he joking? Raul shifted position, stealing a sideways glance at his profile. But all he saw was an indistinct silhouette, outlined against the folds of a deep burgundy curtain.

Francois continued, "Giovanni Verrone was born in a time of darkness, of alchemy and sorcery and I would say many secular beliefs." A distracted "Oh, yes" interrupted his remarks. "Quite beautiful."

Raul's gaze shifted to the distant doorway. Katarina and Philip had arrived at last. And yes, beautiful was the correct word for how she looked tonight. She was a vision in a strapless sheath of lace over satin. Shimmering black that somehow paid a compliment to the green of her eyes. Across her throat she had draped a long satin scarf so that the ends might flow down her back with the soft ripples of her hair. It was all he could do to drag his eyes away before she noticed him staring. It was safer for her not to know that he was here.

"Katarina," Francois called softly, destroying that hope. "Please come here and explain to this gentleman about Giovanni's legend."

Raul glanced again at the man. There was something in his tone, a note of amusement, perhaps, a cat toying with not one mouse but several.

Katarina approached with Philip at her side. Raul felt a jealous growl in his throat but swallowed it and eased himself deeper into the shadows.

It was a futile move. Katarina's eyes registered momentary recognition before she greeted him with a polite nod.

"Yes, what is it you would like to know, monsieur?"

"He asks, do I believe in the legend?" Francois supplied. "I say that I do, and this surprises him."

Philip's brows shot up. "Can't say about him, but it surprises the hell out of me, old man. You actually believe in all that nonsense?"

"Excuse me?" Katarina said, and instantly he qualified the remark.

"Of course I believe in fantasies, love, always have. I think we should do our utmost to make them come true. I'll even grant you that ghosts might wander the earth. But puppets being brought to life?"

Philip shook his head and Raul smiled wryly to himself. Stupid man. For so long Philip had pretended to believe, and yet he was really no different than most people, a skeptic like Raul. Except that Raul had never lied about his convictions, especially not to Katarina.

Annoyance, disappointment, if she felt either Katarina hid it well, turning doubtful eyes to Francois. "You think Giovanni exists?"

"You ask a creature of the night that question?" a new voice put in, and behind his mask Raul rolled his eyes. Pierre now, and Louise. This situation went from risky to impossible. He fell back a bit more, drawing the black cape tighter about his body.

"Good evening, Pierre." Still that hint of humor marked Francois's tone. "You have brought a companion tonight, I see."

Louise smiled. "He likes red hair. I'm here by default, I think."

"Hardly that," Pierre assured. He sent Raul an assessing glance. "Do I know you, Monsieur Phantom?"

"If you do then you have me at a disadvantage," Raul replied calmly, controlling his urge to bolt. He felt more trapped here than in the vaults, a rat surrounded by drooling cats. Ah yes, but two guardian angels as well. Don't forget that, Raul.

"I think maybe we've met," Louise remarked with convincing dispassion. "Last year at the Opéra?"

"Perhaps," he murmured.

Katarina took over, shifting the conversation back to its original theme. Also, Raul noted with a glimmer of amusement, she strived for a clearer view of Francois's enigmatic features. He didn't think she would get her wish.

"Have you always believed in the legend, Francois?" she pressed.

"I have always believed in many occult possibilities."

"He *is* an occult possibility," Pierre muttered to Louise, but he glared at Francois as he spoke, and Raul found that interesting. No hiding of disdain for his partner's eccentricities and only a low chuckle from Francois's throat in response. Quite strange.

Louise affected a shiver. "Puppets walking about, living, breathing—"

"Controlling," Francois murmured.

"Whatever. The whole idea gives me the willies."

"Me as well, old girl." Philip's bright blue eyes ran the circle. "Really, people, this is complete and utter nonsense. Puppets are made of wood. If they walk about, it's only in myth."

"You do not think that puppets of flesh and blood exist, Philip?" Francois's softly spoken words were rich in meaning. But it was Pierre who waved an impatient hand.

"You speak in terms of philosophy now, of symbolic things that have nothing to do with legend. Puppets of greed and gain, of ignorance and uncertain direction. Call them the sheep of modern society and it would be the same thing. It comes to this. Puppets of a metaphorical nature exist, puppets of legend do not."

Perhaps Francois would have argued the point, or maybe Katarina. However, the opportunity was cut short by the sound that suddenly pierced the din of music and voices and laughter.

It was a dreadful sound—a woman screaming in terror. And her scream came from the great hall.

"FIND IT! Catch it! Kill it! Please! Does it crawl on me?"

Katarina's eyes scanned the tiled floor beneath the curving sweep of overhead railing. Nothing. No dead body as she'd been sure there must be. But then, if that was the case, the woman's screams wouldn't have made sense. Corpses couldn't crawl. So what, besides Katarina's skin, could?

Long, warm fingers wrapped around her wrist. "A rat," Raul said softly in her ear. "One of the guests arrived as I did with two white rats on a leash."

Rats on a leash? Katarina shuddered, allowing Raul to pull her into a distant corner of the hall. Her nerves were unraveling. "Okay," she said. "That's it. I'm going home."

"You should."

She looked up but it wasn't Raul she saw, it was a phantom. Not Giovanni, another being of legend in a long black cape. A man with the most hypnotic eyes. She would recognize them anywhere, and so would anyone else who cared to look. He shouldn't be here!

Let's both leave, she wanted to suggest, but that would be unspeakably rude to Philip, who'd done nothing to warrant such treatment. "You think the puppet master's thieves are going to rob this place, don't you?" she asked instead, unable to tear her gaze from his eyes. Surrounded by leather they were only that much more riveting. "But do you also think the puppet master's here?"

"I'm not sure. Yes, if he's Francois or Pierre. No, if he's anyone else at the theater. Only the elite were invited to this party, and I don't see any costumes that would disguise your crew or castmates."

"Well Ian's here, anyway," Katarina started, but Raul placed a forestalling hand over her mouth and dragged her into the shelter of the curving stairwell—into the hardness of his caped body.

"Quiet," he cautioned, then nodded at the periphery of the chaos that still had many of the guests scrambling madly about the floor. "There's Babette. And Ian right behind her." He leaned forward a little. "Can you hear what they're saying?"

Who cared what they said? But Katarina forced her feelings back. "No, but, Raul, look." She tugged on his cape. "Look at her face. She's upset."

She didn't wait for him to object, just took hold of his cape and made her way over to the twosome. The hall was one bright glare of lights, but maybe the commotion around them would be screen enough.

"I cannot do it, Ian," Babette was moaning. "I cannot. Keep him busy, you insist, but all the time I see blood and I think I see the puppet master watching me from every patch of darkness.''

''Don't be absurd,'' Ian snarled, then drew her alongside a potted palm and lowered his voice. ''He can't be everywhere, you know that. In fact, I haven't even seen him tonight.''

''But he is here, yes?''

''I should imagine so. However, he isn't likely to be watching you. Now, where is Armand?''

''He is—'' Babette hesitated, licking her dry lips. ''He is with another. He grew angry with me and went with a duchess to his private suite.''

''His private suite.'' The sigh in Ian's voice pretty much told Katarina where the would-be stolen merchandise resided.

Raul, too. ''No robbery tonight,'' he murmured, and she nodded, relieved in spite of herself. No robbery, no trouble, no chance that Raul would be caught.

''You fool,'' Ian said mildly, then sighed again. ''All right, Babette, come along. As all is apparently lost, I might as well take you home.''

''What about the puppet master?'' Babette whispered, sounding scared. ''Will he be angry with me?''

Ian didn't answer. His hooded eyes looked into the crowd where somewhere, Francois and Pierre both lurked.

''But who is the puppet master?'' Katarina wondered out loud.

Against her hair, Raul shook his head. ''I don't know. But this is for sure, Babette has gotten herself into deep, deep trouble.''

LOUISE'S STOMACH fluttered and she didn't know why. It was early enough, the light rain had stopped and Pierre's limousine wound its way through the streets of Passy like an elegant snake.

They'd left the party almost as one. Francois first, then Ian and Babette, then Katarina and Philip—and Raul had certainly watched that departure in Phantomesque silence—and finally she and Pierre. If a robbery had been committed she knew nothing about it; however, she suspected none had. Something in Babette's distress indicated that not all had gone as planned. That wouldn't please the puppet master one bit.

Louise stole a glance at Pierre, a statue beside her since they'd left Versailles. He didn't speak—did not look pleased—and that jarred.

But no, she was overreacting, spooking herself with speculation. She'd gone out with him last week and not even the tiniest hint that he might be the butcher who'd killed Claudia had surfaced. The general weirdness of tonight's party bothered him, that was all.

He maintained his silence long after they'd stepped from the limousine and ridden the fancy lift to his security flat. And what a flat it was, she thought, looking around. Plush furnishings, plants, a wall of puppets and Picasso paintings. Most impressive.

"A glass of cognac?" Pierre inquired at last.

Thank heaven, he smiled. "Please." Louise arranged herself on the sofa. This very handsome man was someone to want, and she did want him. So forget the crazy notion that he might be the puppet master. Pierre was as sane as they came.

"You didn't enjoy the party," she remarked when he joined her on the soft leather couch.

Was she wrong or did his smile not quite reach his eyes? "Did you?" he asked.

"Not much." She sipped her cognac nervously, then gave herself a shake and reached out to finger the collar of his shirt. "I thought it was rather overdone, but then I should imagine all the so-called normal people escaped early as we did."

"I imagine." He sounded absent. His gaze was riveted to the wall of windows across from them. "I know that Phantom," he stated so unexpectedly that Louise almost dropped her glass.

"A patron of the arts," she suggested, clearing her throat and tightening her hold on the crystal stem. "I've met him before."

Pierre looked sharply at her face. The dark light in his eyes didn't settle her nerves. "Where?" he demanded.

"I'm not sure. At the Opéra, maybe. Yes, that's it. Last year."

Damn Pierre's unrelenting skepticism. "I do not think so," he said slowly.

"You think I'm lying?" Louise returned gently, still stroking his collar, although seduction wasn't her intention at this moment.

"Not lying, mistaken." Catching her fingers in a rather tight grip, Pierre brought them to his lips. It was an idle motion, his mind was far away. "I know this man, I am certain of it. I just cannot place him."

Louise banked her trepidation long enough to make one more attempt. "Pierre," she said, capturing his chin and turning his head. She saw no cruelty in his expression, but there was something. "Forget Phantoms and queer-duck parties. Think about me instead, hmm?"

That won her a small smile, and his attention. The grip on her hand loosened, his thumb caressed her palm, bringing a shiver of anxious anticipation to her skin. This man knew how to seduce, and to scare.

Maybe it was crazy but she sidled closer anyway, untying his hair and running her fingers through the rich brown length of it. Her lips brushed his jaw. "Forget everything, Pierre," she whispered. "For tonight, think only about me."

She broke off quite suddenly as her sifting fingers brought a previously hidden lock of his hair into the periphery of her vision. A tangled strand, she'd thought at first. But her horrified eyes quickly corrected that.

It wasn't a tangle in the braided lock of hair that rested in her icy palm. It was gold threads!

Chapter Seventeen

Raul was cross by the time he returned to the Puppet Theater. He wanted to let out his frustration on someone. Philip Hambleton, the puppet master, it made no difference which.

So what if Katarina had gone to the party with Philip and courtesy dictated that she leave with him. Raul didn't have to like it, or the fact that everyone associated with the Puppet Theater had chosen to withdraw from the freakish affair at almost the same instant. That included Philip, who'd come looking for Katarina just when Raul had been about to take her onto the terrace.

"Go before Philip sees you," she'd whispered, pushing on his chest with her palms. "He'll recognize you for sure in this light."

Not if he was punched in the face first. But Philip didn't deserve that. And so Raul had faded from sight.

"I'll come to the vaults tomorrow," Katarina had promised in parting, but that didn't help much.

He'd watched her go, his fists clenched. Then he'd watched Louise leave with Pierre—God help her if he was the one. And, finally, Ian had told Babette that he would take her home, then he wanted to return to the Puppet Theater.

To meet the puppet master? Raul wondered. Or perhaps to postpone that unpleasant confrontation and consider in solitude what might be offered in Babette's defence. One thing about Ian, he seemed to like Babette. He wouldn't risk his life for her, but he might try a little persuasion to keep her alive.

By taxi Raul trailed them from Versailles, first to Babette's apartment then to the Puppet Theater. Ian walked like a man who carried a tremendous burden, through the side door and up five flights of stairs to his office. Raul caught the theatre door before it closed, slipped in and followed him up.

The cleaning crew worked in the museum at this hour. Unless Pierre or Francois put in an appearance he would be safe.

Halfway down the fifth floor corridor, Ian paused to glance at the now reboarded hallway, then released a weary breath and moved on. Raul wished that someone else would react in this manner, but so far no one had. None that he'd seen, anyway.

Ian trudged into his office, closed and locked the door. Unfortunate, but no real surprise.

Raul heard movement inside, one set of footsteps. No talking, therefore no puppet master. To ponder his options was Ian's intent, after all.

Raul lingered even so, listening as more sounds reached him through the door. A metallic click, a chink of glass, two dull thuds—heels on the desk, Raul assumed—then silence for a short time, and finally Ian's voice.

But only his voice, spoken into a telephone and likely to a highly displeased puppet master.

"You saw what happened?" Ian asked quietly. "Yes, I know she botched things, but she was upset. Couldn't we...?"

Silence again, then a subdued, "Yes, I understand. No, I'm not defending her, I'm merely pointing out that she's done good work in the past. Maybe if I spoke to her..."

A protracted silence this time—and something charging the air.

Raul noted this in mild surprise. Some cloud of brooding evil stretched out to envelop him in the corridor, a sense of corruption so strong it brought a chill to his skin, had his eyes roaming the hall, just in case.

Ian's tone grew tense, nervous. "Is it absolutely necessary?" he asked at length. "Won't you let me talk to Babette one more time?" The plea dwindled off and with a defeated sigh, Ian bowed to the pressure. "As you wish," he agreed. "If you feel we must. Do you have a plan, a way to, er, dispose of her that will not turn suspicion on us?"

Raul strained to hear better.

Thirty seconds later, he was left white-faced and shaking in the hall, wishing to God that he hadn't heard anything.

Yes, they would kill Babette. But no, this time the architect could not be framed. He had disappeared. Another must be set up instead.

Babette Toulon would die this coming Saturday night. She would be murdered at the Hambleton masquerade ball. And the blame would be laid at Philip Hambleton's feet.

KATARINA GAVE LOUISE a cup of strong coffee to drink and a blanket to wrap about her shaking shoulders, and sat down next to her on the sofa. Louise had shown up at Katarina's apartment five minutes ago, shortly after midnight, frantic and babbling about Pierre Fousard, saying things that made no sense whatsoever. Something about braiding his hair, and lifeless puppet eyes.

"Tell me again, Louise," Katarina said, rubbing her friend's trembling forearm. "Exactly what happened with Pierre?"

Louise's voice quavered, but she was calmer now. "He was acting very queer, Kati, as if his mind were somewhere else. I didn't know what to make of it. And I like him, you know, which didn't help." She gulped the coffee, pushing at her unruly hair with her fist. "In my hand," she declared taut-lipped. "I held it in my hand, and I still can't believe it."

Katarina didn't understand. Maybe she was still half asleep. She'd gone straight to bed after Philip brought her home. "What did you hold?" she asked.

"Gold threads! Kati, he has gold threads braided into a tiny section of his hair. Underneath and at the back, you know, where normally no one would see them. Unless, of course, they happened to be cozying up to him as I was."

Startled, Katarina whispered, "But how did you get out? Didn't he try to stop you? I mean—that's very strange."

"I know." Louise pressed the tips of her fingers to her forehead. "Funny thing is, I don't remember much after I saw the wretched thing. Except that suddenly all of his puppets, and he has many by the way, seemed to be staring at me. And then *he* stared at me. And he asked me what was wrong, almost as if he didn't know I'd found the stupid threads. He was acting so strangely." She sighed, letting her head fall forward. "And there's more. He felt he knew the Phantom he saw tonight."

"I knew someone would do that." Too jumpy now to sit still, Katarina began pacing, running her damp palms up and down the arms of her white peignoir. "One problem at a time. What horrible end might this lead to?" Sighing, she said, "Disaster." Then she lifted her head. "Maybe not, though. Even if Pierre figures out that Raul is the Phantom, he still won't know where he's hiding."

"He'll know he's in Paris."

"The party was in Versailles. Anyway, the police are already looking for Raul in Paris. If they don't know he's hiding in the vaults, why would Pierre? Besides, who's to say that Pierre will even make the connection?" A horrible thought occurred to her. "My God, Pierre's the puppet master, isn't he?"

"Is he?" Louise rubbed her eyes. "Who knows? When I saw the gold threads, that was my first thought, too. But after I left I told myself that was total rubbish. I've been swinging back and forth ever since. I mean really, Kati, would the puppet master wear gold threads in his hair?"

Katarina tugged the broad curtain aside and gazed at the jumble of rooftops below. "Maybe. He's crazy you know. He butchered Claudia, and I'm sure he did the same thing to Genevieve. And I keep remembering what Jean told me about the answers being in the legend."

Louise stared, uncomprehending. "What does that mean?"

"I have no idea." Katarina pushed on her temples. She had to reason this out. "Puppets come to life in Giovanni's world. Maybe Pierre thinks he's a puppet, you know, like the Italian merchant."

Louise whispered. "I don't want to hear this. Who's Jean?"

"Someone I met in the vaults. You're sure Pierre didn't try to stop you from leaving his apartment? You'd think if he was the puppet master he would have."

"He might not realize I saw the braid," Louise reminded. "Anyway, the telephone was ringing. When he answered it, that's when I grabbed my bag and bolted. Oh, I made some lame excuse about having a migraine, but mostly I just wanted to get the hell out of there, go someplace safe. Not into the vaults, though I really ought to have. Raul needs to know about this."

"I'll tell him." Katarina paced in front of the window, tapping her elbows nervously. The only light came from the kitchen, the living room basked in a silvery mauve glow. Comfortable a moment ago, it now took on overtones of malevolence and danger, of sickness and heaven knew what else.

A gold braid in Pierre's hair. Francois, whose face nobody ever saw, like the Italian merchant. One dead woman, likely two. Raul in the vaults and a mysterious other man insisting that the solution to all of this lay in the legend.

"Puppets," she murmured. "My God, Louise, I used to think how nice it would be if the legend were true, if puppets actually could come to life. Now I'm terrified that in some mad, twisted way, that's exactly what's happened."

PUPPETS, the person in charge thought in disgust as he strolled serenely into the theater Friday morning. Idiotic caricatures, made of wood. Not real as he was. He touched the gold braid hidden in his hair and smiled. Death to those humans who knew too much. Claudia, Genevieve, Babette...

He stopped there, leaning on a column beside the empty stage and picturing the people-puppets who danced for him every night across the polished floor. "Oh, yes," he whispered, "they make the audience clap, but who really pulls the strings? This they don't know. Even my small band of puppet-thieves knows nothing for sure."

Babette must be told, of course. She must know who killed her. It was no fun to be anonymous at the pleasurable last moment.

Ah, but did he dare murder this one himself? The setup he had planned for the masquerade ball was dangerous. If it did not work, he might be caught. He would make Ian do it. That was the safer way. And Ian would comply, because he was not a total idiot. If he did not obey, he would die.

In actual fact Ian would die anyway, but he was not aware of that.

"Death to those who know," the puppet master repeated out loud, still regarding the stage from the shadows.

He laughed and thought of Ian's face when the delicious moment of discovery arrived. "You can't mean to kill me," he would exclaim in horror. But that was exactly what the puppet master meant to do. Poor deluded Ian, always controlled by someone.

He stopped, closing his eyes. "Put it in order now," he whispered to himself. "Babette will die first, by Ian's hand so that Philip can take the blame."

What would the police make of it? he wondered. Well, undoubtedly they would make precisely what the puppet master wished them to, and that was, if Philip cut up one woman, he must also have cut up the other two. He was a crazy man, perhaps responsible for the rash of recent robberies in and about Paris. The ringleader, or say rather, the puppet master.

Lucky architect, whoever he was. He would be let off the hook. Babette would be dead, and that would leave only a few minor details to clear up. Three to be precise. Ian, Louise, and . . . Katarina.

Ah, but how to blame Philip for these murders? Before they could be committed wouldn't Philip be in the hands of the police? Yes, this was a question to ponder, but solvable, perhaps, by pinning the blame for Katarina's and Louise's deaths on Ian. Leave them for the police to find and have Ian, the puppet master's servant, mysteriously vanish.

The puppet master laughed again in delight. "Enjoy your last few hours, ignorant puppets. For the grim reaper and his knife will be calling for you in the darkness after the masquerade ball."

TWO-THIRTY Friday afternoon. Raul walked undisguised and uncaring through the Place Contrescarpe, an uninspiring little square on the Left Bank. There was squalor here, and the kind of despair that Raul hated, but then despising an unpleasant thing didn't make it go away. He would give them money if he thought it would help.

Did these people have a choice about anything? he wondered. Possibly not. *Did he?* Raul squeezed his eyes closed. Yes, he had a very definite choice.

Out of habit, he checked the square for police. He saw none, but did it matter?

He felt sick inside, ripped apart, disgusted by the debate that raged in his head.

What he'd learned last night had shocked him. Babette would die, Philip would be blamed for her murder. It didn't take a genius to carry that one step further and realize that Philip would almost certainly be blamed for Claudia's death as well.

The situation would be like Raul's, but Philip would be given no chance to escape before the police arrived. The puppet master would see to that. Philip would be apprehended, and Raul would be free. And he could have Katarina, too. His problem would be solved—except for two small details. Babette would be dead and an innocent man would be blamed.

Listlessly, Raul drifted with the flow, past dingy cafés then downhill along the busy market street. Narrow, cobbled, crowded—surely a policeman lurked among the colorful stalls. It was hot and sunny, and he could be easily spotted since his picture must be posted in every city station.

But it would never go so easily for him, would it? Get arrested and like magic, no more dilemma.

He had to choose. Let the puppet master do this monstrous thing, win his freedom and the woman he loved, or do something to prevent this ghastly plan from succeeding and maybe get caught himself.

If charged and convicted he could forget about a life with Katarina.

It was his choice, and he had one day left in which to make it.

He caught the aroma of hot bread and apples. He smelled people and perfume and coffee and maybe an approaching storm. He looked up and saw black clouds bunched over the river. Yes, a storm was coming.

So now the test. How deep did his system of ethics run?

Raul wanted to shake his fists at the heavens, scream at the powers above. The sun bathed his face, but the black clouds were creeping closer. He saw faces of judgment in those clouds, heard voices in them, too. Make a choice, Raul Sennett. Time grows short.

What would he do? He honestly didn't know—and didn't like that feeling one little bit.

"FICKLE CLIMATE," Louise grumbled Thursday evening as she and Babette and Katarina cut through the museum on the way to their dressing room. "Sunshine one minute, pouring rain the next."

"Yes, and always it is so perfect in England," Babette retorted. She sounded crankier than usual to Katarina. "No rain ever, only fog like in the horror movie, *Jack the Ripper*."

Katarina's stomach turned, but then Babette didn't know the whole truth about Claudia's death, or anything about the bloodstain upstairs in that closed-off part of the building.

She shook moisture from her hair. A step ahead, Louise and Babette bickered, each cross for a different reason, but Katarina was too involved to referee. She hadn't spoken to Raul yet, hadn't had a moment today to slip into the vaults.

"Our writers have made changes in the script," Pierre had announced early that morning. "Study them. We will rehearse in half an hour."

In half an hour, for half the day. After that came the tours. Two of the performers were out with the flu. Would

Babette fill in? "Of course not," she'd said. So it fell to Katarina and Louise to substitute.

Five o'clock did finally come, and Katarina was about to bolt when Ian arrived at their dressing room.

"We're having a preperformance meal at Lutèce," he'd announced. "Owners treat. No excuses. Everyone be there."

Everyone was, except for Francois. Even Pierre showed up.

"Trust me, the gold threads are there," Louise had whispered glumly. "I should have such a hallucination."

Then the meal was done. Now they had to dress for tonight's performance. More hours would pass before she could get to Raul.

Babette's high heels clicked on the stone floor. Tap, tap, tap, like the rain and the clock in Katarina's head. Time would crawl tonight. She wanted to see Raul now.

Glass cases blurred in her peripheral vision. Low lights made the museum seem very spooky. Her feet dragged. Maybe she could get sick, run to the vaults. Who would know?

Nicoli seemed to be smiling at her. An illusion only, but what a handsome little puppet. Seeing him made her want to be with Raul even more. Yes, she would get sick.

The idea tantalized her so much that she almost missed what happened in front of her. Babette stopped abruptly. Her mouth dropped open. Her finger came up to point in horror.

Katarina followed the finger, felt Louise's hand on her arm. She saw the question in her friend's eyes, but didn't know the reason for it.

Babette's glassy gaze was fixed on one of the cases.

Katarina searched the displays. She found nothing out of the ordinary inside—until she got to the Italian merchant, or rather until she didn't get to him. She looked around. Where was he? Not in his case.

She gasped suddenly, felt Louise's nails bite hard into her arm. He wasn't *standing* in his case, her shocked eyes corrected, but he was there. His sandaled feet dangled in the air. He was hanging by the neck at the end of a slender gold thread!

Chapter Eighteen

It was a message of death.

Run, Katarina told herself, as she hurried through the passages below the ground. Find Raul, safe in the cool dark sanctuary of the vaults. Don't think. Don't hear Babette's shrieks that summoned everyone from the theater to the museum.

The memories came anyway, the image of a puppet suspended by a gold thread, his wooden neck snapped in two, his little head lolling. It had to be a sign, a symbol of violent death.

But it was the swinging feet that had affected Katarina most of all. Bare, sandaled feet, dangling helplessly. It made the merchant look indescribably vulnerable, made her nerves shudder.

"We are doomed," Babette had screeched. Ian tried to lead her away but she was rooted, transfixed. Terrified. "It does not end here. More awful things will happen. The ghost, he tells us this through the puppet. He is a madman!"

"You are mad, Babette," Pierre said coldly, motioning to Ian to take her out. "This is a prank, nothing more. Everyone go. I will fix it."

More pictures formed in Kati's head. Francois had hovered next to a stone column. Why? Did a smile pass through his shadowed eyes? She couldn't tell, either then or now.

She'd done the play in a trance, scared, shaking, feeling for all the world like a puppet. And how distorted time had become. People, too. A cardboard audience watched, pretty painted faces but entirely unreal. And up on stage a dozen little Pinocchios danced....

She raced through the shadowy corridors. Her flashlight played ahead of her, making weird patterns in the darkness. And then, with no warning, came a collision that left her gasping and stunned, as if she'd slammed into an invisible wall.

But then she heard a voice and she knew. Not a wall or the puppet master, it was Jean, dressed as before and still wearing that same wistful expression on his handsome face.

Katarina pressed a hand to her stomach. "My God, but you scared me." She leaned her back against the cool stone wall. "I thought you were the puppet master."

"Is this what he is called?" Jean's tone was vague. "Murderous puppet is a better term, I think."

A tremor ran through Katarina's limbs. Then she paused. Some nuance in Jean's voice had alerted her. "You know, don't you?" She peered at him but couldn't see much in the dim light. "You know who the murderer is."

He smiled sadly. "I told you, the answers are in the legend. This is all I can say. The rest you must figure out yourself. You and Raul."

Yes, she had to see Raul. But Jean's words unnerved her. If he knew the truth, why would he keep it a secret?

"Proof, Katarina," he said as if reading her mind. "Knowledge without it is nothing."

"You could still tell me," Katarina protested, but knew he wouldn't even before he gave his head that slow, sad shake.

"No, I could not. Do not ask me why. Consider, perhaps, that I inhabit these vaults for a reason not dissimilar to your friend's."

Now that she hadn't considered.

Still, she couldn't let the matter go. "Please, Jean," she began, then stopped, a little startled when he pressed a finger to her lips. Cool touch, it felt strange to her. Of flesh and bone, absolutely, but of something else as well.

"Go now," he said gently. "It is a monstrous thing that unfolds here. You must stay out of it."

"Why?"

"Because it is dangerous."

"I know, but..."

"It is like a piece of poisoned wood, Katarina. Except that it has arms and legs and it thinks. Blood makes it smile, and pain. It has no soul. Do you understand?"

"No."

"Think of the legend, then, as I instructed. But think only. Know with whom it is you deal. He is an evil puppet, in control of a less evil puppet, in control of a legion of greedy puppets."

Ian and a band of thieves—the hierarchy Katarina could grasp. But who was the top puppet?

She hovered uncertainly by the wall. She wanted to grab Jean's frayed jacket and shake him, but she kept still.

"Leave here, Katarina," he went on. "I will do whatever else I can, I promise you this."

Again some vague nuance carried to her brain...

"You're the one!" she whispered, caught between awe and distrust. "You broke the merchant puppet's neck and hung him in his case by that thread. But why? What does it mean? That the puppet master should be punished? That he should die as violently as his victims?"

For a moment Jean's body looked almost transparent, but when she brought the flashlight beam around he was fine. It was a trick of the shadows only.

"It can mean both things," Jean agreed, but left something out, Katarina suspected, some detail he refused to pass on. Her frustration mounted.

"Tell me his name, Jean, please."

"I cannot." Head moving regretfully, he stepped back. "Turn now and go to Raul."

"Turn?"

"He is not here. He has not been here for much of this day. He is troubled inside. He takes risks in this state, foolish risks."

"But how do you—never mind." Katarina strained but could no longer see him in the gloom. "Do you know where he is?"

Surely that knowledge he wouldn't possess.

His voice seemed to come from a great distance. "Just off the Rue Lepic in Montmartre is a small coffee house, a dark room with shabby tables and no name above the door. Three widowed grandmothers own it. Do you know this place?"

"No, but I'll find it." Katarina waited but he offered no more. "Jean?" she asked the blackness. "Are you there?"

No answer came, just a light brush of air across her cheek, a gentle caress and then a whisper of silk that might have been the rustle of his long scarf as he withdrew.

Or maybe it was something else entirely.

DAMN BUT HE WANTED to get drunk. He settled for red wine and misery in a dingy café in Montmartre, an appropriate setting at least for the battle in his head.

No welcome dimming of senses came to him, though, just the bite of the wine and pictures of the Revolution swimming before his eyes. Of himself being led, shackled and blindfolded, through the Place de la Grève to a waiting guillotine. And then the blindfold came off and he realized that the revolutionaries were all puppets, who shouted, "Death to humans!" at the top of their little wooden lungs.

Raul shuddered deeply and drank more wine. Mama Germaine, one of the owners, sat at a crooked table near the back and stitched silently on a piece of crimson cloth. She wore all black.

His eyes blurred the city below, but it was from longing, not wine. In the darkness somewhere was Katarina, his beautiful love. Maybe he wasn't worthy.

Philip's face drifted through a corner of his mind and he sighed. More injustice there.

Babette must die!

No, she didn't have to die, but she would if Raul didn't get his head screwed on straight, and quickly.

The café door opened and someone came in. So much for solitude and only Mama Germaine for company, her presence a balm in a vague, celestial sort of way that he didn't fully comprehend.

He took another drink, heard a soft creak of leather near his shoulder. He glimpsed long legs and high boots, and then a short black leather skirt with a matching leather jacket. None of it interested him.

"Don't you think this is just a little dumb?" a woman's voice asked.

Raul choked on his drink, swinging his head around in disbelief. Katarina's sea green eyes stared down at him. She had a black felt beret perched at a jaunty angle on her dark hair, her hands were in her jacket pockets and there was no smile on her lips.

"My God!" He looked past her, half expecting ten members of the Paris police force to storm in. "What are you doing here? How did you find me?" Because if she could do that then surely any decent police inspector could, too.

He shoved his chair back, grabbing her wrist and pulling her against him. There was no sway in his stance. Not drunk yet. "This is very dangerous," he said in a low voice. "How—?"

She twisted on her arm. "Jean told me," she said through her teeth. "Raul, let go. You're hurting me."

Raul slackened his grip instantly, bringing her wrist up to his lips and kissing the tender skin inside. "I'm sorry. How did you know?"

"Coffee, mademoiselle? Wine?" The oldest of the sisters hobbled out of the kitchen with a cane.

"Coffee, please," Katarina said hastily.

Behind him, Raul caught a soft murmur of words, but when he looked Mama Germaine's head was bent down, her attention focused on her stitchery.

Raul sat Katarina down, holding her chair for her politely as though he hadn't seconds ago nearly snapped the bones of her wrist in two. He hadn't meant to; he wouldn't hurt her for all the world. But it was bad, her coming here like this. She put herself in direct danger searching for him. What if the police spotted them together? What if the puppet master did?

Raul felt sick inside and instantly pushed his wine away. It was suicide to be drunk now, fatal for Katarina, and her safety he refused to jeopardize. Thank God she was here, though, he couldn't help thinking.

"Who is this Jean?" he began, then it hit him how she was dressed and confusion darkened his eyes. "Why are you wearing leather?"

She leaned forward. "I was trying to be inconspicuous."

Raul pictured her miles of shapely leg, high black boots and short, short skirt. Hardly inconspicuous. "Kati," he said, but she stopped him, reaching out to touch his hand. His fingers curled automatically about hers, clinging to them.

"I didn't want anyone to recognize me," she said anxiously. "I had to talk to you. So when Jean said you were here—and I don't know how he knew, he just did—I decided to come. Louise says that Pierre thinks he's seen the

Phantom from the Louis-St. Desmond party somewhere before."

Raul closed his eyes, feeling for a moment like he'd been kicked in the stomach.

Katarina's fingers dug in. Her tone grew urgent. "That's not the worst of it, either."

There was more? Raul listened to her story, trying not to stare at her black tank top.

"Louise saw gold threads braided in Pierre's hair," she revealed. "And we found a broken puppet hanging in its museum case. Well, that was Jean's doing, but the point is, he knows who's running this macabre show."

Raul frowned. "Who's Jean? Where does he get his knowledge?"

She sighed. "I wish I knew."

More questions formed in Raul's head. How could Jean have directed Katarina to this café, when Raul hadn't known he would come here himself? He'd wandered aimlessly all through the afternoon and wound up on this street. Had Jean followed him? Did he work for the police?

"No," Raul said out loud.

Katarina waited until a cup of café au lait had been set before her, then she leaned farther forward and demanded in a whisper, "No, what? I saw the merchant, Raul, if that's what you mean. It was creepy."

It was nothing, Raul wanted to shout. His fingers tightened around hers. *Say it,* his conscience commanded. *Confess to her the kind of man you truly are.* But he could only dip his head and stare at the dregs of his wine.

"The clock approaches midnight," a quiet voice remarked from behind. Mama Germaine's lips moved but her eyes remained on her sewing. "Two policemen come here at five minutes past the hour every night, sometimes earlier."

Only midnight? was Raul's first reaction. Then he realized what she was telling them. No thought of why, or what she, like Jean, might know that he wished she didn't. She warned him of danger. They had to get out.

"Maybe she saw your picture in the newspaper after Claudia died," Katarina suggested once they'd reached the street.

"And didn't believe the story?" Raul was confused by Mama Germaine's attitude of sympathy, and very aware of Katarina's long legs, her luscious body covered with tight black leather. Another torment for his soul.

A car cruised past and she took his hand, whispering in his ear, "It isn't safe for you on the street. Let's go to my apartment."

"And become forever lost," Raul murmured, numb now right through. Then smiling in faint remorse, he nodded and kissed her cheek.

HER ROOMS WERE DARK, warm, inviting, above ground. Raul smelled oregano and suddenly wanted to whisk her off to Rome for the best pasta and veal in spicy red sauce that could be found anywhere.

But they were in Paris and it was a beautiful night in spring. Heat and humidity hung in the air. In the distance, he saw a domed cathedral and lights flickering. Life unfolded here even deep into the night.

The Marriage of Figaro drifted up from below.

Raul smiled and relaxed, not enough, but then his conscience still pulled at him. What would he do about Philip and Babette?

"Do you want light?" Katarina's hand hovered over the lamp switch. Her body was a seductive silhouette against the city's golden glow.

"No," Raul said, and her hand fell.

"What about food? Madame Gerot downstairs brings me fresh bread every other day. And I have cheese in the fridge. We could make a fondue."

Raul forced his eyes to her shadowed face. "That would be nice."

She studied him for a long moment—he couldn't see her expression—then came to where he stood beside the puppet stage and brought him over to the sofa. "What is it, Raul? Beyond the obvious, I mean. Is it that I could find you at the Three Sisters' Café?"

"Is that what it is called?" he said with faint humor.

"Don't change the subject. Does the gold braid in Pierre's hair upset you? Or is it a separate thing?"

"A separate thing," he admitted slowly, carefully. He tried to say more but the words got stuck in his throat. "I'm sorry, Kati, I can't explain it. I think it's very interesting what you tell me about Pierre and the broken puppet." So was Jean, he wanted to add, but why bother?

He brushed his questions aside and stared into Katarina's large eyes. He saw so much there. Love? Maybe. He could hope for it anyway. But maybe he shouldn't hope, because he was so badly torn up inside. What would he do?!

"You aren't going to talk to me, are you?" Katarina said softly. "Why not?"

Her fingers combed through his hair. He loved the sensations this small act aroused, feelings that slowly began to wipe away the horrible darkness.

"I don't want to talk, Kati," he answered her.

That was the truth and more, because something was coming clear to him now, some perverse and complicated aspect of his and perhaps every human's nature.

He needed to know it all, needed to be tempted, taken right to the edge. He had to let everything he felt for this woman out. He had to let go, love her to the limit, realize how incredibly good it could be for them. And then he would decide. He would find out then what kind of person he really was.

"Raul, what is it?" she asked again. "You look so miserable."

A lovely haze poured through the window. Heat and shimmering wetness, a thousand different scents wafting in on pastel points of light. And there was music, too. Soft, very elegant, a Gershwin tune.

Raul stroked her cheek, let his fingers slide along her throat to the curve of her black top. She caught back a quick breath but didn't stop his hand.

"You really don't want to talk," she murmured, her lips full in the pale light. "I thought..."

"Don't think, *chérie.*" Raul inclined his head, touching his mouth to her warm skin and the swell of her breast barely visible above the clingy cotton fabric. "Forget. Empty your mind of everything evil. There are no puppets, only you and me, and nothing more to the world than that."

An unoriginal statement, but then no words would really be right. How could he ever say what he felt for this woman with mere words?

He felt his mind deserting him, drifting away to another place. He tasted her soft, warm skin beneath his exploring mouth, so salty and sweet. Her fingers wound around the ends of his hair, pulling him forward. Her breath came in short bursts. He felt his own skin begin to warm, the blood in his loins pounding, making him hard so fast that it was a painful thing. Hell and heaven together.

Was it right to do this?

Raul paused for a second, torn. A tiny scrap of conscience clawed at him, of doubts that had nothing to do with love but with something else, of questions not yet answered and the idea that maybe he was wrong, that maybe he should have made his decision first, or told her about it at least.

Panic formed in his head, his limbs, at odds with the rest of his body.

"Oh, no you don't."

Katarina's voice was a sweet soothing sound above the dull throb of blood in his ears. Gently determined, she cupped his face in her hands, lifting his head, forcing him to look into her eyes with his frightened ones.

"No second thoughts, Raul. No thinking, period. You made the rules, not me."

Her lips came closer with each word, driving him crazy with anticipation. Excitement shimmered inside, scattering his confusion. What did anything matter except that he loved her?

She brought his mouth to hers, kissing him thoroughly with her lips and tongue, a slow, erotic delving that reached right into his soul.

He felt the barriers dissolve. It would be impossible for him to describe the hot little ripples that shot through him. He could only enjoy it all, let it build inside him, the heat and the hunger together, the currents of pain that stung at times and brought an ache to his entire body at others.

It was luscious, the feel of her pressed tightly against him, of her hands flowing over his arms and shoulders then down his chest to his waistband.

"Love you, Kati," he said against her mouth.

Tangled thoughts swarmed in his head, but always around a central point of light. That's where he was, where her kisses took him, to this warm, peaceful place. But there were other things here than peace, such as her fingers on his skin, making him tingle all over, shudder and get harder and then to want to crush her against that hardness, to press himself into her.

He shifted on the sofa, letting her pull the drab army T-shirt over his head. And then he found her mouth in a wet, hungry kiss that made it all the more necessary for him to feel all of her.

She was soft and vulnerable beneath the pressure of his lips. The leather of her jacket was a sleek pelt under his palms. It hid everything and nothing. Raul drew it off, slanting his mouth across hers and deepening the kiss with his tongue.

She was hot, wanting. And there was an exquisite pain in his lower body, stabbing, throbbing, telling him to rush, but he kept it deliberately slow.

She tugged on his fly while he stripped away her skirt, her boots, her stockings. Not as smoothly done as he would like, but it didn't matter. And then his hands were caressing her waist and hips, locating the lacy band of her panties.

A gasp broke suddenly from Raul's throat as Katarina's mouth left his and slid wetly to his ear. She took the lobe gently between her teeth and sucked on it, her breath coming warm and seductive into his ear. He struggled for control. He couldn't think, only feel, want more.

"Kati..."

Her name was a gasp on his lips, a desperate sound. He went on instinct, rising and moving until his body hovered above hers in the silvery darkness.

She worked impatiently now at his zipper, pushing at the worn denim until it was out of the way.

He couldn't go slowly, and somewhere in the back of his mind it came to him that she didn't want slow. His fingers slid along her silky thigh, then quickly inside her, and this time it was Katarina who gasped.

No more waiting. She clutched at his shoulders. Her body was soft beneath him, yielding, demanding. In his ear, she whispered things, disconnected words and then an urgent, "Now, Raul. Please, now."

That was the last thing he remembered hearing. But two things his mind did grasp. One, that all of this was as it was meant to be. And two, that he was no longer lost, no longer feeling as though he were being jerked about at the end of a string. He was nobody's puppet. He was all right and he loved Katarina. And if only for this one brief moment in time the evil that was the puppet master didn't exist.

Chapter Nineteen

Katarina felt floaty, dizzy as if she'd been drinking. She felt hot from the inside out and a little bit wild. Actually, a lot wild.

Her fingers dug right into Raul's skin. The skin on his shoulders and neck was like silk, hard, but so smooth, a layer of satin over bone.

Raul shifted his weight, and she gasped. He swallowed the sound easily. His hand continued its intimate exploration, his fingers deft as he learned her body, her every response to his every touch.

She couldn't breathe.

She felt dreamy, drowsy, but not really. She stretched out for that distant and elusive something, kissing him with a fierceness she hadn't known she possessed. There was no fear in her with Raul—and so many levels of sensation she couldn't keep track of them.

His fingers slid deep, deep inside her, a sudden thrust, answer to the hands that searched and found the heat between his legs. She arched her neck, a cry forming in her throat. Her nipples were hard, wonderfully sore where his skin and the small patch of his dark chest hair rubbed against them.

Her fingers closed about him convulsively. She heard him jerk back a startled breath. Off and on he kissed her mouth.

Sometimes it was her neck. And sometimes his lips closed about the tips of her breasts, his teeth and tongue teasing the nipples, making them harder still.

She couldn't stand the waiting. "Now, Raul."

She said his name, probably screamed it. She couldn't hear herself, only her pounding heart, the blood in her ears.

But she heard Raul. She knew that his mouth was on her and she couldn't think. Then he kissed her lips one more time and her body became a mass of sensation.

Her head thrashed back and forth as her hips arched upward. Delicious shudders of pain rushed through her. She clenched her teeth, her whole body. She felt Raul move against her, the loose curls of his hair caressing her cheek, his hands beneath her, lifting her, matching her rhythm.

She clutched fiercely at his taut shoulders. She wasn't going to let this feeling slip away. It was out there, that nebulous something, and she was going to get it.

The scent of Raul's hair was heaven, his skin and the salty warm taste of him. And then it happened. That stretched-out moment that went on forever, except that forever was only one small second.

"Oh, God!" She clenched her teeth. "Raul!"

She held him tightly, hung on, moved against him, moved with him, clung to him. Good, so good. She groaned and just let the feelings come. No, not feelings, one feeling. Love.

But what, exactly, did that entail?

THE SUN SUGGESTED a big orange ball just coming up over the city. It sent soft beams through a haze of departing cloud and early morning mist. Damp heat hung in the air, making the ends of Raul's hair curl.

He stood naked at the bedroom window, the curtain pushed back, one hand resting on the frame as he stared at a waking Paris. He didn't see it really. But he did see Katarina when he turned his head to gaze at his long-limbed love, still sleeping soundly in a bed that looked to have been visited by a hurricane.

When had they come to this room? Sometime deep into the night. They'd made love again and again, like it was a marathon, but it wasn't that, no, not that at all.

Raul let his head fall back, squinting up at the ceiling. So now he knew. He had crawled right to the edge last night and then tumbled over. It had been so very good with them.

Closing his eyes tightly, he groaned, a low rumble far back in his throat that sounded like an animal in pain, which he was.

He pressed his forehead to the window. He heard the cotton sheets rustle but didn't dare look at her. Time to decide. No more pushing away this struggle in his head. No more avoiding it. Did Babette die tomorrow night or not? Did Philip take the blame for her death or not? Did he lose Katarina? Did he even have her to lose?

Questions on questions crowded in. His head hurt, the rising sun stung his eyes, making them water. He felt sore all over—Katarina's doing and he loved the feeling—but he felt deflated too, sad, and those feelings he did not love as much. Because he knew what they meant.

His decision was made.

IAN'S STOMACH twisted itself into little knots. His mouth opened then closed then dropped open again.

"But I couldn't possibly!" he exclaimed, white-faced. "Kill her? Me?" He put his hands up as if to ward off an advancing beast. "No! I can't do that."

The person in charge merely glared, calmly, and that always scared Ian to death. There was no talking to him when his face got this hard. But kill Babette? Might as well ask the puppet master to become a humanitarian. He could not do it!

Today, tonight, whatever it was, they sat at a back table in a horrible club.

Ian was white and shaking, and all the puppet master had to offer was an unfeeling, "You will do as I say, or you will die. Is that clear to you?"

Ian blinked at his untouched Singapore Sling with its yellow-and-green parasol and bright red cherry, hearing again the words spoken to him a full hour ago.

"You will kill Babette," instructed the puppet master coldly. "It is too dangerous for me to do it."

And it wasn't for him? Ian had almost shrieked.

"Please don't make me do this," he begged. "Please."

An icy hand clamped down on his wrist. In every sense the puppet master truly was a bloodless fiend.

"Philip Hambleton will take the blame," he reminded above the thump of rock music. "It will all be perfect, as I want it to be, except that I shall not be the one to do the killing this time." A dreamy light filled his eyes. "Think on it, Ian. All the loose ends tied neatly up. Say goodbye to Philip, the puppet master—though no one knew it—and hello to a better life than your limited imagination could possibly envision. The Hambleton name in disgrace, Babette no longer a threat, and both of us free. No more puppets or puppet masters. As I say, perfect. And all with one twist of the knife."

Ian's stomach gave a sickening lurch. His white cheeks went whiter still. There was no blood in him right now.

It was the puppet master who ended the conversation, who stood and stared down at Ian's frozen features. "Do not torture yourself," he remarked with an edge of mockery that made Ian want to strangle him. "You will kill Babette, and that is that. I will get rid of Katarina and Louise. So you see, I do most of the work, anyway."

The puppet master patted Ian's cheek. It was an act of mockery, but thank heaven there were no more comments. He simply drank down Ian's warm, fruity drink and chuckled to himself.

Ian paused. Somewhere in that chuckle lurked a raving madman. This person would turn on him in a minute. A terrifying thought, but true.

Ian pressed his sweaty palms together. He must think matters through with absolute clarity, proceed with the greatest caution. Because if he didn't, Ian knew he would die.

"I CAN'T ABSORB all this, I'll explode," Katarina said out loud. Her head reeled as she struggled to understand, to sort things out and speculate.

What was it Raul had said to her?

"The puppet master wants Babette dead, and Philip is to take the blame."

The world had gone mad.

She walked alone, far away from the Puppet Theater near an old stone barn and a collection of other half timbered buildings. The Seine flowed in front of her, Paris stood far to her left. Grass grew here and weeds and little pink flowers in the cracks of an ancient stone walkway.

There was blue sky above, a breeze on her face, and two men fishing about thirty meters away. There was greenery everywhere.

She walked slowly, her long, Indian cotton skirt swishing against her ankle boots. It was hot today. Maybe her brain would melt. She pulled at her tank top, unable to think straight. After sheer bliss last night with Raul, who could blame her?

Blame. Now there was a word. It brought a chill to her skin. Poor Philip. Like Raul, he was to be made the fall guy for a murder. Poor Babette, too, another name on the puppet master's hit list. Katarina shuddered deeply. She hoped that hit list was very short. After all, how many deaths could they hope to prevent in one night of masked merriment?

Assuming, of course, that Raul's plan would work.

Katarina sighed and kept walking, her face raised to the burning sun. She'd seen pure misery in Raul's eyes when he'd told her about overhearing Ian's telephone conversation Wednesday night. Guilt, as well. But why?

"Because this shouldn't have been a problem to begin with," he'd told her.

"But that's ridiculous," Katarina had said, wrapping her arms about his hurt body. So this is what love entailed, was it? "You're human, Raul. No one expects you to be a saint. Anyway, you made the right decision. You want to help Philip and Babette...."

Yes, absolutely, Raul had made the right decision, but now Katarina swallowed hard around her own guilt.

"I say that and you still love me?" Raul had asked.

She'd kissed him. "What's not to love? Everybody hesitates..."

The words came back to her now. Ah, Raul, you should be inside my head right at this moment. Talk about unsaintly thoughts.

Because she wanted Raul free. She wanted them to be together. And there was such an easy, tempting way to ensure that goal. Turn a blind eye. Sacrifice conscience.

"No!" Katarina said out loud in a harsh whisper. She clenched her fists at her sides, angry with herself for ever contemplating such a vicious thing. If Luther looked down at her from heaven, he'd be so disappointed.

Don't disappoint him, then. Get it straight in your mind, Kati. Raul has a plan. Go to him. Help him finish it. Make it work. Then it will be good for everyone.

Except for the puppet master.

"WHY?" SOFIA DEMANDED, her nimble hands fussing with the soft folds of Vignette's dress.

It was 7:00 p.m. Friday evening. Raul, sitting idly on the low wall that overlooked the lower chambers, roused himself from his thoughts to glance at her. "Why, what?"

"Why save Babette?"

"Damned if I know." Raul sent her a distracted smile. "I just can't let another person die."

"And so you will put your life in danger to stop this." Sofia tottered over, holding Renato. She waved his golden head in Raul's face. "You seek to save this Philip, too. I think he's not worth the saving."

"You don't like Philip?"

"I do not like pretty men. I do not trust them. Once I knew a young marquis who was beautiful. I fell in love with him. It was not a good time to do this, of course. Many citizens were starving, living in squalor, but I did not see this, only him. But then one day we met a country beggar, and he asked us for a small coin because he was so hungry. I thought, I have many coins, I will give him some. But my marquis said no, I should not throw my money away and he took out a pistol and he shot this man. Then he put the pistol away and he offered me his arm and asked me sweetly where would I like to have our picnic lunch."

Raul frowned. "That's terrible, Sofia. But what has it to do with Philip?"

"He is spoiled and weak. Women like his pretty face. He has never had to be more than this. You wish to help him, but to do this you must have his cooperation. He must help you back. How do you know that he will do what you need him to do? Maybe he will crack under the pressure."

Raul studied her consideringly. "Why would he crack?"

"Because he always has been sheltered. Too much has been given to him. But one day it might not come so easily and then what will he do?"

"I don't understand."

She hit his shoulder with Renato's head. "This pretty one is not a person to trust. Maybe he is good, maybe not. What I'm saying is that you should not depend on him when you do not really know him. Do you understand?"

Smiling a little, Raul kissed her wrinkled hand. "Yes. But I have no choice. The puppet master must be caught before anyone else dies. This man is for sure a monster. I need Philip's help, Katarina's even more, and Louise's. I don't think Philip will crack under the pressure, but if he does then we'll have to do something to compensate."

"I think you take a great risk, my young friend. I am going now, deep into the vaults. I will call out for Giovanni's ghost and plead with him to help you. Do not argue with me, I will do it anyway. You could die tomorrow night, and then I would have nowhere to go when I am done forever with these vaults." She hesitated, peering at him. "I can come and live with you and the pretty young one with the long dark hair, can I not?"

In spite of the horror set to unfold around them, Raul fought the amusement that wanted to tug at his lips. "Yes, Sofia, you can."

It brought a cackle of delight to her throat. But did he speak the truth? What did he really know of Katarina's feelings? Not enough to presume that she would marry him once this nightmare ended.

And what if Philip did crack!

A thousand dark doubts rushed in on the heels of that thought. He realized distantly that Sofia was leaving.

Raul rested his arms on his raised knees and bowed his head. Let her go, he had to think. No, not about the buried finger or the bloodstain upstairs. Not even about Katarina in the way he would like to. Think schemes, and traps.

He'd spoken briefly to Katarina and Louise about an hour ago. Katarina looked sun-kissed. Her walk this afternoon must have been a long one. They couldn't talk, though, not with Louise there. They each had things to do. Katarina would talk to Philip and then after the performance tonight she and Raul would speak again.

His plan wasn't yet complete. Who knew if it would even make sense in the end? He was an architect, he didn't weave counter murder plots for a living.

His insides felt like ice as they had for most of the day. Too many thoughts crowded into his head.

"It'll work," he'd said to Katarina and Louise earlier, and meant it. He loved Katarina with all his heart, and she was very close to the evil now. Too close. That bothered Raul.

Had Babette let more slip to her than she should? Did the puppet master know that? Did he want her dead, too?

Panic slid through Raul's bloodstream, but he gritted his teeth, fighting tremors of terror.

"Look to the legend, Raul Sennett. The answers are there...."

Raul's head snapped up. Who'd whispered those words to him? "Who's there?" he asked out loud.

His eyes combed his own chamber and then the darker ones below. But there was only silence.

He left it that way; he wasn't sure why. He didn't question the voice or himself. And yet he knew he wasn't prone to hearing things. Not here and not in the Puppet Museum with Katarina on the night of the backstage party.

He settled back. These whispered warnings should unsettle him. To think that someone watched, and knew the vaults better than even Raul had come to know them. That this unseen person would choose to remain a shadow—all of it should disturb him. But it didn't. And for the life of him, Raul couldn't understand why.

Chapter Twenty

Alone in the darkness, in the stuffy black silence, the puppet master sat, on the bloodstain that was all that remained of Genevieve Capri.

Love the blood, he thought dreamily. Love to make skin crawl. Dark, evil, vicious, bloodthirsty. That was him.

"I am a monster, a fiend, a butcher. I am in control of all things."

He laughed so hard then that tears ran down his cheeks and his eyes smarted. Careful, though. People lived up here by day, and sometimes that day stretched into the night. Other things wandered, too. A curious cat for one. Nuisance animal.

He stood and lit a candle, walking around the bloodstain. Eerie, dancing steps carried him around this symbol of death. He savored the feeling that crept over him, crawled into him. "I will kill Louise because she is a threat. I will make Katarina watch. She will see that I am in control of all things. Then I will go to work on Katarina. Goodbye, my beauty, for you, too, threaten my existence, and this I cannot allow.

"You should never have listened to Babette," he said into the darkness. "For all I know she might have told you everything. I dare not take that chance."

He released a long anticipatory breath. A new life beckoned, absolute freedom. No more ties to this theater, to puppets or to people of power. No more strings attached. He would be gone from here, a dark evil thing roaming loose in a world of pumping hearts and rich red blood. He would control them all.

He clasped his hands together.

"Thank you, Giovanni Verrone..."

"LOOK TO THE LEGEND." From behind his back, Katarina wrapped her arms around Raul's neck. She pressed her cheek to his hair and sighed. "I wish I knew what that meant."

It was late, past midnight, which was to say it was masquerade ball Saturday. They'd come to the place by the river where Katarina had walked that afternoon. Here they would talk and plan, and try to understand what Katarina's mysterious Jean meant—that the answers to all of this resided in Giovanni's legend.

The scent of green grass and flowing water, of Raul's skin and his hair, washed over her. It was difficult to concentrate. The moon was out, a pearl whose rays spilled like a pale curtain over the countryside. How peaceful it was here, and Raul had procured a basket of food from somewhere.

"We'll have a picnic at the witching hour," he'd told her when she'd come to the vaults after the performance. "Away from this place, though, Kati. I'm tired of stone walls and the dark of an underground world. It's beginning to feel like hell. And now the shadows are speaking riddles to me, telling me that my fate will be controlled by a legend. I can't accept this."

But if it could help...

"There's got to be something in the fact that puppets come to life," she said now, her arms still tight about Raul's neck. "Something in the legend." She set her chin on his shoulder. "Gold threads in puppet's hair, gold threads in Pierre's hair."

"An Italian merchant puppet posing as a human, tricking a human," Raul added. He stroked her hand with his fingers, leaning back into her. "A man-puppet who remains always in the shadows, or at least can't be clearly seen by Giovanni."

Katarina bit her lip. "Sounds like Francois. I think I'm lost."

"Forget the legend," Raul advised her. "It is a fascinating story, nothing more."

"No, it *is* more, Raul. Jean said so, and I believe him, whoever he is."

"Possibly the puppet master," Raul suggested softly. "We know nothing of this person, Jean."

Katarina shivered but shoved the idea away. She would not believe that. "Well, at least the planning's done. I only hope and pray this idea will work, that whatever the puppet master intends to do won't happen, that we can stop it before it has a chance to develop."

Raul's nod was silent and Kati went on, "I talked to Philip earlier today about the part he'll be playing. I'll tell him the rest of the details tomorrow." She sighed. "I wish he wouldn't look so hurt every time we speak. I wish I could figure out the legend."

"If we're successful," Raul reminded her, "the legend won't matter."

Jean's words wouldn't go from Katarina's mind. Pushing them to one side, she hugged Raul. "This plan has to succeed.... But what if it doesn't?" Panic fluttered in her chest. "No, it has to," she stated, and felt Raul's fingers curl about her hand.

He turned to face her, his eyes large and dark and disturbing, more than enough to drive somber uncertainties away.

"It'll work," he promised.

But how could he know that? He rubbed her chin with his thumb, then steadied her jaw with his fingers and set his mouth on hers.

It was a deep kiss, wonderfully thorough and consuming. She gave in to it, let her worry slip away. What could it help?

He lifted his mouth, smiling down at her, his features shadowed, beautiful. "Have you ever made love in the loft of a medieval French barn?" he questioned softly. A little dazed, Katarina shook her head.

"Not in this lifetime." She looked at the ancient structure behind him, a mass of soot black stone. It brought another black thing to mind and a fearful chill to her skin.

"Don't think of this mad creature," Raul said, kissing her again. "What will be, will be. But not tonight. For this moment we're together. Alone. There's no puppet master, and nothing more we can do to stop him."

Katarina let the darkness slip away, but her brain protested Raul's words. There was more to be done, more that she could do with what Luther once called her magic eyes. She could unmask the fiend, she was sure of it.

The answers were buried in the legend.

SATURDAY MORNING, sunup. A haze enshrouded the city, curling around the Cathedral of Notre Dame. Ian stood before the west face portals and stared. They said the two side portals were carved by the devil—in other words, by the puppet master in his current form.

The heat haze wafted over Ian's face. Once, long ago, he'd thought to challenge the devil, to do something either really good or really bad, to defeat the beast or to better him. Look where he'd wound up—serving the damnable creature.

He'd never realized that the devil was insane, although probably he should have. A master of tricks and deceit. A genius, yes, but twisted into a tangle of black knots and thirsty for blood.

"Crazy vampire," Ian murmured faintly. "And I am your left-hand puppet-demon."

For today. But what about tomorrow?

Sweat formed on Ian's skin beneath his linen suit. He stared at the Portal of the last Judgment, looked above the tympanum to the carvings that represented the weighing of souls.

"What soul?" He almost laughed, but really wanted to cry. "The good go to heaven, the damned to hell. What have I done?"

"You will kill Babette, Ian!"

He flinched physically, looking with desperation to the carving of Abraham, who symbolized heaven. "Help me," he pleaded. "I can't do this. But if I don't, he'll kill me. He's evil right through. He has no soul."

The haze began to lift, a curtain being drawn back around the cathedral and in Ian's mind. He'd thought to defeat the devil once, why not take up the challenge again?

"Because he'll kill me. He'll cut me up. If I do as he orders, maybe he won't. I must obey him. For my life I must do this. I'm his servant, his puppet, I can be nothing else. For my life..." he finished, tears streaming down his cheeks. "God forgive me, I want to live."

But could he live without his soul?

IT WAS LATE AFTERNOON when Raul descended into the gloom of the theater vaults. Sweet Katarina, he couldn't believe he'd left her.

What did he sacrifice to be noble? Because if they failed tonight he would surely be condemned to hell. He might also have Babette's death on his conscience. And Philip's.

He shoved back his hair, squinting into the unnatural darkness of his subterranean chamber. Something white and folded lay on his cot. Another note from Sofia. He took a bottle of water and a loaf of bread to the wall, settled there and started to read.

Dear sexy young friend with the beautiful dark eyes:

What a morning it has been. So puzzling, and you were gone for all of it. I hope you were with the pretty girl. I know she was not in the company of Philip because I saw him sitting on the edge of the stage, drinking a bottle of something that made his eyes look very funny. He laughed and said things like, "I will go to South America, I think. Yes, that would be the perfect place to begin a new life." He also said "she" had nerve to not want him and what a mistake her not loving him would turn out to be when he left here for his new life. I did not know he had money of his own, did you?

"No, I didn't," Raul said to the note, then he paused. A new life for Philip was news to him. Something twisted in his stomach. Maybe Sofia was correct, and this man could not be trusted. Could tonight's plan work if Philip Hambleton was not the person he seemed? Raul searched his mind. How much had he asked Katarina to tell this man? Not everything, but possibly enough to endanger them all.

No, he couldn't think this way. He must believe the plan would work. There was no reason to distrust Philip. Raul read on.

Nothing more did I see or hear, except that the man who clings to the shadows stood far back in the theater. And then the shadow-man went away and the bundle of black fur came to sit on the stage and stare at Philip's eyes that did not look right at all.

I left then and came back to the vaults. I go now to look for Giovanni. I will find him tonight, I feel this deep inside me.

But I might not find you before you go to the party. So be careful. Do not trust anyone you do not know well. This is Sofia's advice to you, all the seventy-four years of her wisdom.

"Sixty-four," Raul murmured, refolding the note and shoving it under the puppet Jo-Jo's little feet.

Head resting against the wall, he closed his eyes and sipped his water. Be careful, Sofia said. Yes, he must be that and more. Because tonight the puppet master would be unmasked. The puppet master who was both a murderer and a madman.

KATARINA FUSSED with the hard plastic mask that covered her entire face, then ordered herself to stop fidgeting. So what if she was hot and the lights in the Hambleton mansion glared and the humidity made her feel like she was breathing under water. She played a part tonight, and she must execute it to the letter or else...

She strolled through the crowded ballroom, nervous, but she wouldn't show it. A grand, ornate room spread out around her, a vast sweep of marble and gold with elaborate mirrors for walls, crystal chandeliers and tables loaded with food and alcohol.

For the moment she was Jo-Jo, the jester gnome. But very soon Jo-Jo would fade unobtrusively away, and she would resurface as Renato, which just happened to be the puppet disguise Babette currently wore.

"You are both clear on this?" Raul had asked earlier of Katarina and Louise. "You each know what you have to do?"

Two nods.

"And what of Philip?"

"He'll be dressed as Renato, same as Babette," Katarina reported. "Frilled shirt, and breeches and boots. Golden hair."

"We'll float about as is for one hour," Louise went on, "always with our eyes on Babette and Philip, while you, Raul, watch Ian who will undoubtedly be the most difficult to keep track of since, like approximately half the other guests, he'll be dressed as the mysterious Italian merchant."

"Including Pierre and Francois," Katarina put in. "I found that out this afternoon."

And it wasn't a promising development, she reflected now, sidling up as close as she dared to where Babette stood beside a table of champagne.

Because Katarina knew Babette's mannerisms, her costume and masked face were not a problem.

There was also salvation in these suffocating masks, she acknowledged, inching closer. Unless you knew a person well, no one could possibly know who was who beneath them. And so when Katarina assumed Babette's costume, so long as she also adopted her distinctive gestures, nobody would be able to tell the difference.

Katarina let her mind go slowly back over the plan.

One hour would pass. Almost that much had. Louise would lure Babette out of the ballroom. Immediately Katarina would slip away, only to return five minutes later wearing Babette's disguise, that of the puppet Renato. Over to the champagne table she would drift. In the meantime, Raul, also costumed as the Italian merchant, would divert Ian's attention. God willing, the switch would be made cleanly.

Exactly fifteen minutes later, Renato-Philip would ask Renato-Katarina to dance. Across the marble floor they would glide. Then Katarina would suddenly pull away from Philip, apparently angry, maybe a reaction to an offensive remark. The guests would have to decide that for themselves.

Katarina would storm out of the room. Philip would follow close behind her, shouting, saying that he was sorry.

They would go to the garden and then beyond it onto the vast sprawling grounds of the Hambleton estate, down the winding path to the white-columned gazebo. But not inside; rather, they would take a left turn to the majestic twin oaks with their connecting wrought iron bench. They would stand there in a lovely patch of moon and floodlight, visible to anyone who might follow but not to the masqued masses in the ballroom. They would argue in low voices, inaudible to all except the birds above, but resolve nothing it would seem. Finally Philip would throw up his hands and leave while Katarina flounced out of the light and into the darkness of the gazebo....

Katarina trembled slightly. That's when things would get really tricky. Because that would be the puppet master's golden opportunity. Surely a chance he wouldn't pass up. It was too perfect. Kill the person *he thought* was Babette and frame the departing Philip.

In the ballroom, still dressed as Jo-Jo, Katarina shivered deeply. From the corner Ian watched Babette closely.

Where was the puppet master? Who was he? These were the frightening questions, unanswered, though heaven knew Katarina had dissected and examined every part of Giovanni's legend today.

It had something to do with those life-giving gold threads and the Italian merchant, she was sure of it. It might also have to do with the gold threads braided into Pierre's hair or the fact that Francois never let his face be seen.

None of this told her much, though. Maybe Jean from the vaults was as crazy as the puppet master. But she knew deep down that wasn't true.

"Five minutes till I lure Babette away. I wish I could figure out where Pierre and Francois are."

Louise glided over to where Katarina waited on the rim of the dance floor and stood back to back with her. Puppets walked everywhere, many like Louise done up as Mignon. Katarina had to struggle to concentrate. It was so hot. Her head was swimming. Where in the legend were the answers?

"There are at least fifty Italian merchants here," Katarina remarked. "All cloaked and masked. Maybe Raul knows which ones are which."

Louise sipped on her tonic. "Hope so."

Katarina glanced around. Her nerves were stretched to the limit, like piano wire, and just as finely tuned. Maybe that's why the room had begun to look so distorted. There was too much to take in for a mind that was suddenly absorbing everything. Heat, light, color, people, masks, eyes behind masks. She even noticed a persistent fly that was buzzing around the harpist's head.

"You all right, love?" Louise broke through to inquire. Dragging herself back, Katarina nodded.

"Fine. Where's Philip?"

"Dancing with a duchess. Two minutes left."

"You'd better go."

"On my way." With crossed fingers Louise tapped Katarina's shoulder. "Good luck to all of us. Except the puppet master."

Closing her eyes, Katarina murmured a fervent, "Amen."

Chapter Twenty-one

The puppet master's plan was a clever one, but this was still a nightmare.

Ian fought with conscience and panic as he watched Babette. How could he do this?

"It will be fine," the puppet master had promised hours ago from the safety of his darkened theater office.

Easy for him to say that when he was in no danger of anything.

"You wear the disguise of the Italian merchant," he'd said. "So do many others. You will quietly take Babette aside, instruct her to find Philip and bring him to you. Upstairs is good, unless a more appropriate setting presents itself. You tell Babette that her locating Philip is part of my robbery plan—a robbery that will not take place tonight, although Babette does not know this. Out of fear she will comply. And then it becomes very simple. You take Philip to an empty bedroom, you knock him out, you take off your merchant's robes under which you will be wearing a puppet-Renato disguise—this precaution against any unlikely witnesses—you go to another bedroom where you will have told Babette to wait for you, you bring her to the room where Philip is, you kill her, you put the knife in Philip's hand, you put on your merchant's robes, you rouse Philip to near consciousness and you leave. The authorities will take it from there."

"But how?" Ian asked.

"Think, idiot," the puppet master snapped. "They will discover things about Philip that will lead them to believe he was the person in charge of the robberies. I will plant evidence of this in his theater dressing room. They will conclude that he intended to rob his own parents. His motive, revenge against Papa's suffocating hand. And of course personal freedom. No question as to why he would feel the need to kill Babette, whom everyone knew to be on the verge of hysteria lately. She was one of his puppets and a threat to him, so he killed her. Unfortunate for him that this time he was caught." A smile formed on the puppet master's lips. "So you see, Ian? It is as simple as I say."

"Simple, yes, if everything falls neatly into place. But what if it doesn't?"

"Then you will have to improvise," the puppet master had informed him coldly. "Use your brain. You do have one, do you not?"

A vicious resentment filled Ian's mind and his body at this memory. Right now as he stood here in the ballroom, he truly could kill, but not Babette.

He probed for the gun beneath his robes—his own precaution—and found it, together with the knife provided by the puppet master. A knife belonging to Philip, no doubt. Ian's heart sank. What monstrous deed would he perform tonight? The devil's work done by the demon's hand. Oh, please, God, forgive me for this dreadful sin.

SHADOWS PERMEATED the vaults and the chamber inhabited by Raul Sennett. Sofia crept in with the second to last puppet in her hand. Nicoli, or as she saw it, Giovanni. She went to the niche where the other puppets sat. The originals. Had she told this to her sexy young friend?

She held Nicoli in her hands, then carried him with her to the cot, tucking her legs underneath her and sitting him down opposite. Maybe she could contact Giovanni through the puppet.

"I know you are here," she said to the puppet. "Why do you not reveal yourself to me? You know who the evil monster is. But you do not tell the police."

Sofia started. Did she hear a voice? It wasn't shock that formed her expression; rather, it was triumph and delight.

"I knew it," she whispered, then cackled with glee and patted Nicoli's head. "At last you talk to me, Giovanni. Why did you wait for so long?"

"I had my reasons."

She got no sense of where he might be hiding. Maybe ghosts could not be seen. Or did he hide from her on purpose?

"You must help Raul and Katarina," she instructed.

"Help them, why, Sofia?"

He sounded weary, young of voice, yet old of soul.

"Help them because they are special," she answered. "And do not say why to me again. You know they are special just as surely as I do."

He didn't deny her words. "I have done all that is possible for me to do. I cannot go to the police."

"Why not? Is that a rule for ghosts?"

"It is you who call me a ghost, not I."

"You are a ghost," she maintained. She picked up Nicoli and set him in the dip of her peasant skirt. "Will you help them?"

"I have already."

"In what way?"

"I cannot tell you."

"Why not?"

"Because I do not wish to."

"Then you are a mean ghost."

"I am what I am. The truth begins to surface. Plots unfold at this moment. It is not for me to direct the course of these events. This is God's jurisdiction. What will be, will be."

Sofia batted the puppet's little head. The voice did not issue from its mouth, but she could not hit the air. "Make sense," she ordered. "Do you see the future?"

"No."

"Then we are the same and there is no reason for you not to interfere."

"There is a reason. And we are not the same."

Sofia gave the puppet's head another swat. "You are a stubborn ghost. Uncooperative. Help them."

"I have. The answers are in the legend."

"Answers to what?"

"To many things."

"I do not understand."

"I know. But I think you soon will. Call to me again when you are ready. I will return then."

She did not completely trust this voice. It belonged to Giovanni, did it not? "What do you mean?" she demanded, then clutched a startled hand to her sweater. "I'm not going to die, am I? You are not really Death sent to talk to me in Giovanni's voice, are you?"

No answer, just a forlorn, "Call to me when you are ready, when you understand." His voice faded into the blackness. "Remember, the answers to everything are in the legend."

Sofia sat back on the cot and swiped fretfully at Nicoli's puppet head. "Ghost of legend, what do you know? I have understood everything for a very long time now."

THE SWITCH had been made, cleanly, Katarina prayed. She danced now with an uncharacteristically stiff-limbed Philip. Did Ian watch? She couldn't see through the waltzing bodies. The orchestra played the *Blue Danube.* She kept count, floating through smoke, past the bandstand.

Yes, there was Ian, over by the French doors. Do it now, Kati, she thought. Stop dancing. Pull away from Philip. Good. Now pause, give your head an insulted lift. Slap his face. Come on, Philip, her mind said. React, or you'll get hit.

Philip's fingers locked on her wrist. Was that real anger in his eyes?

Pull away, she thought. Now turn and march out. Push at the woman in the Vignette wig. You want to get noticed now.

Philip's playing his part, shouting Babette's name. He's apologizing. Sorry, she thought with a sigh. Your apology is not accepted tonight.

Keep stomping across the marble floor, Kati. Go through the double doors. There's another group of people in the entryway. Shove them aside. Babette would do that. Mutter a French swear word, as well.

Stalk down a carpeted corridor, out another set of glass doors to the rear terrace. Good, there are people here, too. They're glaring at you. They can hear Philip calling to you from behind.

"Babette, don't go. I'm sorry. I shouldn't have said those things. Babette!"

A thread of impatience crept into his voice. Nice touch, Kati decided.

A tremor of revulsion went through her. She thought now of the puppet master. Did he follow them? Did Ian follow, too? What if Ian grabbed Philip while the puppet master grabbed her? What if he stabbed her and then Raul, who was sure to be right there?

A deep shudder passed through her body. She must follow the plan, walk quickly down the terrace stairs with angry strides, follow the path, past the marble fountain, the cherubs and big trees with a grouchy carnivorous look to them, oak trees that seemed to want to grab her and bite.

Panic started up inside her, tiny ripples far down. She must keep them down. Raul would come. Maybe he'd caught the puppet master already.

The party noises died out now. Nature had taken over. She heard singing bugs, frogs and the tinkle of fountain water. Up ahead she saw the gazebo. It looked like a ghost house, gauzy in the moonlight that came and went with the shifting clouds. Fingers moved across its pearly face.

Okay now, stay calm, she told herself. The twin oaks are right here, and the bench. The gazebo's to the right. But don't go there yet. You have to fight more with Philip. Who knew what lurked in the shadows.

Fingers on her arm yanked her around. Philip's eyes seemed to blaze with anger beneath his Renato mask. Did she smell Scotch on his breath? Her teeth clenched. Drinking, at a time like this? Philip, are you crazy?

She began counting to thirty, then pulled free of Philip's grip, annoyed now.

A sudden attack of breathlessness hit her. She didn't imagine it. There were things creeping along the path, shadows darker than the night. They wore robes. Her eyes went to Philip's mask. Did he see them? *For heaven's sake,* she thought, *stop glaring at me and look.*

Twenty-seven, twenty-eight... Finally the thirty seconds were up. And there was Philip, gesturing that he was going to leave her, alone, with the robed shadows. She controlled a shiver. Raul!

There was no way to stem the panic now. She tasted the fear in her mouth, felt a chill on her perspiring skin. Raul hadn't wanted her to do this, but she'd insisted. She had to be the bait. Louise was too tall, too thin.

She ordered herself to stay calm, to play the part. Do it, Kati. Walk to the gazebo, go through the columned entrance. But it was so dark in here, latticed shadows and then total blackness.

So it came at last, the moment of truth. A figure sat to her left, the silhouette of a woman. She mustn't look at it. The scent of Babette's perfume clung to its clothes, clung to hers, too. She had to ignore it all, tiptoe quietly past. The shadows approached. Be very quiet now. Pretend you're a ghost.

She took one quick glance back, unable to confine her curiosity.

What were the robed shadows doing . . . ?

IAN'S BODY TENSED. This was it. Babette entered the gazebo. Philip, God help him, was unconscious, lying beside a thick hedgerow. One swing and down he'd gone. A glass-jawed aristocrat. Ian could take pride in his punch—if only in that.

He crept forward, eyes straining. Sweat poured into them. This was not the puppet master's plan, his frightened brain cried. There were no bedrooms in sight and he'd never even spoken to Babette. He couldn't, not with that idiot dressed in merchant's robes suddenly babbling at him in Spanish, calling him Count Brumir as he pumped his hand, holding him captive while Louise and Babette exited the ballroom.

There was no way to escape the idiot. The man just kept on shaking Ian's hand, refusing to let him lift his mask and prove that he was not in fact this Count Brumir.

But, thank heaven, it had been all right. Louise and Babette had come back. There was no mistaking Babette. She'd stalked straight to the champagne table, her perfume hanging like a cloud around her.

She'd danced part of a waltz with Philip, had an argument of some sort with him, then made an indignant exit. Now she was here, her shoulders hunched as she wandered into the gazebo. Alone. Maybe this was better than a bedroom, but Ian didn't like to improvise.

He liked to kill even less.

The knife bumped against his ribs as he tiptoed across the grass. The gun, too. His skin was soaked with sweat. His heart pounded like a drum.

He crept up two steps, still on tiptoe. There she was, a Renato silhouette. He smelled the Chanel perfume. She sat on a bench in the corner. How very dark it was in here, but that was Babette all right. Was she upset, crying?

He sneaked forward, a demon-rat with a knife clutched in his fingers. Ice-cold blood slid through his veins; sweat stung his eyes. Please understand, Babette. I don't want to die.

He crawled closer. And then he was there, and his arm and the knife were going up. All on their own they seemed to rise, like someone pulled a string from above.

A grimace deformed his lips. I'm sorry, Babette, so very sorry.

Down came his arm, arrow straight. The blade plunged into her neck. It made a horrible slicing sound, made Ian want to throw up. But he couldn't. He wasn't done yet. He had to remove the knife, and put it in Philip's hand.

Babette had not made a sound, not a single movement. Was this right? Did people die so easily?

He pulled out the knife, paused, then stared at it. It was dark in here, yes, but the blade glinted even so.

Something wasn't right about it. The metal gleamed like polished steel. It was a shine of silver, not red.

The nausea stopped in his throat. Where was the blood? All people bled when they were stabbed. Where was Babette's blood?

Again his hand felt attached to a string. It grabbed the blond wig, and the plastic mask, ripping them off. His eyes strained, nearly popping as he yanked the body around.

Lifeless black eyes stared back at him, glinting dully in the darkness. Ian flinched. He went cold inside and out. He started to laugh, then to cry. He stepped away. He wanted to tear out his hair.

This was madness! Sheer lunacy. He'd just killed a puppet!

Chapter Twenty-two

Katarina stared, numb, mesmerized, at what she saw.

"Go, Kati."

Raul's voice in her ear was a whisper. He gave her a push. But go, why? She didn't understand. There was no danger here.

They were hidden behind a chestnut tree, the place she'd literally crawled to after passing the set up puppet in the gazebo. It was all part of the plan. Draw the puppet master in with bait, provide victim and opportunity. It was too perfect to pass up. And he'd gone for it all the way.

"Kati..."

Raul whispered another warning, but she didn't want to leave. He'd gone to the security people at the party, told them to come and help him catch a killer on the grounds. Wasn't that them out there, those dark shadows closing in on the puppet master in the gazebo?

There's no danger, Raul. But the man hiding under the mask, the mad killer, connected somehow to Giovanni's legend, his identity she had to know.

Raul gave her one last gentle push as he left the shelter of the tree. The robed figures moved now through the shadows, closer, and the man in the gazebo knew it. He saw them, spun around, knife in hand, blade up. He was poised to kill.

There was jerkiness to his motions, however. He looked like a man yanked about by an unseen puppeteer. Katarina's skin crawled.

"Come on, Kati." Another voice came into her ear. It was Louise this time. "Let's go to the back of the gazebo. We'll be safer there."

A rush of adrenaline rejuvenated Katarina's body. "No. I have to see this. Maybe it's stupid, but I have to know."

"You're crazy." But Louise stopped tugging on her arm. "Okay, let's do it then."

Together they crept closer. Louise was behind her, it would be okay. Ahead of them were Raul and Philip.

She glanced back. The security guards were there.

"Stop!"

A growl burst from the gazebo just as Katarina got there. The man with the knife was speaking.

"Who is it?" Katarina wondered very softly.

"He sounds familiar," Louise whispered.

"Quiet, he'll hear you. Besides, I can't hear him if you talk."

Katarina leaned closer, entranced. He kept shouting while he hopped about like a marionette gone mad. It was an eerie, unpredictable dance.

"My God, I think it's Ian!" Louise whispered very loudly. Katarina heard the shock in her tone, and knew she was right. It was Ian. Not the master.

Disappointment slid through her, until she realized that the figure had leapt up in the air and landed facing them.

"My God, he heard me!"

Louise's grip on Katarina's arm tightened. Both man and knife were pointed right at them. He was inching forward, creeping like a rat. A scream rose in Katarina's throat. Where were the security guards? Raul!

"Let's get out of here!" Louise hissed.

Katarina nodded, stammering, "Y-yes, l-let's do that right n-now."

"Come on!" Louise tugged urgently on Katarina's jacket. "Hurry!"

Katarina couldn't believe it. "I can't hurry," she said, her voice shaking. "I'm caught."

"Kati..."

Time was the strangest thing. It took forever for two seconds to tick by. Forever, and a flash. One moment, both knife and man pirouetted jerkily inside the gazebo. Next, there was a loud splinter of latticed wood, and suddenly an arm about her throat, squeezing off her oxygen, and Ian breathing hot and heavy down her neck as he hauled her up tight against his robed body.

"Stay away," he snarled.

"No, don't," she tried to scream, but he cut her off with pressure from his arm.

Astonishment more than terror streaked through Katarina's mind, and her body. The fear would come, though, after the shock wore off.

Be smart, Katarina, she told herself. Use the moment. Stomp on his foot, poke his ribs, scratch his hands. Bite them.

Voices seemed to swirl in front of her, a nonsensical babble. She had a sensation of being carried backward.

Something jabbed her under her chin. Panic began to claw at her. Her nerves felt hot like little wires. Her breath was short in her chest, uncatchable.

Another jab, then she heard Raul's voice, saw him approaching. Then her eyes blurred. She couldn't breathe!

"Let her go, Renshaw," Raul said, as if from a great distance. "We know you're not the puppet master. Help us catch him. Nothing will happen to you if you just let Katarina go."

"Yes, Ian, please let me go!" Katarina fought for air. *Let me breathe at least,* she pleaded in silence.

Fire burned in her lungs. What was that hard thing under her chin? The knife? No, it wasn't sharp enough for that. What then?

"Keep away," Ian growled. "Or I swear I'll shoot her."

A gun! Oh, God, no, her mind begged, Ian, please don't shoot!

"I'll do it, I will."

She heard the hammer being cocked, and then a slight sob in her ear. Still they gravitated backward, and all Katarina dared do now was pull at Ian's arm, struggle to breathe.

"He'll kill me, don't you understand?" Ian rasped. "I can't turn him in. You don't know him. He's deadly. He has no feelings for anyone. I'm just a puppet to him. He told me I had to kill Babette. It was too dangerous for him to do it. He wouldn't even come tonight. But I didn't want to kill her. I didn't want to kill anyone."

He shouted at them, but never stopped hauling Katarina across the lawn. Where were the security people? They must have cleared out because they thought he would shoot her before they could get his gun.

Ian breathed in short spurts now, whimpering, slackening his stranglehold just a bit. Katarina gulped lungfuls of air.

"It's his doing," Ian cried. "He's the master, the monster, the cause of it all."

"Then take us to him."

A stranger said that, a man's voice that Ian didn't seem to like. He made a rumble in his throat, possibly a release of some kind, because he changed suddenly, snapped. All his anger seemed to surface, and his demeanor shifted. His arm became a steel band across Katarina's windpipe.

"No!" His growl was pure hatred. "I won't take you anywhere." The gun barrel twisted under Katarina's trembling chin. "I'm sick of it, all of it. Rob, kill, cover up. Do this for me, Ian. Do that. Of course I treat you like dirt. You're nothing. I'm a genius, your master. The puppet master. I cut women into little pieces, that's how I control. It makes me better than you in every way, a brave, fearless butcher. You could never do these things. Never, never, you pathetic puppet."

Fury radiated from him, an explosion of pent-up emotion. It felt like a glow. And then he stopped dragging her. Katarina prayed. Grab him, someone! Raul!

The shadows didn't stir. Why?

She heard the nightmare sound, a sharp click of metal. The pressure on her throat was released, then a quick shove and the world tilted sideways. She hit padded leather.

"Drive," Ian snarled.

The gun blocked her vision. Her cheeks were chalk white, they had to be. Her blood had evaporated, and her saliva. She couldn't even swallow.

Her eyes stared blankly at his face. Her stomach was hollow, there was no life in her fingers, or her voice. "Drive where?"

"I'll direct you." He sounded weary now, as if exhaustion pulled at him. But he still waved the gun under her nose.

"Start the engine, Katarina. We're going to see the puppet master."

A ROAR OF DENIAL rose in Raul's chest, then burst from his throat. This couldn't be happening, not any of it!

Philip clutched at his arm, breathless, scared. He was drunk. The car was pulling away, a brown Saab. There were millions of them in Paris.

Raul clenched his fists, trying to think. He felt ghostly, sick. Ian was taking her to the puppet master. Pierre and Francois hadn't come to the party. Raul had checked; he'd made a point of learning that.

Security swarmed behind him, but no police. It was pointless to involve them. They wouldn't have believed. They would rather have slapped the cuffs on Raul's wrists and been done with it. But they couldn't do that now, could they? Ian had stabbed a life-size puppet. It was hard to get more murderous than that. He'd talked, too. Security had heard him. He'd said the puppet master made him do it. It was too dangerous for the leader to kill Babette. He hadn't even come tonight.

A burst of engine noise broke the air, and the smell of exhaust. Finger clouds stretched over the moon. The Saab was a disappearing shadow. Kati!

Agony burned in Raul's throat. The Saab was fading from sight. The nightmare had grown to monstrous proportions.

Knots of panic dragged at his muscles. He had to shake Philip off, had to swallow the sickness and think. Where were they going? To the theater?

He twisted his head around, saw the line of cars beside him. Security milled about, confused.

Idiots! Raul squeezed his eyes closed, then snapped them open. "Get away from me, Philip," he snarled.

He shook off the limp hand that kept pawing at him and began to run. There was a Jaguar with keys in the ignition, a car begging to be stolen.

He twisted the key, felt the roar of power. No one tried to stop him. Good. He was in no mood to reason.

"Where are you going?" Louise screamed at him, her fists pounding on the window. "Let me come, Raul."

"All right, come, but get in now."

There was a scramble of feet, the faces of a thousand puppets flashing before his eyes. Glass eyes, cold, mad. Who in the legend had been so mad?

He gritted his teeth, shoving the car in gear. He knew Ian would go to the theater. He had to stop the puppet master from killing Katarina.

IT WAS REALITY uncontrolled, her nightmare coming true.

Katarina couldn't believe this. She was being dragged through the Puppet Museum by Ian Renshaw in merchant's robes at midnight. Hell was here and now and all the little demon eyes in the underworld watched from inside the puppet cases.

"Ian, wait," she begged. "Don't!" Dig in your heels, she told herself. Be an anchor on his arm. "Please don't do this."

"He's probably upstairs," Ian muttered. He made no acknowledgement of her pleas. "Upstairs, dreaming of blood."

"Whose blood?" Katarina whispered. She felt sick now, as well as terrified.

She made one last desperate appeal. "Why are you doing this, Ian? You know what he'll do to me."

He came to a dead stop, so abrupt that the arm wrapped around Katarina's throat nearly choked her. "He'll kill you."

Her fingers plucked ineffectively at his sleeve. "I know."

"He'll use his knife on you."

"Yes, I know." I don't want to hear it, though. "Couldn't we both just leave before he sees us?" Whoever *he* was...

"I don't—no!" Ian wore a hood, and a mask, but even with the barriers his mouth felt close to Katarina's ear. "I want to live, Katarina. I'm sorry."

His free hand stroked her hair. Her eyes flew open. Where was the gun?

Stay calm, Kati. Breathe. The gun must be inside his robe.

He was hauling her again, past a collection of tall island cases. How gloomy it was in here. The legend raced through her mind. Giovanni created Mignon, a beautiful woman-puppet. But he'd wanted to make her real, or to put his soul into Nicoli. Then the mysterious Italian merchant appeared with his magic threads of gold. He knew the secret, of course. He was a puppet himself!

More glass cases passed. Get the gun from Ian....

"Ian wait, I can't—you're choking me."

"You might prefer it that way." He didn't let up or even break his stride.

Marble eyes gaped at her. No life in them, no feeling.

Tiny electric shocks rippled through her. Where had she heard that, "no feeling"?

The eyes multiplied. Weak shafts of light hit them, giving them a spooky look. How could she get that gun?

Something soft sounded on her right. She twisted her head around. She saw puppet cases only, and eyes.

But one set blinked!

Her panic unleashed itself now. Live puppets? The legend coming true? The world was insane!

A silky whisper of motion reached her. Ian still bruised her throat with his grip. A staircase loomed, seldom used. She looked fearfully sideways. How could puppet eyes blink?

Something flew through the darkness, brushing her cheek, bringing a strangled scream to her throat. Amadeus!

"What...!"

Ian let out a startled cry. The cat was hanging from his robe, clawing its way up to his shoulder.

"Run, Katarina..."

An invisible voice spoke to her. "Jean?" she whispered.

None of this was real. She must get away—but get the gun first. Ian's arms flailed, groped for the cat. She had only to reach into his robe.

One flailing arm cracked her hard across the cheek. Tears of pain stung her eyes.

"*Leave the gun,* Katarina. *Run...*"

The voice came again. But run where, she wondered, searching the gloom. Up the staircase? There were corridors everywhere up there and blessed darkness. She could hide in a maze of shadows.

"Get him off me!" Ian shouted. "His claws are sharp."

Katarina bolted. Thank heaven for leather boots and breeches. She could run easily in them.

The circular staircase went up precisely ten steps. She followed a twisty hall and then ran ten steps down. Where was she? Would the puppet master be waiting wherever she went?

Terror gave her stamina. It felt like she breathed some foreign substance. Oh, Raul, where are you?

Tears slid down her cheeks now. Her teeth chattered. Her skin felt like ice. This was a monster movie come to life. Raul, I can't think.

She spotted a door to her left, pushed through it. A tunnel of darkness spread out behind it, like Giovanni's beloved vaults.

What had the merchant said? If he could make it so, all puppets would be human and all humans would be puppets. In other words, there would be no more reality.

She felt dizzy now. Exhaustion gripped her. She stumbled, hit a wall and her head. The pain brought her back.

She shoved through another door, stopped and let her eyes adjust. She was in the theater. The orchestra pit stood ahead and seats to her right. How had she gotten here?

It didn't matter. Find an exit. The nearest one was behind the stage.

She hoisted herself onto the apron, raced across the polished floor, slipped a little but caught her balance. She could see the wings. Only a few more yards . . .

She hit something hard, a wall of black granite. The impact shattered her thoughts, left her mind and body in a fog. Then hands gripped her arms.

"What are you doing here, Katarina?"

Francois!

"No!" She panted. She pushed frantically at his robed chest. "Let me go!"

"What is the problem?"

Pierre joined him. He came up behind her, not so much in the shadows as Francois, but dressed the same way. Two identical Italian merchants.

She worked her head around, saw Pierre and then Francois. They were unmasked.

"What is wrong, Katarina?"

Francois spoke, but he didn't release her arms. She tried to hammer on his chest, to hurt him. She had to get away.

He only changed his grip, bringing her closer to him. She snapped her head back, glaring at him. You're crazy, both of you, she wanted to tell him. Partners in business and in murder.

She heard herself gasp instead. Horror swept through her, hot, blinding prickles of terror, and sudden comprehension.

She couldn't see Francois's face, but in his hair were braided several threads. Gold threads, just like the merchant in the legend.

A scream of denial and terror burst from her throat. "No! Stay away from me!" She wrenched free. "This can't be real!"

Pierre's fingers clamped onto her wrist, jerking her around. "You are hysterical, Katarina."

Yes, she was hysterical, and desperate. She raised her fingers to scratch at his face.

That's when she saw it, the thing she dreaded most. Of course it would be there, the same golden braid in Pierre's hair!

She sprang backward, away from both men. She tripped but didn't fall. Somehow she scrambled for the far wing, then ran as though Satan chased her across the stage.

Two sets of feet pounded behind her. Partners in all things, she realized, different, yet united in their insanity.

She ducked now into a labyrinth of props and backdrops. Be quiet, she told herself. You can lose them in the mess. Crouch down. Hide. Control your terror for just one more minute. Raul will come. He'll bring the police. He'll know where Ian went. He'll figure it out.

Voices reached her, muffled by velvet and canvas and wood. Katarina strained to hear them.

"Where did she go?" Francois whispered.

"You ask me?" Pierre said impatiently. "She almost scratched my eyes out."

Francois, angry now for the first time that Katarina had ever heard, said, "Find her, Pierre."

And Pierre, like a sarcastic adolescent replied, "As you wish—master."

Chapter Twenty-three

"Kati!"

Raul burst through the theater's side door. He ignored the surprised watchman and Louise's quick explanation behind him. He tore off the merchant's robe, down to a black T-shirt and pants, then took a deep breath.

"I have seen no one, mademoiselle," the watchman stammered. "Except for the messieur's Fousard and Lupier."

Raul winced, and grabbed Louise's hand. *Find Katarina* was the shout in his head. Don't let Ian make a gift of her to the puppet master.

He started to run. Through the shadows, around one corner then another, down an aisle, through a door—

Straight into the robed body of Pierre Fousard.

THERE WERE MORE STAIRS to climb. This set was hidden behind an old door in the prop room. Katarina's knees wobbled, but she dared not stop. She must go up, where Pierre and Francois were not—she hoped.

Prayer and hope were all she had. This nightmare couldn't continue forever. But would it end with her death?

"Only puppets die tonight, Katarina."

The voice spoke to her again! It sounded sad now.

She looked around, almost stopped. But no, she couldn't do that. She had to keep going. Maybe she was a puppet and didn't realize it. It sounded absurd but both Pierre and Francois wore gold threads in their hair. So define reality tonight.

She heard no more whispers on the stairs, just the pelt of her boot heels. She couldn't keep up this pace. Her head was starting to feel funny, light, fuzzy. It was such a narrow staircase and it sort of zigzagged around. It even ended once, and she had to grope her way down a dusty, dark passageway, but there were more stairs waiting.

Maybe she should have gone down, into the vaults. The monsters lived up here. Was she crazy, climbing the stairs to a realm of fiends?

Her head spun. Katarina paused, leaning on the cracked wood railing, fighting for air. Her hair fell in her eyes. Her mind was a tangle of legend thoughts. Who are you, Jean?

Did the answers lie in the merchant's role? Puppet destroying human, driving human to the brink of madness, that was logical. The merchant had no feelings, no soul! What a scary concept.

Dread hung over her like a giant bird. She forced herself to move. There *was* an escape. She was not a puppet.

She pitched forward as the stairs ran out. She'd reached a level surface now, there was only one direction to take. She groped through the darkness, then choked off a scream as something wound itself around her ankles. She heard a soft meow. Her body sagged against the wall. It was only Amadeus.

She stroked the silky ears. "Be quiet, though, Amadeus," she warned. "I have no idea where we are." She looked around. "Just pray we don't bump into Ian or the puppet master."

The cat went silent, no more meows in the darkness, only the rapid beating of Katarina's heart. There was a dead weight in her chest and stomach. Her limbs felt stiff, like wood. She wished someone would wake her up.

A barrier sprang up suddenly in front of her. She couldn't believe it for a moment. The corridor had ended. It was a trap!

Her fists hit the wall in a small gesture of futility. A sob broke from her throat.

Tears rose in her eyes, her lower lip trembled. But then she thought, *No! I will not give up!* And she brushed away the unshed tears. Come on, think. What is this wall? It doesn't feel like stone. Maybe there's a door.

With her hands, she examined the panels. They seemed familiar. She frowned, trying to recall that night with Raul. They'd been sneaking around. Yes, after the backstage party, the hidden staircase, the wardrobe, Ian's office—that was it! But then came the gruesome rest of it. The cat, the puppet, the boarded hallway, the room—the bloodstain. She shivered. But she didn't have to see any of that tonight. Oh please, Ian, don't be in your office.

She sensed a tiny rift in the silence behind her. It was just Amadeus. How did these panels come out? Slide or. . . ?

A hand closed firmly over her mouth and she gave an instinctive jerk. The hand had come out of nowhere. A man stood behind her. She couldn't scream!

Shock raced through her as his arm caught her waist, pulling her back into him. His burlap sleeve scratched on her cheek—she knew he was wearing a merchant's robe. And it wasn't Raul, because he wouldn't grab her like this.

She twisted harder, terrified, angry. Let me go, you monster!

"Be quiet, Katarina." He whispered in her ear, a firm, even command from one accustomed to giving them. "Do not fight me."

It was Francois Lupier. The man whom Pierre called "master".

Katarina fought with all her strength. But his hold on her merely tightened. His mouth moved against her hair.

"Do not struggle," he warned in an ominous tone. "On your life, do not make a sound." He gave her a shake. "On your life, Katarina Lacroix."

CLAW MARKS made Ian's hands bleed. Katarina was gone. The puppet master was here somewhere, but his orders had not been carried out. Babette still lived.

Ian's chest began to heave. "He'll kill me."

But with those words came a sudden clarity of vision. Good Lord, what had taken him so long? There was a solution, a perfectly simple one.

"You do have a brain, don't you, Ian... ?"

The puppet master's question came back to haunt him. Ian almost started to laugh. A brain, yes. He had the power to think, to act, to kill the fiend that would surely kill him. He could take on the devil and win. Why hadn't he thought of this sooner?

Giddiness made him dizzy. He moved through the darkness with purpose. He had the knife in his pocket, and the puppet master was here somewhere. Upstairs? He needed only to find the beast, to catch him off-guard. To use the knife and kill him...

"VERY STILL NOW," Francois cautioned.

They were inside Ian's office wardrobe. One thin door stood between Katarina and possible freedom. Why didn't Amadeus jump on Francois?

The man held fast but didn't strangle. She worked her head around a little, tried to see his profile, his eyes. Were they glassy, like a puppet's eyes? Did he think he was a puppet?

He squeezed her waist for compliance, a subtle threat. Be still, be quiet. One wrong move and he would use his knife on her for sure.

The hand on her mouth eased her head back around. "Open the door a little," he instructed. "Make no sound."

A tremor ran through her. She was his puppet. Oh please, she prayed, let me wake up. Don't let this be happening.

A tiny moan escaped from her throat, bringing a stronger pressure on her waist. Then she heard something. A click. The door to Ian's office was opening. The figure of a man was creeping in.

The hand was a clamp on her mouth.

"Make one sound and you will die," Francois promised so softly it might have been telepathy.

She stilled her struggles, waiting.

The figure paused on the threshold. It seemed to gather strength, perhaps courage. It talked to itself.

"No more," it said through its teeth. Was it Ian? "Not ever again, you devil puppet master. Tonight it is you who die."

That was all he said. And then he was no longer in the doorway. He was streaking across the carpet to the desk chair, a high-backed chair that faced the window.

No, wait, Ian, Katarina wanted to cry. The puppet master's not in the chair. He's in the closet!

She could no longer restrain herself. She clawed frantically at Francois's hand, kicked him. He would kill her anyway.

Her teeth sank into Francois's finger. "Ian," she started to scream, but the name caught suddenly in her throat.

Again she felt that sense of time stretching into infinity, yet passing so swiftly that a century might have been only a second. Strange, though, how her mind could take it all in. Every sight and sound, even the fact that she still fought with Francois. Maybe time overlapped or lagged or just got so confused that it created a vacuum. Because what happened next made no sense at all to her.

She was making all kinds of noise with Francois in the armoire. Her foot even managed to knock the door wide open. But Ian didn't notice that—almost like it wasn't happening. He'd wrenched the chair around, so now the back of it faced Katarina, and all she could see was Ian standing there, looking down, his knife poised to strike.

But strike who? Pierre?

But then in her side vision, three shocking other figures appeared at the office doorway—and that was when complete confusion took over her mind.

She panicked, biting Francois's hand, hard. Finally, it left her mouth. But the name she would have screamed died on her lips. Astonishment slowly widened her eyes.

"No more, you monstrous butcher!"

Ian shrieked this. But at whom? Pierre stood in the doorway with Raul and Louise. Francois stood in the wardrobe behind her. And Ian held the knife...

"You murdered Claudia and then Genevieve. You would have murdered Katarina and Louise. You would have had me murder Babette. And then what more would you have done?"

"You know the answer, Ian. You do not need to ask me."

Katarina's entire body froze. This was unreal.

"I won't let you control me anymore. I won't let anyone control me. Do you hear me, Mother?" he shouted upward. "I do what I want to do."

"Shut up, Ian," the figure in the chair snapped. "You will do as I say."

"Butcher." Ian's eyes glowed. "Anyone who threatens you, you kill. You love to kill. You wait for the chance. You want to see people's blood spill because you think they try to bleed you. Well, I'm the one who always gets bled dry, told what to do. No one listens to me. Well, no more, fiend. Never again!"

In a rage, Ian yanked the chair around another half turn. Now Katarina could see the occupant, the puppet master, clearly.

That feeling of being trapped came once more, of being caught in a moment without beginning or end. The second man's voice was familiar. She knew it. She closed her eyes. "God help us," she whispered.

In a flash Ian's arm came down. "Die, devil puppet master!" he cried. "Die!"

The room, and Katarina's head spun. There was no sense in this, yet strangely it made perfect sense. Horrible, perfect sense.

The answers were buried in the legend. The merchant puppet had tricked a human. He'd controlled a human.

"Die. Die. DIE!"

This was not legend but it was real, it was happening. The human here was Ian. And sitting in the chair, being stabbed and stabbed, was the puppet master, the puller of strings, with little gold threads braided into his hair.

"Die, devil!" Ian screamed. And raising both hands be brought the knife down one last time on the figure before him. He plunged it deep into the little wooden heart of the Italian merchant.

For the second time that night, Ian murdered a puppet.

Chapter Twenty-four

"Mama? It is Babette. I am in very big trouble. Mama, are you there? I love you, Mama, I want you to know that, to believe me. Mama, can you come to Paris . . . ?"

It was over, finally over. Katarina sat on the edge of the stage, merchant puppet in hand—and told herself the nightmare was finished. Babette was on the phone in the background, about to be taken to the police station. She was now a confessed thief and, as the officer in charge put it, "We're not sure what other charges will be laid, Mademoiselle Toulon, but you must come with us to the station. We shall straighten this matter out there."

"A trade for her testimony," Katarina said to Raul. "I hope they're not too hard on her. Greed's not much compared to murder. Anyway, it's done now, more or less. No more puppet master, right?"

"No more puppet master, *chérie,*" he murmured, holding her from behind as so many others had done tonight. Ah, but this person loved her, and she loved him and that made all the difference.

"But it was weird, you know," she told him, "that final moment in the armoire. One minute I was Francois's prisoner, the next I was free. And I don't know where he went because he wasn't there when I got out and came over to you. Only Amadeus was there. I mean, I know Francois is talking to the police now, but if he knew about Ian before, and I think he did even if he's denying it now, then how did he get that knowledge? And why didn't he act on it?"

"Maybe he had no proof," Raul suggested. "Or it could be that Francois prefers, for reasons of his own, to stay out of the spotlight."

"Like a vampire?" Katarina asked. "Or a wanted man? And what about Jean down in the vaults?"

Raul kissed her cheek. "You forget, I never met your Jean."

"I know, and that's another weird thing. You should have run into him sometime. You'd have known him for sure, Raul. He looked like you, and Nicoli. I wonder..." She hesitated, then shook the idea away. Too farfetched. "Oh, and then," she said, "there was the voice I kept hearing tonight, maybe the same one you heard in the vaults."

"Imagination, Kati. Echoes of thought, nothing more."

"You think so?" With a shiver, Katarina snuggled back into Raul's warm chest. "Well okay, let the inexplicable remain that way. All I care about is that I love you. I only wish I could tell you how much."

He smiled. "I think I know."

She shivered again, only this one wasn't so pleasant. "Did you hear Ian, Raul," she asked, "after he stabbed the puppet?"

"He wanted his mother."

Katarina squeezed her eyes closed, picturing Ian's distorted features, his tears. He'd been laughing, crying, shouting, "I did it, Mama, I killed the monster. He is gone forever, this devil puppet master who murdered Claudia Clercy and cut Genevieve Capri into little pieces." Then his voice had dropped, down to a stage whisper, as if he confided some great secret. "Genevieve found a letter written by Claudia. It revealed the puppet master's identity. I had to kill her. I couldn't let that come out."

Opening her eyes again, Katarina said with a sigh, "Poor Ian."

She looked around the stage area. Police swarmed the theater, alerted by the security guards at the Hambleton estate. What a nightmare evening; what strangeness in the air.

"I also asked Pierre about the gold threads in his and Francois's hair," Katarina told Raul.

"And what did he say, *chérie?*"

"That they were nothing. Just a gimmick. It's funny, though," she said. "Have you ever noticed how Francois and his cat are never in the same room together?"

He offered her a tired smile and an indulgent, "More mysteries, Kati?"

"No, God no. I've had enough mysteries for ten lifetimes, I think. Anyway, Francois couldn't have occult powers. But speaking of unsolved things, what did you mean when you talked to the police about a finger you buried in the vaults? It sounded positively disgusting."

"It was." He pulled her closer. "Amadeus brought it to me one night."

"Amadeus again?" That cat was smart enough to be a human. It had stolen from a cabinet the very merchant puppet into which Ian had put his murderous dark side. She bit her lip. "I know this sounds absurd, but do you think Amadeus did that intentionally?"

"No. But I think that Genevieve Capri's body will be found in many pieces like the one he brought to me," Raul said on a somber note.

Katarina groaned. "Dear Lord, Ian. How could you...?"

"It wasn't Ian, *chérie,* not really. It was a part of himself that could no longer stand the constant humiliation, the thought that everyone treated him as an inferior being, a person to be walked on and used. You heard him. Even his own mother treated him this way."

"Interesting how these complexes always come back to the mother." Katarina paused. "So you're saying he took his anger and resentment and hatred for people and put them all into a little puppet. I mean, that phone call you thought you overheard was really Ian talking to his puppet, right? Ian talked and the puppet answered into his head." She twisted around. "Do you know I heard the police say that he even rented an apartment in Passy where the puppet master could go but Ian couldn't." Katarina shivered, turning back around. "Puppets can't commit murder, though, Raul. Did Ian dress up like the Italian merchant sometimes? Is that what Claudia and Genevieve discovered, why he killed them?"

"That will probably come out under investigation, but it would seem to be the case. I think at times he was Ian and at other times the puppet master. And occasionally when they would go to a public place, and he'd have the merchant puppet in a bag or in his coat or perhaps even sitting next to him, he would be both."

"That's really horrible. Poor, deluded Ian. No," she corrected. "Poor Claudia and Genevieve—and almost Babette, Louise and me. And of course Philip, the intended fall guy. By the way, where is he? Do you know why he was so angry tonight?"

"He knew that he could never have you."

"That accounts for hurt, Raul, not anger."

"He was going to be set up for the murder, Kati. He finally came to realize that he has no control over his life. No money of his own, no true goals, and then he learned that he was to be blamed for a murder." Raul shrugged. "It's natural that he should become enraged. Maybe now he'll take control of his future, go to a new place where his father isn't and make a name for himself."

"I hope so. But what about Ian? Will he ever—you know—get better?"

"I don't know how minds work, Kati. I'm sorry, I wish I did. Maybe now that he's killed the puppet master it'll be better for him, but that's for a doctor to say."

"Yes, but a doctor didn't hear him shouting, 'I killed him! I did it. He's gone! Forever gone!' And a doctor didn't see that smile on his lips when the police officer holding him called him Ian, and he looked over and said so innocently, 'Yes, that's a fine name, Ian Renshaw. You may call me that if you wish....'" She looked back. "If you *wish*, Raul?"

"Let it go, Kati," he advised. "You can't help him now."

A tremor ran through her body. He was right. Let the dark thoughts go. The police officers were approaching. It was time to leave this place and tell their stories at the station.

Turning, Katarina kissed Raul's cheek. "I love you," she said solemnly. Then she smiled and whispered, "Is there a Puppet Theater in Barcelona?"

"No." Raul's beautiful dark eyes seemed amused. "But soon there will be a man who loves you and wants you in Barcelona with him."

"Live in the real world?" Setting the puppet down, Katarina pulled his mouth onto hers. "If you're reality, Raul, I'll be there. From this night forward."

"Forever?"

She nodded and thought maybe Luther did, too. "Just like Mignon and Giovanni," she said. "Only we'll be real."

IT WAS THE FIRST TIME in many years that Sofia had worn anything resembling a gown, but tonight she did it. Deep rose pink taffeta. Very old and lovely.

Quietly she came into Raul's soon-to-be-vacated living quarters, set the puppet Nicoli in the niche with his companions and regarded the single empty space that remained. Only Mignon was missing now.

A shaving mirror hung on the wall. She put a folded note on the cot, then peered into the reflecting glass. Gray hair stuck out of her kerchief. Her blue eyes were surrounded with wrinkled skin. Old, like a prune. Some immortality!

Something appeared then. Another reflection, a narrow-featured young man with dark sexy eyes and a wistful smile on his lips. It was a familiar face, close to that of her new friend but not quite his.

This man wore a long silk scarf and a shabby tweed coat as he had done so often in the past. Yes, he was very much like her new friend who would shortly leave this place of darkness forever. Perhaps they were related in some way, these two souls. Connected . . .

She let the idea go, smiling slowly at the man's reflection. Reaching up she carefully removed her kerchief and allowed her long gray hair to spill about her shoulders.

"The merchant was wrong," she said, though she had never thought she would. "Humans should be humans. Puppets should be puppets. This is the right and proper way, is it not?" Gently she fingered a tiny braid in her hair. Slowly she began to undo it. "I understand what is real, Giovanni." A teasing light came into her blue eyes. "Or do you call yourself Jean?"

His smile changed, it lost its tragic quality. As she pulled the slender gold threads from her hair, he took her hand and brought it to his lips.

"They will call me Nicoli, my love. From this moment forward. Forever and forever, Nicoli . . . and Mignon."

Epilogue

Sofia's final note

To my beautiful young friend:

You will come to these vaults one last time, I am confident, to collect your belongings and to say good-bye to me. You will not find me, however. Not Sofia.

Most important to me is that you promise to take away from this dark world all of these original puppets that I have brought to you and that now sit—every one of them except for the Italian merchant whom Giovanni did not create—upon these stone shelves.

Let them live with you always, because I know that you and Katarina will be together when you leave here. You will be Giovanni and Mignon as they would have been had Mignon been a human and not a puppet brought to life. There is a difference that I have come to understand but that I cannot explain or you will think me insane.

You will be happy, I am certain. Some things are meant to be, some are not. You and she are meant to be.

I go now to live as I should have from the beginning. Giovanni was wrong. Puppets are puppets and people are people. Only tragedy results when the two become connected.

Remember me always. The woman you met in the vaults below the Puppet Theater. Sixty-four years old, and a terrible liar....

I do not lie, though, to tell you both that I love you, that I will be with you forever in spirit.

Goodbye, and please do not forget to take the puppets away with you. They are my final gift to you. The complete collection—for this very night Nicoli and Mignon have joined their old friends. They are what they should always have been, two puppets made for each other. You see? They hold hands. And you can tell for sure that they are the puppets Giovanni created by looking at Mignon, at the tiny gold threads she holds in her fingers.

And what precisely does this mean, you ask? Well, my friend, it means simply that Mignon's story is done. She has come home at last.

Love for always,
M

AMERICAN ROMANCE®

A Calendar of Romance

What better way to conclude American Romance's yearlong celebration than with four very special books that celebrate the joy and magic of Christmas and Hanukkah, on sale now!

Be sure to complete your Calendar of Romance collection with the following titles:

#421—*Happy New Year, Darling*
#429—*Flannery's Rainbow*
#437—*Cinderella Mom*
#445—*Home Free*
#455—*Sand Man*
#461—*Count Your Blessings*
#425—*Valentine Hearts and Flowers*
#433—*A Man for Easter*
#441—*Daddy's Girl*
#449—*Opposing Camps*
#457—*Under His Spell*

If you would like to order any of the above titles, send your name, address, zip or postal code, along with a check or money order (please do not send cash) for $3.29 each for #421 and #425 or $3.39 each for #429, #433, #437, #441, #445, #449, #455, #457 or #461, plus 75¢ postage and handling ($1.00 in Canada), payable to Harlequin Reader Service to:

In the U.S.
3010 Walden Avenue
P.O. Box 1325
Buffalo, NY 14269-1325

In Canada
P.O. Box 609
Fort Erie, Ontario
L2A 5X3

Please specify book title(s) with your order.
Canadian residents add applicable federal and provincial taxes.

COR-F